WANTING MORE

A KIMBELL TEXAS SWEET ROMANCE
BOOK FOUR

ANGEL S. VANE

BonzaiMoon Books LLC
Houston, Texas
www.bonzaimoonbooks.com

This is a work of fiction. Names, characters, places and incidents either are the product of the authors' imaginations or are used fictitiously, and any resemblance to actual persons, living or dead, business establishments, events, or locales is entirely coincidental.

Copyright © 2023 by Angel Vane

All rights reserved.

CHAPTER 1

ARREN

"You owe me ten thousand dollars," Wiley Alexander says, like a loan shark calling to collect on a debt that is years past due, and if I don't pay up, the next step would be busting my kneecaps.

Except I don't owe him a single cent.

Wiley continues, "Don't think about using a cash app. I want a wire transfer directly to my account at Bell Bank. You know the number."

I rake a hand through my hair and take a deep breath.

"What are you talking about?" I whisper into the cell phone as I zigzag through the crowd of wealthy Texans dressed in expensive ball gowns and pristine tuxedos. The ballroom of the Post Oak Hotel in the Galleria area of Houston is decorated with black, silver, and gold balloons, streamers, and flowers for the annual New Year's Eve celebration. The who's who of wealthy philanthropists are in

1

attendance, anxious to squeeze in one last donation to bolster their tax returns before the end of the year.

But fundraising for my not-for-profit organization isn't the reason I'm here.

I need their influence and connections more than cash.

"The bet we made on Christmas Day. Don't act like you forgot," Wiley says.

"Has falling in love scrambled your brain?" I ask. "We didn't make a bet. We made a pact."

"Same thing," Wiley said. "I held up my end of the bargain and told Zaire how I feel about her. Now, I'm living my happy ending. What are you doing, Darren? Hmm?"

I maneuver past a group of women who don't bother to hide their stares and point as I walk by. They beckon for me to come over, probably wanting an autograph for their son, brother, or dad, plus a selfie with me to post all over social media. I give them a quick smile, then point to the phone as an apology for not stopping and push the double doors of the ballroom open.

Wiley continues his assault. "You were supposed to tell Jasmine you're in love with her."

I wince.

Tell my best friend I've been hiding that I've been totally in love with her for as long as I can remember and risk her wrath. Or, worst yet, her apathy?

Not high on my to-do list.

But he's not wrong.

I did promise Wiley I'd come clean with Jasmine.

"All you've done is make excuses," Wiley chides. "It's almost midnight. Time is running out."

"I don't remember there being a deadline," I say, passing through the brightly lit, expansive hallway. Shiny Rolls Royce luxury vehicles are parked under spotlights inside the hotel. "When did we ever discuss doing it before the end of the year."

"Right now, when I realized you're dragging your feet again! I'm adding a cash penalty, so you'll take it seriously. Your future is at stake. That's worth at least ten grand. Maybe eleven," Wiley says with a chuckle. "Where are you anyway? I heard music."

"I'm at the New Year's Eve gala at the Post Oak Hotel trying to get support for the kids' football league," I say. A year ago, I gave my foundation the mandate to create a youth football league for children with physical and mental disabilities. While volunteering at a rehabilitation center, I overheard a few kids complaining that they don't get to play "real" football like the other kids. After receiving a report on special needs youth football teams operating in Texas, I realized the kids were right.

And I vowed to do something about it.

"How's that going?"

"It's not. I've taken photos and got a lot of agreement that my program serves a need in the community, but nobody feels comfortable partnering with the project," I say glumly.

"So you're good enough to get an autograph from but not to go into business with? Seriously?"

"People outside the sports world aren't as forgiving of my past. They have long memories, and being affiliated with me could make them look bad. A few folks admitted that to my face."

"But you're innocent," Wiley says. "After all these years, that's the only thing they remember when they see you? I don't understand it."

"Neither do I," I say, then rip the bow tie loose. "Maybe it's how my dad made the whole situation disappear that leaves a bad taste in people's mouths."

It left a bad taste in mine, for sure.

The renowned college football coach with a record number of national championships couldn't allow his reputation to be tarnished by my scandal. So he wrote a check with too many zeros to make it disappear.

"Guess they think the settlement makes you look guilty."

"And even though I wasn't guilty, it's the stain I wear daily. A fact of my life. I hate to see the kids suffer because of it," I say.

"They're not going to suffer. We'll figure out how to get what you need … after you tell Jasmine you love her," Wiley says, returning to the same broken record he's been on over the past week. "This is the woman you've loved since you were six! Don't you think twenty-five years is too long to keep that secret from her?"

I glance at the curving staircase toward an empty library on the second floor, then head up to get some privacy.

"Six-year-olds don't know anything about love," I say, although I'm not entirely sure that's true.

What I do know is I was born with twisted and bowed legs that affected my ability to walk. By the time I went to school at Excelsior Prep, I could walk but only with the aid of forearm crutches, and even then, my gait was slow and uncoordinated. That made me the primary target of bullying by the other kids until the day Jasmine Jones joined my first-grade class.

She was taller than all the boys, with a chubby body, a pretty smile, and ponytails that swung back and forth as she walked. I was utterly smitten with her and had written her name on the back of my notebook with a heart around it.

Wrong move.

That one act gave Timmy Quinn, Jimbo Barnes, and Byron Magee another reason to bully me. During recess, they stole my crutches and threw them into the bushes. I fell to the ground, unable to get back up.

And Jasmine saw the whole thing.

We made eye contact across the lawn, and everything changed for me.

Jasmine marched over to the boys and punched each one of them, leaving them howling and clutching their bloody noses. I couldn't help but laugh as she grabbed my crutches and handed them back to me.

I looked at her like she was my very own Wonder Woman come to life.

Jasmine gave me a bright smile showing off her missing center teeth and said, "They won't bother you anymore. Come on. It's snack time. I hear they have oatmeal creme pies today."

She didn't help me up.

She didn't look at me with pity.

She didn't make me feel like I wasn't normal.

She waited patiently as I stood, then walked with me to the cafeteria.

We've been inseparable ever since.

Wiley says, "I don't know why I bother with you. I had the most amazing experience ringing in the New Year with Zaire on Copacabana Beach. I should still be holding her in my arms, but I made an excuse to grab us some food so I could call you."

"Look, I appreciate you pushing me—"

"Do more than appreciate it, Darren. Talk to Jasmine. I hope you don't wake up and regret not telling her how you feel. That would be the worst, but it'll be your own stupid fault. Don't say I didn't warn you."

"What's that supposed to mean?"

"You think Jasmine is going to stay single forever? Sure, she was focused on her career for years. But now she runs the ER department at the largest hospital in Lasso County. She's professionally successful. What do you think she's going to focus on next?"

My stomach sours.

As close as I am to Jasmine, there's always been one off-limits topic —our respective dating lives. Neither of us could bear to hear details of the other's romantic exploits. Sure, she could scroll through my social media feeds over the years and see pics of my ex-girlfriends, but I doubt she cared enough to stalk me. All Jasmine would've found was a long line of women who were the opposite of her. Women who didn't stand a chance of taking her place in my life or my heart, no matter how long I may have dated them.

Since we moved back to Kimbell five years ago, neither of us has been in a relationship.

But what if the next boyfriend is around the corner for Jasmine?

What would I do then?

I've been so focused on not ruining our friendship by revealing my feelings that the thought of losing her to another man hadn't crossed my mind.

And what man wouldn't want Jasmine?

She is beautiful, with gorgeous brown eyes, a breathtaking smile, and a body with curves in all the right places. She could easily have any man she wanted.

But could she want me? Could she be willing to risk our friendship for love? Should I go another year without knowing the answer to that question?

I pinch the bridge of my nose.

"Fine. I'll talk to her tonight after she gets off her shift at the ER."

CHAPTER 2

J ASMINE

PUTTING THE CAR IN PARK, I GLANCE AT THE LINE OF CARS in the driveway of my childhood home and swallow down the dread and ... embarrassment. This is not how I want to spend New Year's Eve. The alternative would be crashing some big shindig that has a live band, confetti and a balloon drop at midnight. But stuffing my size eighteen body in some sequined contraption and stilettos to attend that kind of party is at the bottom of my "fun times" list.

Right now, that sounds much better than walking into Evelyn's house. Especially when she's in there with my Aunt Lisa and Aunt Mary, doing the thousands of things they usually do to prepare for the New Year's Day feast.

What I should be doing is hustling around the emergency room at

St. Elizabeth's Hospital, treating the myriad of idiots, fools, and morons who make stupid decisions like shooting guns into the sky, being irresponsible with fireworks, getting into fights, jumping off rooftops or driving drunk to ring in the New Year. All the while, praying I won't need to save the life of an innocent person in the wrong place at the wrong time who happened to cross paths with those jerks.

The ER is my kingdom, and I'm its undisputed queen, ruling with somewhat of an iron fist.

Until tonight, when I was ripped from my throne and kicked out on my hiney by the very people I rule over, day in and day out. All their protestations about it being for my good did nothing to improve my mood. But I took their well-meaning actions to heart and assuaged their panic by doing as I was told.

This time.

Stepping out of the car, I smooth the stretchy fabric of my form-fitting knit dress over my ample hips and practice sucking in my stomach a few times. Long ago, I realized these dresses were infinitely more comfortable than squeezing into scratchy, tight cotton scrubs or wearing business suits. And since I'm the boss, no one can stop me. Plus, the look is smart underneath my white coat, especially since I have dresses in many colors and designs.

Trudging up the hedge-lined sidewalk that leads to the front door, I have a moment of hesitation. I could be in my apartment, sitting cross-legged on my couch with a half-gallon of Blue Bell Cookies and Cream ice cream soothing me as I watch celebrations of the New Year happening around the world.

There's still time.

But what would I tell my team when I return to work in two days? They forced me out of the ER so I could spend the holiday having fun with people I love. I gave my word, so that's precisely what I will do.

My pace slows as I get closer to the door.

As I pulled out of the hospital parking lot, I thought of spending the evening with ice cream and Darren, my best friend. As

8

unbelievable as it is, my best friend is a hulking, six-foot-six former professional football defensive superstar. We are an unlikely pair, but it works for us as others try to move in on my territory. Others being that goofball, former playboy Wiley Alexander who, every chance he gets, mouths off about Darren being his best friend. While that may be true, Darren has never made it a secret I'm his number one friend—now and always.

But Darren is in Houston at some swanky New Year's Eve party. He was suspiciously vague about a date, which means he's probably there with another gorgeous model dancing the night away before the clock strikes midnight, and they have the obligatory, mind-blowing kiss to bring in the New Year.

Good for him.

I want him to be happy.

So, with my first option not available, it only takes nanoseconds to weigh my other options.

The family crew comprised my overprotective, lovable, lady-magnet brother, Hendrix, and my equally infuriating and overprotective cousins, Jaxon, Maxwell, and Lennox. When I'm not with Darren, I'm in the company of these fine men, who all happen to be working this New Year's Eve. Add to the list my other brother, Braxton, a spy for the CIA, who is in parts unknown and unavailable to hang out with his baby sister.

Pivoting away from my usual hang-out buddies, I try the friend route. The list of friends I can call up and hang out with quickly dwindles to one—Mya Young. She's the first girlfriend I've had in a long time and has given me a glimpse into how fun it would've been if I'd grown up with a sister. But Mya's engaged to the love of her life, Ronan, and they are doing family things with his twin boys tonight. Sure, she'd welcome me over in a heartbeat, but spending New Year's with the perfect family is enough to make me gag.

That leaves spending it with my mom, Evelyn, who would never turn her back on her youngest child, and my aunts, Lisa and Mary.

I huff a breath, then use my spare key to enter the house. The stench of chitlins almost knocks me out as I dry heave in my mouth. The soft rumble of the stinky soul food staple boiling floats from the kitchen. Evelyn will batter and fry them tomorrow, which is why the house is sacrificed to the odor tonight.

I go to the kitchen, suck in my stomach, and paste on a bright smile.

"Hey, Evelyn." I make a beeline for her.

Her arms are submerged to the elbows in a sink filled with collard greens. My mom jerks her hands from the water, spraying droplets across the kitchen, then grabs a towel to dry them.

"Hey, baby! I wasn't expecting to see you tonight," she declares with a beaming smile. "Why aren't you at work?" She asks as she wraps me in a warm hug.

The hug becomes the salve for my irritation, and I let the healing wash over me.

"I got kicked out."

Gasps ring through the kitchen as the three women's eyes grow wide as saucers.

I stifle a laugh. "My team rearranged the schedule so I could get a couple of nights off since I worked Thanksgiving and Christmas."

The women glance at each other with relief.

"That's sweet of them, but maybe they could've told you earlier so you could've made plans," Evelyn says with a huff. "What's the point of doing that a few hours before midnight?"

"Seriously!" Aunt Lisa chimes. "How's a girl supposed to wrangle up a New Year's Eve date with short notice?" She shakes her head and purses her lips.

"Well, I'm glad Jas came to ring in the New Year with us," Aunt Mary says. "It's been too long since we've seen you."

"You saw me Sunday at church," I remind her, then lean over to hug and kiss her.

"That don't count," Aunt Mary declares.

I cross behind the table and hug and kiss Aunt Lisa. The table is littered with giant bowls of soaking black-eyed peas, raw oxtails, pork chops marinating in a dry rub, and mounds of collard greens which my aunts are cutting with surgical precision, then twisting the leaves to remove the center stem.

Walking back to my mom, I ask, "Anything you need me to do?"

"A surgeon's hands are for saving lives, not cooking food. Go sit down and prop your feet up," Evelyn says. "I'll whip you up a green smoothie as a snack. It helps with weight loss."

"It does," Aunt Mary says, giving me a sweet smile. "I drink one every night. I've already lost five pounds this month."

"You should double up, Jas. You got a whole lot more than five pounds to lose from what I see," Aunt Lisa adds, reaching over to pinch my belly, which I'd forgotten to suck in.

I swat at Aunt Lisa's hand, then roll my eyes. Crossing my arms over my chest, pushing my F cups higher, I say, "I don't want a smoothie, Evelyn."

"Well, if you change your mind, let me know." She gives me a look like I'm a fool for not drinking a smoothie that could help me with my "problem."

Losing weight is the furthest thing from my mind. Sure, I've gone up a dress size or two in the past few years, but I'm a healthy woman. I'm not pre-diabetic, my blood pressure and cholesterol levels are normal, and I walk from the back of the parking lot to the hospital every day when I go to work. That's equivalent to three thousand steps, round trip.

There's no reason for me to go on a diet—

"Jas, losing weight will help you get a man," Aunt Lisa says. "Go ahead and drink that smoothie."

My mouth falls open.

"Stop that, Lisa. There are plenty of fat women with husbands," Aunt Mary says, giving me an encouraging nod.

I cringe.

"Sure, but Jas has to do more because of the other things that will hold a man back from wanting her," Aunt Lisa says.

"Excuse me? What do you think is holding men back from wanting me?" I ask, insulted but also mildly curious.

I have been single for … forever.

Evelyn glances at my aunts, then says, "You'll want to sit down for this, baby. Here comes some cold hard truth."

CHAPTER 3

J ASMINE

Now is not the best time to ruminate on my pitiful relationship history. The fact is, I've only had one serious relationship my entire life. This was with Lance Bassett, a fellow alum of Excelsior Prep who went to college, then law school, worked at a prestigious law firm in Chicago, and then recently returned to Kimbell as the go-to local attorney.

Lance is a nice guy. A great guy, actually. When he returned to town a few months ago, we briefly entertained the idea of rekindling our romance. We had managed a complex long-distance relationship while I was in medical school and he was in law school. After we graduated, our careers took us to different cities. He wasn't willing to compromise his path, and I wasn't ready to compromise mine, so we split amicably. That didn't mean we couldn't pick up where we left off since he'd relocated back home. But it became apparent after a couple of dates we'd grown apart and were better off as friends, leaving my string of consecutive years without a man firmly intact.

I turn my attention to the elder women of my family and ask, "Why do the three of you think men don't want me?"

Aunt Lisa, as expected, is the first to share her opinions, unfiltered and blunt. "You're too smart and successful, Jas. No man wants a woman who is smarter than him or makes more money than he does."

"And because you've accomplished so much, your standards are high. Men can't handle the pressure of trying to meet those high standards," Aunt Mary says.

"You know how confident and assertive you are," Evelyn adds. "You don't back down from anyone or anything. Men can't handle a woman who expresses themselves strongly like you do."

Aunt Lisa continues, "Not to mention you don't need a man to take care of you. You know men get their value and worth from being able to take care of their woman. You being you robs them of that."

"And your stature in the community is intimidating. The whole town respects and looks up to you, which means any man you date will be living in your shadow," Aunt Mary adds. "No man will stick around long in that situation."

"That's why you need to use a woman's secret weapon," Aunt Lisa proclaims. "An attractive body is like kryptonite to a man. He'll overlook all those other things to have you on his arm."

I lean forward and glare at each of them. "You're joking ..."

Confused stares pass between the three women as if everything they said was the gospel instead of stereotypes that need to be obliterated.

"First of all, any man intimidated by my intelligence or career is not the man for me. I have no time to mollycoddle some man's ego." Prickly heat creeps up my neck. I continue, "Second, I will not waste my time trying to lose weight for some guy to want me. What they see is what they get. If men can't accept me for who I am, on the inside and the outside, then maybe I'm better off single."

A strange look passes between my aunts and my mom, who raises an eyebrow. Laying the dishtowel on the counter, she walks to the table and sits beside me. She places a hand on my shoulder and says, "Jas, you only feel that way because … you have Darren."

"What?" I screech. "What does Darren have to do with any of this?"

"He's your crutch, Jas," Aunt Lisa announces like an indictment. "You use that man and your friendship with him as a substitute for a real romantic relationship."

"It's not fair to either of you that you use Darren that way," Aunt Mary says.

"I am not using Darren!" My hands fly into the air.

Evelyn says, "In my daughter's defense, I think she and Darren are using each other. He's too scared to date again after that sweet girl he was dating dumped him. He never recovered."

I roll my eyes, remembering Cassidy Mitchell, the so-called sweet girl. She was a thorn in my side, forcing me to scale back on the normal routine of my friendship with Darren so she wouldn't feel threatened by me. Still, I felt terrible when their relationship ended, especially since a part of me knew I had played a role in driving them apart. I still fill a twinge of guilt about that.

"And she dumped him because of those horrible accusations that physical therapist made about him. What did he do after his daddy cleaned up that mess for him?" Evelyn asks a question we all know the answer to. "He moved back to Kimbell because Jas suggested he come home. And he's spent too much time with you ever since. You're like his old, beat-up, worn comfort blanket. Familiar and safe. He uses you to avoid risking his heart again."

"This is ridiculous!" I say, feeling defensive, although I'm not sure why.

"It makes sense, Jas," Aunt Mary interjects. "Don't dismiss what we're saying so quickly. Think about it."

"If you and Darren didn't have each other, both of you would've gotten back out there and found love again by now." Aunt Lisa jabs her finger toward my face. "Well, at least Darren would have. You need to work on your body before you can snag a man."

"That's enough, Lisa," Evelyn says, giving my aunt a warning glare.

Aunt Lisa ignores the rebuke and continues, "Your friendship with each other stops both of you from finding your real soul mates. Both of you could be happily married by now. But you're not." She looks at Evelyn. "Is that better?"

My mom nods her approval.

"Let me get this straight," I say, squeezing the bridge of my nose. "You think Darren and I being best friends has stopped us from finding real love with other people?"

All three women nod at me as if this is obvious.

"I don't know how either of you have time to date. When you're not at the ER, and he's not at the fire station or working with his charity, the two of you spend all your time with each other," Evelyn says. "What man wants to compete with Darren? What woman wants to put up with him hanging with you all the time? This friendship is holding both of you back."

"Evelyn! You know I'd never do anything to stop Darren from dating someone. He wouldn't do that to me either. Our friendship is not why we haven't found love with other people," I insist.

Aunt Lisa shouts, "Jas, no man wants to be compared to a best friend who won a bunch of Superbowls!"

"I don't think it's healthy either," Aunt Mary adds, then squeezes my hand.

I open my mouth to dispute them, but no words come out. I feel like I've been sucker punched. What's worse is I'm beginning to believe they are right.

Could I be missing out on finding an epic love like Evelyn and Dad?

Even after my father made questionable medical decisions for his patient and landed himself in jail, it hasn't weakened their connection. Evelyn visits him every week in Huntsville without fail, refusing to be separated from the man she loves.

Could my friendship with Darren mimic a love match enough to keep me content? Is it the same for him?

I stand up and grab my purse. "It's time for me to go."

"Please don't leave. We didn't mean to upset you," Evelyn says, trying to block my path to the foyer. "But I want you to face the truth."

I hug my mom, then say, "Y'all have given me a lot to think about."

My voice is glum because I do my best thinking … with Darren.

CHAPTER 4

ARREN

WHEN WAS THE LAST TIME I HAD SWEATY PALMS?

I rub my hands against my tuxedo pants, wishing I'd stopped by my house to change before driving to St. Elizabeth's Hospital. Showing up in a tuxedo to tell Jasmine I love her is over the top. Makes it feel like a monumental declaration, which I suppose it is.

Honestly, not one part of me believes Jasmine returns my feelings.

She hasn't given any sign of interest in me other than as her best friend. She treats me no different than her brother, Hendrix, and her cousins, Jaxon, Maxwell, and Lennox. The only difference is we are always together.

Any free time either of us has, we find ways to be with each other.

She's hands down my favorite person in the world.

I don't just love Jasmine.

I like her.

I like talking to her, going out with her, teasing her, and sharing my life with her.

And that's saying a lot.

My best friend isn't known around town as the friendliest woman.

She's brash, brutally honest, and impatient. Never sugarcoats and delivers the cold, hard truth whether people are ready for it or not. She rubs a lot of people the wrong way, but everyone agrees she's the best doctor this county has, and that makes up for her prickly personality.

But that's what always drew me to Jasmine.

Her no-nonsense, confident, self-assuredness forces everyone to accept her as she is. Jasmine doesn't worry about making people like her or doing things to fit in. Her motto is to accept her as she is or don't accept her at all.

I accept her.

I want her.

I love her.

It's about time she knows that.

She may not see me as a potential love interest yet, but maybe I can change her mind. Show her how perfect we are for each other.

Pushing my hands into my pockets, I stroll through the automatic doors of the emergency room and walk over to the nurses' station. The place is quiet—a good sign there hasn't been any tragedy on the roads so far.

Nurse Avril Judson looks up as my steps echo in the cavernous hall. She smiles, then a slight frown creases her forehead.

"You okay, Darren?" Avril asks. "Did you hurt yourself?" She checks me over, likely looking for gushing blood, a gaping wound, or dark bruises to patch up.

I lean over the desk and say, "Nope. Here to see Jasmine. Can you tell her I'm here? Or is she with a patient?"

"She's not working tonight," Avril announces.

Now it's my turn to frown.

"She told me she was."

"Yes, but that was before we surprised her with a night off," Avril explains, bubbling with excitement. "She was so stunned when we told her."

"Wow, that was nice of y'all."

"Did you know she worked every single holiday this year?"

I knew that, and it's one of the things I scolded her about. Not having a husband or kids doesn't mean she has to sacrifice all of her holidays so those with families could be off. Especially the holidays when I wasn't on shift at the fire station and wanted nothing more than to spend that time with her.

"I'm not surprised," I say.

"All the nurses got together and asked a few other doctors to work tonight so she could have the last holiday of the year. We were able to surprise Jasmine when she came back from a quick dinner in the cafeteria."

"I'm sure she didn't take that well," I laugh, imagining Jasmine fighting her team to keep working despite them wanting to show their appreciation by giving her a night off.

"Nope. We had to push her out of the ER," Avril says, laughing. "She looked so lost and confused, like she didn't know what to do! But we marched her out to the parking lot and forced her to leave."

"And I bet she was fuming mad when y'all did that," I say.

"You know it."

"Any idea where she went?"

"I'm guessing Baker Bros. It's Kimbell tradition and so close. It's the best option to celebrate on short notice."

I nod, though I disagree entirely with Avril.

There's no way Jasmine wants to spend the night celebrating with the packed crowd at Baker Bros BBQ. She's much happier spending time with family or close friends in a low-key setting than at some splashy, crowded party.

But if she didn't know she would have the night off, I'm guessing she went back to her apartment to watch the New Year's Eve celebrations with a pint of Blue Bell Cookies and Cream. It works out in my favor. Confessing my feelings will be much easier if it's the two of us in her apartment than here at the hospital with her whole team around.

"Thanks," I say, squeezing her hand. "Hope it's a slow night. Happy New Year."

"Me too," Avril says but looks skeptical. "Happy New Year, Darren."

Minutes later, I'm racing down the packed streets of Downtown Kimbell toward Belvedere on the Lake, where Jasmine lives on the top floor of the newest apartment complex in town.

I grab the key card from my pocket and let myself into the gated complex, driving through the narrow roads until I reach her building, nestled at the back of the property. Pulling into a spot in front of the stairs leading to her door, I jump out of my Range Rover and stare at the parking space on the left of me.

The empty parking space.

The space where Jasmine's silver Audi A4 should be parked.

But it's not here.

I kick myself, wondering if she could've gone to Baker Bros after all. Maybe she was feeling festive and wanted to party, especially since she thought I would be ringing in the New Year in Houston.

A wave of disappointment rumbles through me.

To be sure, I rifle through the keys on my key ring until I find the one to her apartment, then jog up the steps and let myself inside. Walking into the dark living room, I flick on the lights and glance around. Two oversized framed jerseys are prominently displayed in her living room. The black and gold Pittsburgh jerseys I wore in each Superbowl were signed by me.

"Jasmine, you here?" I call out as I walk over to the jerseys.

Silence.

I reach toward the frame and run a finger over the glass, circling the message I wrote to her.

Jasmine, I could never be me without you. Darren #98.

Turning away from the memorabilia, I fall backward onto her couch and text her.

DARREN

Hey where are u

I stare at the screen for seconds that turn into minutes.

I wait longer, and after ten minutes pass, I give up on getting a response and wrack my brain on options of what my best friend would do with her unexpected night off.

The next thought has me doing a drive-by of Evelyn's house. But I decide not to go in when Jasmine's car isn't parked outside. The last thing I want to do is cause her mom undue worry. I shift the SUV into park at the stop sign and send a group text to the Joneses.

DARREN

Hey y'all know where Jas is?

Hendrix is the first to respond.

HENDRIX

ER. Duh!

Her team gave her the night off.

LENNOX

Really? That's nice of them.

MAXWELL

She's not at home?

Nope

JAXON

Should I be worried? I can get some black and whites to search for her

Too early to panic

LENNOX

Just texted my mom. She was at Aunt Evelyn's earlier with them but left. She was upset.

HENDRIX

Well we can all guess where she is then

MAXWELL

Right

Yep. I'll text y'all when I see her.

Tossing my cell phone onto the passenger seat, I race through the winding streets of Kimbell. My foot is heavy on the gas pedal as the clock ticks closer to midnight. My heart tightens, panic gripping me as I feel time running out.

The ultimatum from Wiley weighs heavily on me like a ticking time bomb that could banish me to the friend zone for eternity if I don't tell her I love her before the New Year.

My heart thumps erratically in my chest as I speed down the unmarked road lined with towering pine trees. I don't bother pressing the brake as the wrought iron and stone gate slides open in time for me to roar past with a wave at my long-time guard posted up in the gatehouse.

I jerk the Range Rover to a stop behind Jasmine's Audi, parked in front of the stucco and hill country limestone Victorian-style mansion I call home. Another glance at the clock sends adrenaline shooting through my veins.

Three minutes to midnight.

I fling the door open and race through it like the devil is after me, eyes fixed on the winding staircase. My feet pound the steps as I take them three at a time, chasing after the ticking clock counting down to the New Year echoing from the movie room upstairs.

The cheers and whistles from the television get louder as I reach the doors. I shove them open with a loud bang and step inside.

My heart leaps in my throat at the sight of Jasmine lying on her favorite chaise, arm dangling toward the nearly-finished pint of ice cream.

She looks impeccable. Black wavy locks brush against the satiny smooth deep brown of her graceful neck. Sleeveless fitted dress clings to her curves, soft, inviting and revealing a hint of her thick thighs. But her mouth captures my attention. Lips brushed with a hint of glossy pink and full, open in surprise. A vision of beauty that leaves me breathless and sure that she belongs right here with me … always.

The countdown chant begins.

Ten … nine … eight …

A smile plays at the corners of Jasmine's full lips as she sits up on the chair. Her brown eyes light up and search mine, lashes fluttering as she runs a hand through her black tresses.

"Hey, I thought you were ringing in the New Year with the rich folks in Houston." Her intense stare shifts from excited to suspicious.

She places the ice cream on the side table and walks toward me.

Seven … six … five …

"I was until I realized I wanted to spend it with …" I move closer to her until we are only inches apart.

Four … three … two …

"You," I say.

The cutest look of confusion crosses her face as I lean toward her, erasing all distance between us.

One.

So … here goes nothing.

CHAPTER 5

J ASMINE

HOLY SMOKES!

Is this really happening?

Is my best friend actually kissing me?

I force the thoughts from my mind and focus on the feel of his lips, so soft and warm. The sweetness of his breath mingles with mine. Time stands still as if nothing else exists at the moment except us. As much as I try to resist, I melt into his embrace and lose myself in the glorious sensation. Electricity tingles along my skin, and my knees turn to jelly. If Darren's arms weren't wrapped around me, hands exploring all my curves as he presses his body against mine, I'm sure I would've turned into a puddle of goo and melted to the floor by now.

But reality comes crashing in.

What does this mean?

Are we crossing a line?

Is our friendship ruined?

The questions come hard and fast, but I still can't bring myself to pull away. His lips feel too good kissing mine. Or maybe it's been too long since I've kissed a man, and I'm being self-indulgent.

Warning bells and red flags go off in my head, distracting me from the out-of-this-world sensations.

I pull away, breaking the kiss.

Darren gazes at me with those incredible blue eyes filled with hope, passion, and ... desire.

I'm stunned by what I see and what happened between us. The most incredible kiss I've ever had in my life. Not that I've kissed many men, but this one has caused me to forget every other one I've had.

Who knew Darren could kiss like that?

Well, the long list of models, singers, actresses, and cheerleaders he's dated over the years, plus the Kimbell girls he dated at Excelsior prep and a few strippers sprinkled in ...

I stop my analysis as the cold hard truth of the situation washes over me like a bucket of ice water.

Evelyn, Aunt Lisa, and Aunt Mary were right about us.

Darren and I are using each other as substitutes for love, and I have to stop us before it ruins our friendship.

I groan and push away from him.

His presence fills up all the space in the room. The humble confidence and massive defensive lineman muscular body, which he's kept up after not playing professional football for the past six years, draws me to him like a magnet. But I need to resist. This is my best friend.

"What's wrong?" Darren asks, concern etched on his handsome face. The face I've stared into millions of times before looks brand new to me now. The thick strands of short auburn hair slicked into a style appropriate for a holiday celebration. The chiseled square jaw, smoothly shaved, showcasing his olive skin tone. The lips that left me breathless. But more than anything, it's the pale, translucent blue eyes staring back at me, asking more than his words indicate. Questions for which I have no answers.

"This is wrong, Darren!" I shout at him, then shove him in the chest, keenly aware of his rock-hard, sculpted pectoralis major. My push doesn't budge him, to my chagrin. I press my hands on my hips and point my finger in his face. "What are you thinking? You are not supposed to kiss me. I'm not supposed to kiss you. We are friends. Best friends! Super close and maybe ... too close?"

"What?" Darren reaches for me, but I side-step his grasp. "Don't say that. There's nothing wrong with how close we are, Jasmine."

I shake my head, my frustration mounting as I try to make him see reason.

"Don't you see what we're doing, Darren? This isn't right. Both of us have avoided relationships for years. Maybe we had good reasons to take a break initially, but now it's gone on for too long."

"I know—"

"Boy, shut up and let me finish," I say, grabbing his hands and pulling him down onto the chaise beside me. Have his hands always been this large and strong? Geez, what's with this guy? I close my eyes and try to focus. "We can't keep using each other as relationship crutches."

"Relationship crutches?" Darren frowns, his eyes searching mine. "What are you talking about?"

"We don't try to find real love because we have almost everything we want in a relationship with our friendship. But almost isn't good enough for me, and it's not what I want for you either." I lace my fingers with his and squeeze his strong hands. "We both deserve happiness and real love."

"I agree with you. I just think—"

"That's why I created a New Year's resolution for us."

Darren exhales slowly, his expression pensive. "Why do I have a feeling I'm not going to like this?"

"We need to push each other out of this comfort zone. This bubble we've been living in has stopped us from finding love again,"

I say, the words rushing from my mouth. "Look, I'm not dumb. I know you've dated women since you moved back home. Occasionally, someone will show me you and your date in some photo on social media and try to pump me for information I don't have. But you don't let any of those relationships grow to something deeper."

Darren slides his hands from mine, then caresses my arms. "There's a reason for that—"

"I know. I lived it with you. Losing your football career and then being accused by that cow, Pippa, of sexual assault was like one devastating blow after another. I saw firsthand the effect it had on you. How it changed you in ways I don't think you understand."

"I'm not denying I changed, but going through all of that ... with you by my side ... brought me some clarity," Darren says, closing the distance between us.

"You leaned on me when you should've leaned on your girlfriend. Cassidy couldn't understand why I could get through to you, and she couldn't. When y'all broke up, I know you felt like it was easier to not give your heart to anyone again," I say.

"Is that what you think?" Darren's voice is devoid of emotion, and it breaks my heart to hold the mirror of dysfunctional past relationships in his face.

"Hey, I'm not beating up on you. I'm in the same boat," I say, leaning back on the cushions. "I have literally had one boyfriend my entire life. It's pitiful. When Lance and I broke up, I was blindsided. I didn't see it coming. I hoped he loved me enough to stick around, but he didn't. I tried dating after that, and nothing ever worked out." I shrug. "Focusing on my career and hanging out with my best friend was easier." I reach over and squeeze his hand. "But we can't use each other anymore."

Darren pulls me toward him.

I hold my breath, wondering if he will kiss me again.

Wondering ... not hoping. I can't hope. This is too confusing.

Curiosity flashes in his eyes as he says, "I understand everything you're saying. From the outside, it seems plausible. But I need to ask you one question. Can I do that?"

I huff out a loud breath. "Fine. Ask."

"Did you feel anything when I kissed you?"

A smile almost erupts on my face, but I press my lips together ... hard ... to stop it. How do I respond to this question? I can't lie to Darren. He's my best friend. We don't lie to each other. So, I'll have to tell him the truth.

"Boy, you are an amazing kisser, which I'm sure the hundreds of women you've kissed over the years have told you. So, it shouldn't surprise you that I think the same," I say.

Darren bites his bottom lip in the sexiest way, and I almost smack the look off his face. I snatch my hands from his grasp. "But we're friends. Best friends. But friends. I don't want to confuse things or be some substitute you use because we're so comfortable with each other. There is a woman who is ideal for you, Darren. But she ain't me."

He looks away, and I can't read the expression on his face.

I want him to tell me what he's thinking. Despite my impatience, I force myself to give him time. Seconds turn into minutes before he looks back at me.

"So, what is this New Year's resolution you've thought of?" he asks.

My smile grows big as I bounce on the chaise. "We will find our one true love in the New Year. We'll be dating accountability partners. Now, I don't want to hear the mushy details of your dates. I'm surely not going to share mine, but we'll keep each other honest and at least push each other to go on dates every week. Every week, do you hear me?"

Sadness crosses his face, then disappears quickly.

"Weekly is a lot." Darren shakes his head and collapses back on the chaise.

"Yes, for me, it is. For you, not so much. Are you going to sit here and lie like you don't get dozens of direct messages to your social media accounts asking you out?"

"So what if I do? Isn't quality better than quantity? I don't know those ladies. Not sure I'm compatible with any of them."

"You won't know if you don't try."

"How are you going to try?" Darren asks, suddenly more interested. "Are you going to join Wiley's dating app or something?"

"Of course not!" I shudder.

"So, again, how will you find dates every week?"

"Referrals from friends, including you. There must be some single football player friends of yours who might be a good fit for me—"

"No way. I'm not setting you up on dates with my friends or former colleagues. You can forget about that."

"Fine. Then, I'll ask my other friend, Mya, to help me." I stick my tongue out at Darren. "What do you think? Are you willing to try this resolution out with me?"

Darren stares at me with those gorgeous blue eyes, and I almost forget to breathe. Almost. He's going to make some girl a fantastic husband one day. Whoever she is better appreciate him, or she'll have to answer to me.

He leans forward and responds, "For you, I'll do anything."

CHAPTER 6

J ASMINE

"DOMINO." I SLAM THE PLASTIC RECTANGLE ETCHED WITH five dots on either side of a bold line onto the picnic table, then shake my head. "Have y'all always been this bad?"

Lennox rolls his eyes as he grips the nub of a pencil to write down my score. "Only when you're playing."

"When is Darren getting here?" Maxwell cranes his neck to stare across the rolling lush green lawn dotted with towering pine trees. "Love you, Jas, but we do much better when he plays instead of you."

The bright winter sun breaks through the canopy of leaves, casting a patchwork of light and dark shadows onto my parent's backyard. The weather is mild, in the low sixties, with a slight chill in the late afternoon breeze. I wrap my cardigan tighter around me and push my mostly uneaten plate of food to the side.

"I have the perfect distraction for my little sister," Hendrix proclaims proudly, placing a heaping bowl of peach cobbler onto the picnic table in front of me. He bends over and kisses my head before sitting next to me. Without saying a word, he extends a spoon toward me.

I shake my head. "I'm not hungry." My stomach is in knots. I feel like I may be sick.

My answer gets Jaxon's attention as he peers up from his bowl of black-eyed peas but doesn't say a word.

"Alright, spill it," Lennox demands. "You're kicking our butts in dominoes all the while picking over your food all day. The only thing you ate was the collard greens because, well ..."

My brother and cousins say in unison, "They're the bomb."

"Peach cobbler is your favorite, Jas," Hendrix lowers his voice as he nudges me. "I added a scoop of Blue Bell cookies and cream, like you like it."

"Which is gross," Lennox adds. "But so you."

Jaxon fixes his deep brown eyes on me, and I instantly get why he's the best detective at the Kimbell Police Department. If this was what it was like to be interrogated by my cousin, no wonder the perps fess up and fast. He tilts his head toward me and asks, "What's up?"

Such a simple question, but all I have are complex, complicated, and confusing answers. I'm not sure I want to get into everything that happened on New Year's Eve with them, but how else can I explain why I'm not acting like myself?

Maxwell reaches into the cooler, grabs five bottles of Elm beer, and passes them out.

"I'm not drinking that," I say, pushing the beer bottle away.

Hendrix wraps an arm around me. "Don't remember you having a problem drinking that bottle of Harlow-Rose Cabernet Sauvignon."

"Wine is different. She gave it to me for free," I say, wiggling from his grasp.

"How'd you manage that?" Maxwell asks, raising an eyebrow.

"I was the bigger woman and gave her some advice, which turned out to be wrong." I sigh and let my body sag over on the picnic table. "I shouldn't have wasted my time. But I got the wine as a thank you and drank every last drop. But beer is gross," I say, gazing past Lennox toward the fence gate. I've been on pins and needles waiting for Darren to arrive. I'm not sure if he will show up after what happened between us last night. It's got me in a funky mood.

Jaxon flips the dominoes face down, then moves them across the table in a circular motion to shuffle them for the next game. "Answer my question, Jas," he demands.

I suck in a deep breath, then say, "I'm going to start dating again."

And with that atomic bomb, the eyes of my family bore into me. The breeze ceases, and the birds stop chirping. Silence rings in my ears. Heat blazes across my skin. Sweat rolls down my back.

"Why?" Lennox is the first to speak up. "Is it your biological clock? I thought you said that was a hoax."

Maxwell reaches for my hand and squeezes it. "You're still young, Jas. You have plenty of time."

"Do y'all realize I haven't been in a relationship since Lance?" I ask, looking at each of them.

The lackadaisical nods cause my skin to prickle.

Lenox scrunches his nose. "Y'all were not a good fit. It's better things didn't work out with the two of you."

"I don't like this," Hendrix says, his voice louder than necessary. "I don't like it at all." My brother shifts to face me. "Who are you going out with? When do I get to meet these dudes?"

I look at him like he's lost his mind. "So, it's okay for you to go on dates, but I can't? Talk about a double standard."

Hendrix drags a hand down his face. "I want you to be happy. I'm not trying to stop that, but dating is hard. There are creeps out there. Men who don't have your best interests at heart. Ones who want to use you for your money or your body but don't want anything deeper. I should know."

"Oh, why? Because you are one of those creeps? You're such a player, and you're scared I will date a guy like you." I place my hands on his shoulders and shake him.

"Right. Which is why I need to approve these dudes before you go out with them," my brother says. He's dead serious.

"Not going to happen." I turn away from him.

"Where's all this coming from?" Jaxon asks, taking control of the conversation.

"When I was hanging out with our moms last night, they told me I need to shed a lot of pounds if I want to snag a man. According to them, being smart and successful is a turn-off, so I need to lure a man with a banging body, which I currently don't have," I say, unable to hide my ire.

Lennox bursts into laughter. "When will women stop taking advice from other women about what men think? Please tell me you didn't take anything they said seriously."

I glance down at my manicured nails and shrug. Usually, my weight isn't on my radar, but since last night, it's all I've been thinking about … amongst other things, like my best friend kissing me. My voice is low when I respond. "Well, I have been single for a long time."

Maxwell leans forward, his forearms resting on the table. "You don't need to change yourself for anyone, Jas. Your size doesn't matter," Maxwell says. "Sure, clinically, you're probably over—"

"Obese," I deadpan. "By every medical measure, I'm an obese woman."

"Nobody pays attention to those stupid measures to pick a date," Hendrix said, unable to hide his anger. "You're wonderful the way you are."

"And you're biased," I tell my brother.

"Listen to us," Maxwell agrees. "You're pretty with a nice figure that any man with eyes would find attractive, not repulsive. Your weight is not why you haven't been in a relationship for years."

"Well, according to our mothers, I haven't been in a relationship because I'm using Darren," I say, shame flooding me.

"They said that?" Lennox asks, scoffing. "Using him how?"

"As a relationship crutch." I shrug. "They think because we're so close, we use each other as a substitute for finding real love."

"That's stupid!" Hendrix barks. "Stop listening to their outdated opinions. They don't know anything."

Lennox adds, "Sounds like something Momma-Lisa would conjure up. You can't trust my mom."

Maxwell nods in agreement. "I'm sure our mom didn't make things any better, although she was probably nicer about it than Aunt Lisa."

I glance at Jaxon, who is noticeably quiet, staring at the pine needles bristling on the trees.

"Jaxon," I say, giving him my full attention. "What do you think?"

Jaxon is quiet for a long moment as we wait for his assessment. Finally, he says, "Probably some truth to that."

His words reverberate in my head, echoing like a chilling verdict.

And the kiss Darren and I shared at midnight reinforced the theory with cold finality. This was worse than I thought.

"That's what I was afraid of," I admit. "So, now I feel better about what I did."

"What did you do?" Hendrix asks.

"She decided we would have a unique New Year's resolution." Darren's voice booms from behind me, sending a flurry of butterflies scurrying across my skin. "Find love."

I avoid eye contact with my best friend, ignoring the excitement coursing through me.

After getting him to agree to the resolution last night, I wasted no time rushing back home instead of staying over like usual. The kiss that shall never be discussed again dictated I put distance between us.

"So, she's dragged you into this foolishness, too?" Lennox asks.

Darren eases onto the bench to my left. I glance over and relax as he smiles at me. It's Darren. My best friend. There isn't a hint of discomfort from what transpired last night. I don't need to be worried. We are still us.

"Got enough food on that plate?" I tease.

"If I'm going to deviate from my nutritional plan, I might as well go big, right?" Darren says, poking me with his fork. His plate overflows with ox tails artfully arranged on top of a heaping bed of collard greens. A bowl of black-eyed peas rests next to the plate. He points to my bowl of uneaten dessert. "Your ice cream is melting."

I glance at the bowl of peach cobbler and melted ice cream, then grab the spoon. Hendrix grips my neck, then rubs my back as I take a bite.

"So, what's the plan for finding love?" Lennox asks. "Please tell me you're not joining Wiley's dating app."

"No way. We're going to use our network of family and friends." I point to all of them. "The goal is to meet someone during the week so we can have a date on the weekend. We'll check in with each other to make sure we're not slacking … " I cast a side-eye at Darren, who seems enthralled by his collard greens.

"Now, here are my rules," Hendrix announces as if laying out a town-wide decree. "At least two days before the date, I need the guy's name and details of where you're going. I'll get that over to Jaxon to run a background check on him. If he clears it, then you can go on a date."

"What!" I screech, then look to Jaxon for support. I'm surprised to see him nodding his head.

Jaxon says, "It's a good plan. We'll all feel more comfortable checking these guys out first."

Lennox adds, "It's either that or I'll do surveillance to ensure you get to your date and back safely. What'll it be? Detective background check or personal police escort."

Darren bursts out laughing.

I hit him in the arm, then wince as my hand throbs from his rock-hard muscles. "Fine. Background check it is."

"And I have a great guy for your first date," Maxwell says with a wink.

Darren coughs, dropping his fork as he fumbles for a bottle of Elm beer. He takes a few swigs, then clears his throat. "You do?" His brows furrow in a disappointed scowl.

"What? Worried I'm going to find love before you?" I ask, wrapping my arms around him. He stares at me with a burning intensity, sending sparks of electricity down my spine. I drop my arms and put distance between us. Turning back to Maxwell, I ask, "Who is it?"

"Randall Jefferson, the substitute trigonometry teacher at the school. He's already passed background checks to work with kids," Maxwell nods at Jaxon, who looks pleased. "Since he's new to town, he's looking to make new friends."

"I'm game," I say, injecting extra enthusiasm into my voice.

"Great. I'll set it up and then text you his number," Maxwell says, looking too proud of himself.

I sneak another glance at Darren.

His face is a mask of cold steel.

CHAPTER 7

ARREN

"That's what she said?" Wiley asks, directing the hose toward the mid-sized sedan engulfed in billowing flames. Traffic on the county road leading into Kimbell stands still as drivers and passengers leave their vehicles to gawk at the scene.

I wipe the sweat from my brow and shift the hose in my grasp, giving him more slack. A cloud of white smoke surrounds us as the foam isolates gasoline from oxygen to prevent a dangerous explosion.

I can't see Wiley's face, and that's a good thing. The last thing I want is to see the pity in his eyes.

"That sums it up," I yell over the noise of the extinguisher hose. "Kiss was wonderful, but it doesn't change anything. We're friends," I say, swallowing the words past the lump in my throat. "There was no point in pouring my heart out to her after that."

I step forward, following Wiley toward the front of the car now that the flames near the back and the gas tank are doused. He's making quick work of the fire. Near the road, Luke Diamond and Nate Bell drew the lucky sticks and direct cars around cones at a safe distance past the blaze. Our A-Shift firefighter captain, Ronan O'Reilly, stands in the field behind the burning vehicle, comforting the driver and her three small kids. No doubt he's thinking about his twin boys as he calms them down.

The family looks shell-shocked as they watch their car and whatever belongings they left behind go up in flames. EMTs arrive on the scene and trudge across the grass to check them out for any injuries.

Wiley tugs on the hose, and I release more for him to drench the car's roof with the foam. He glances back at me and says, "Don't tell me you're giving up already."

His words sting. "There's nothing to fight for. Jasmine isn't interested in me romantically."

"You don't know that for sure," Wiley insists.

"Yes, I do," I mutter as the last of the flames dissipate. "Jasmine has it in her head we've been using our friendship as a relationship substitute minus the romance. So she's made a New Year's resolution for us to date other people so we can both find true love."

"Ouch, that sucks." Wiley steps back to inspect the scene. Satisfied all the embers are out, he drops the hose.

I retract it as we walk back to the fire truck. "Tell me about it."

"But still not a reason for you to give up so soon," Wiley says, piling the pressure on. "Do you believe Jasmine's theory? You think you're using her and not in love with her?"

"Of course not." My response comes quick and definitive.

Every part of me knows my love for Jasmine is one hundred percent real. She's not a substitute for anything or anyone. She's who I want. We're perfect for each other. Maybe if she wasn't so stubborn, she could allow herself to explore whether our friendship could evolve into something deeper and more intimate.

I continue, "But I'm not sure how to convince her, especially since she's come up with this bogus New Year's resolution for the two of us."

"What New Year's resolution?" Luke asks, walking over.

Behind him, Nate drags our second hose over. He sprays the area with water to cool down the road and the grassy field near the smoldering car. A standard part of our process to prevent hot spots from reigniting.

"Jasmine and Darren are going to find their one true love this year," Wiley says.

"Not a bad idea," Luke says, rubbing his jaw. "When was the last time you were in a serious relationship, Darren?"

"Cassidy, right?" Nate asks, then glances over at me. "When was that? Five years ago?"

I nod, ignoring the guilt triggered by memories of my ex.

"Whoa, that's a long time," Luke laughs. "Well, it's about time for all of us to follow Ronan and Wiley down Love Lane. I'm sick of them being the only blissfully happy ones in the firehouse."

"Tell me about it. If I have to listen to one more call between Wiley and Zaire debating who loves each other more, I think I'll gag," I say as Wiley tosses his gloves at my head. I duck as they land on the road.

"Ronan's no better now that he and Mya have set a wedding date. Our calendar is filling up with pre-wedding activities over the next few months," Luke adds.

Nate says, "That may be a good way to meet someone, Darren."

"Speak for yourself," I counter. I have no plans to go out on dates with anyone. I'll do enough to give the appearance I'm dating, but there's no point in me wasting another woman's time when my heart belongs to my best friend.

"So, will you and Jasmine help each other find dates?" Luke asks, his green eyes dancing with interest.

I frown.

"I wouldn't mind seeing what could spark between me and the good doctor," Luke says, nodding as if the idea is starting to resonate with him.

My hands clench into fists at my side. "You and Jasmine aren't compatible."

"Why not? I'm a good guy," Luke says.

I have to shut this down. Now. "I'm not letting you date Jasmine, so put that out of your mind."

"Shouldn't she decide if we date?" Luke presses.

I blurt out, "No."

There must have been something in my tone that causes Luke to recoil visibly.

Nate unexpectedly comes to my rescue. "You know Darren isn't going to let his best friend date any of us. That would be … awkward. Just as bad as if you tried to date my sister, Willow."

Luke grudgingly agrees, then says, "Well, let me help you find your first date. I have it on good authority Mirielle Rodriguez has been interested in you for a while."

"And by good authority, do you mean gossip from Blossom Thomas?" I ask, surprised by Luke's suggestion. Luke, Mirielle, and Blossom have all been members of the board of my not-for-profit organization for years. In all that time, Mirielle has never personally shown any interest in me. At least not that I've noticed. And in all honesty, I've been too wrapped up in Jasmine to care whether any other woman was interested.

Luke crosses his arms over his chest. "I won't reveal my source. But I do think you and Mirielle could hit it off. Think about it."

"Yeah, I might do that," I say, but I have no intention of dating anyone but Jasmine. I need to figure out how to change her mind about this relationship crutch theory.

CHAPTER 8

J ASMINE

MYA GULPS HER ORANGE JUICE, PROBABLY TO HIDE HER amusement at my New Year's Eve story, then says, "And what did you do after that?"

"Proved their point by going to Darren's house to watch the New Year celebrations on his gigantic movie screen with a pint of ice cream," I say, running my hands through my hair. "He always keeps my favorites stocked. I needed culinary comfort."

"When did ice cream fall into the culinary category?" Mya laughs.

"Stop it. I'm having a mid-life crisis here," I say, shaking my finger at her. My pancakes sit virtually untouched. I've been talking nonstop since Mya showed up with the twins at Gwen's Country Cafe. Declan and Finnegan are building a fort out of Legos at a kid-sized table. Their distraction allowed me to catch Mya up on my dumpster fire of a non-existent love life.

"Sorry, girl. So, it makes sense to me you'd want to talk to Darren about your mom's theory. What did he say?"

I grab one of Mya's biscuits, pinch off tiny pieces, and then throw them in the syrup, drowning my pancakes. "I didn't tell him. At least not right away. He showed up at his house seconds before midnight and kissed me!"

The spray of orange juice splatters across my face, and I almost gag.

"Did you spit on me?" I yell, reaching for my napkin. "Mya, that's gross." I rub the napkin across my face, then go into my bag for hand sanitizer to slather on my skin. "If I get sick from your germs, I'm ending our friendship."

"He kissed you?" Mya's voice hits a higher octave.

Before I can answer, Declan runs over to me and tugs on my arm. "Dr. Jasmine, can you check my head and make sure I didn't crack it open again." He looks worried.

The interruption couldn't have come at a better time.

I can't believe I let it slip to Mya that Darren kissed me. What was I thinking? I kept that part out of the story when I told it to Hendrix and my cousins, yet it toppled out of my mouth so easily with Mya.

"Well, of course, I can. Cracked heads are my specialty," I say, eliciting a laugh from Finnegan. Declan turns to glare at his brother. I ask, "What happened? Did you fall?"

Declan shakes his head.

"Did your brother hit you with a toy?"

Declan shakes his head.

Finnegan frowns. "Of course not. I didn't touch him. He's worried that his head isn't fixed from his fall. I check every morning to make sure it's not bleeding."

"Every morning?" I glance at Mya, whose expression is a mask of concern. Finnegan nods proudly.

Leaning over, I grab Declan by the waist and sit him on my lap. "Do you know why we let you leave the hospital after you fell off that statue?"

Declan nods. "Because the doctors wrapped my head like a mummy to make it stop bleeding."

"And?" I prompt.

A confused scowl crosses his face.

"Why did your head stop bleeding?" I ask.

Finnegan comes closer, leaning over the table as if he's also keenly interested in the answer.

Declan shrugs.

"The bleeding stopped because we sewed up the crack in your head like closing a zipper," I say, then run my fingers on the scar on the back of his head, mimicking the motion.

Declan laughs, wiggling on my lap as he grabs my hand.

"Do your pants come unzipped on their own after you zip them up in the morning?"

"No!" Declan and Finnegan say in unison. Both boys check their flys to be sure.

"Right. Your head isn't going to come unzipped, either, unless you do something to it," I explain.

Finnegan looks at me with wide eyes, then asks, "Like falling down on his head again."

"That's right," I say, then give the boy a high-five.

"I'm really careful now, Dr. Jasmine. I'm not jumping from statues anymore. I promise," Declan says, then crosses his heart.

"So you don't have to worry about your head cracking back open. Got it."

"Got it," Declan says, then wraps his hands around my neck in a tight hug. His sticky, syrup-covered fingers move along my neck, and I resist cringing.

Mya clears her throat. "Alright, go finish your breakfast. We have a long drive to the Houston Zoo, and I'm not stopping for any snacks."

"Okay!" The boys say. Declan jumps off my lap. Finnegan grabs his hand, and they skip back to the table near the kitchen, cluttered with Legos and the half-eaten plate of silver dollar pancakes.

As soon as the boys are out of earshot, I say, "Does Connor know about this?"

"He's still out of town working with Doctors Without Borders. I don't think Ronan has had a chance to reach him yet."

I lean forward, lowering my voice. "Tell Connor what's been happening when he gets back. He'll know what to do." One of the best things for Ronan's twin whirling dervishes is having an uncle who's a pediatrician.

"You think Declan has PTSD or something."

I raise my eyebrow. "How long has Finnegan been checking his head every morning?"

"It's not only Finnegan. He makes me and Ronan do it, too. As much as Declan has returned to his old self, we still see changes like that in him. I'm so worried."

"Girl, take that boy to a child psychologist so he can work out his fears about what happened. The last thing you want is him being afraid to take chances in the future because of one mistake he made at five years old."

"You're right. I'll talk to Ronan about it tonight," Mya says, then leans back in her chair. "Now, back to the kiss between you and Darren. How was it?"

I roll my eyes.

Mya is a good friend, but I have no problem withholding this information from her. The last thing I want to admit is that the kiss blew my socks off. But what did I expect? I haven't kissed a man in years. I haven't dated in years. Of course, the first kiss I've gotten in all that time will feel monumental.

And Darren's lips on mine were like pure heaven.

I say, "Ridiculous. There's a reason best friends shouldn't kiss each other. It's weird."

A look settles on Mya's face that I can't read.

Before she can probe for more details about the kiss, I say, "I told him the theory, and we agreed we will do whatever it takes to find real love in the new year. That means going on dates weekly, making an effort, and not settling for substitutes."

Mya perks up. "Do you have a date for this week?"

"As a matter of fact, I do. My cousin, Maxwell, is setting me up with a substitute teacher working at Kimbell High School. Some guy named Randall."

"I know that guy." Mya's face scrunches into a cute frown. "He comes to my afternoon yoga in the park classes."

"What's wrong with him?"

"I'm not sure he's a good fit for you. He's boring," Mya says. "But I know someone else that would be much better." She whips her phone out of her purse, then taps the screen a few times before placing it on the center of the table.

I glance down at the picture of the man and almost forget to breathe.

Snatching the phone, I say, "Ohmigoodness, who is this magnificent specimen." My mouth drops open as I take in his flawless caramel skin and the alluring light green eyes staring back at me. His face is defined and decidedly masculine, with a chiseled square jaw and a prominent nose. Waves of close-cropped black hair add a sexy look to his already stunning face.

"That is Troy Renault. He used to work for Kincaid Real Estate with Zaire but then got poached by Jimbo Barnes to be the COO of TimberLuxe," Mya says, her eyes dancing. "I am completely in love with Ronan, but I can't deny this man is gorgeous! I snapped this picture of him when he was at my cross fit class last week. Going to use it on my website to lure more clients."

"This man is not going to want to date me." I drop the phone and push it across the table toward her.

"Why not?"

"Look at him and look at me," I say, waving a hand over my excessively curvy body. "He's ripped, and I'm allergic to working out if you can't tell. Hot boys don't date fat girls."

Mya looks at me like I've lost my mind. "Jasmine, you're beautiful. Any guy can see that. The days of men wanting stick skinny women are in the past. Men love women in a variety of shapes and sizes."

"That's the lie they tell fat girls. I can get a guy that looks like Randall. One that looks like Troy ... that ain't happening."

And one that looks like Darren is definitely not happening.

I freeze.

Where did that thought come from?

I cannot allow myself to think about my best friend that way. It's a recipe for disaster and what my mom and aunts warned me about.

"Is that a challenge, Dr. Jones?" Mya asks, crossing her tattooed muscular arms across her chest.

"Girl, please." I shake my head.

"I'm going to prove you wrong. Troy is a successful, intelligent, and handsome man who needs an equally successful, intelligent, beautiful woman. That's you," Mya says, rubbing her hands together. "I love playing matchmaker. At my old gym in Round Rock, I helped six couples get together. I'm going to help you and Troy get together, too."

CHAPTER 9

D ARREN

I STARE AT THE FOUR FACES SITTING AROUND THE conference room table: Blossom, oldest daughter of Mrs. Williamson, the town's planner of community events, Mirielle, a rodeo barrel racer and local sensation, Idris Gibson, the ranch hand manager for the Baker Farm owned by the Baker brothers, and Luke, my good friend and fellow firefighter. Idris and Blossom had been instrumental in pushing me to narrow the priorities of my foundation toward special needs youth and sports since both were raising sons with developmental disabilities. Luke jumped on board because his do-good personality couldn't resist. And Mirielle ... I'm not sure what drew her to the foundation, but her connections with the media have been invaluable.

The monthly board meeting for my charitable foundation is usually lively, with lots of banter. But today, they avoid eye contact with me.

The mood is decidedly somber.

Not much different from the storm that brews inside of me.

When I agreed to Jasmine's New Year's resolution idea, I thought I'd have plenty of time to change her mind. She hasn't been on a date in years. Why would she be able to quickly find a date now?

That is until Maxwell opened his big mouth and set her up on a date with some nerdy teacher. I try to tell myself there's no way Jasmine will fall for that guy. But even if she doesn't, there will be more guys. More dates. And she will find someone eventually because she thinks we're using each other to avoid a relationship. I don't know how to get her to see the truth—that we're perfect for each other.

Trying to push Jasmine on the topic will make her double down on her mom's theory. My best bet is to play along for a while. Once she sees the dating pool is full of frogs and not princes, maybe she'll be open to giving me a shot.

Idris clears his throat and glances over at Mirielle. "Why don't you cover the good news first?"

I glare at him. Idris avoids confrontation like the plague, which tells me whatever they are keeping from me is worse than I can imagine. I give a quick look at Luke, who looks confused. He's not in on the bad news, either.

"That's fine with me." I lean back in the leather chair and turn to face Mirielle.

She gives me a hint of a sexy smile, batting her eyelashes as she holds my gaze for a few seconds too many. Well, I guess Luke was right. Mirielle is borderline flirting with me as she grabs her notebook from the table, dragging out her news with dramatic flair. I smile despite myself. She's attractive with sparkling hazel eyes and chestnut brown wavy tresses. If my heart was open to finding someone, she would be on my shortlist.

Mirielle pumps her fists in the air. I jump from her abrupt movement as she says with bubbly excitement, "We're going to be featured in Texas Monthly magazine!"

Luke, Idris, and Blossom clap and cheer.

"We are?" I perk up.

"They want to do a feature on me for the rodeo. I made it a condition of giving them an exclusive interview." Mirielle winks at me. "You're welcome." She reaches into her oversized luxury purse and passes out stapled papers to each of us. "Here's the article they'll run two months from now. It's pretty glowing. The journalist interviewed Idris and a few of the kids. It's a feel-good story and great exposure."

"This is the kind of publicity we need to get people to focus on the good we're doing with my foundation," I say, reaching for the papers. I skim the article and let out a whistle, happy the journalist didn't sneak in a jab about my past. There's no mention of the unexpected end of my football career or the scandal that erupted as I recovered from the injury. Mirielle undoubtedly had a hand in ensuring the article focused on the kids and not me. "I appreciate this, Mirielle."

"You can thank me by taking me out to dinner tonight," Mirielle says, twirling a strand of hair around her finger. The sassy, flirty tone in her voice is undeniable.

I hesitate for a long moment.

Luke kicks my shin under the table.

Groaning, I force myself to respond. "Yeah, I can do that," I say, feeling hot under the collar.

Luke's scowl is replaced with a smug, pleased look as he glances back and forth between me and Mirielle.

"Great." Mirielle beams.

"The good news is done. What's the bad?" I ask, anxious to know what we're up against.

Idris's face goes ashen. He shifts in his seat, then takes a deep breath. "Child Protective Services notified us this morning that they'll be performing a surprise inspection of our football practice sessions with the kids."

"What? Why?" I ask.

Idris says, "They've received some calls. They said a lot of calls, actually."

"What kind of calls?" I demand.

"People concerned about the kids," Idris says.

"You're the coach. You run a tight ship. All the volunteers are certified by USA Football. Our program passed all their stringent rules and was declared safe. We aren't putting the kids in danger."

"That's not the focus of most of the calls." Idris swipes a hand along his hairline, which is beaded with sweat.

I sink back in my chair, realization hitting me like a sledgehammer. "What is the focus of the calls?" My voice is low and strained as I fight the surge of anger.

"You know, with your past and everything. People kind of want to make sure the kids aren't exposed to an unsafe environment."

Luke leans forward. "What were the complaints?"

"Well ..." Idris's voice trails off.

Blossom fills me in. "Concerns about the sexual assault charges filed against you a few years ago—"

"The cops never charged me. There was no evidence to support her claims because I didn't do it," I say, my voice rising.

Blossom shrugs, then adds, "Also, a few of them referenced the women you've been linked to since then—internet models, many who earn their living on sites where men pay to see them strip online. They're concerned by who the kids might be exposed to because of your romantic relationships."

"I didn't date any of those women. I don't know them. They were trying to capitalize off Pippa's lies against me," I insist.

Since I moved back to Kimbell, every woman I've gone out with was set up by my agent for public relations purposes. Each woman knew the deal, took the obligatory photos, and expected nothing more than mutual positive exposure in return. None of them had ever been on any stripper sites.

"Who Darren chooses to date is irrelevant. He's not bringing women around to the practices or letting them engage with the kids," Luke says.

"I think that's what CPS wants to confirm," says Blossom.

I can't deny I made boneheaded decisions after discovering I'd never play football again. Kissing Pippa, then pushing her away when she wanted more, is at the top of that list. Lashing out at Cassidy for not believing I didn't cheat on her is a close second. But I never imagined I'd still be haunted by that time in my life five years later. It's like people won't let me move on from my past.

"Are any of the complaints coming from parents of our kids?" I ask, flummoxed by the double-whammy of allegations when all we've done is put the kids first.

Blossom says, "I talked to each of the parents. None of them complained. They all thought the allegations were unfounded."

"You have the full support of the parents and the board." Mirielle reaches over and grabs my hand. Her fingers lace between mine and squeeze gently. "Let CPS do their investigation. I can help you brainstorm a PR strategy to combat this negative publicity ... when you pick me up for dinner tonight."

CHAPTER 10

ARREN

My heart lurches in my chest as Jasmine walks out of her bathroom. Her curvaceous hourglass figure is on full display in skinny jeans that hug her hips, amplifying her sexiness to new levels. I regret hanging out with her before her date with the nerdy teacher.

Although, I won't lie and say I'm not pleased she's acting more like she's going to have a root canal than going on a date with a man she's interested in.

"What do you think of this shirt?" Jasmine asks, turning from one side to the other. "I have to make sure I suck in my belly if he's looking, but I think the ruching is slimming, don't you?"

"What is ruching?" I lick my lips, loving how stunning she is in the shirt with a plunging V-neck. I flip over onto my side to get a better look at her. I've been lounging on her bed, with my favorite pillows balled up under my head as she fluttered around the apartment, getting ready for her date over the past hour.

"You know, this ..." she says, grabbing at the fabric gathered together in a ripple-like effect. "It's supposed to mask all the bad parts of your body."

"You don't have any bad parts of your body."

Jasmine raises an eyebrow, then rolls her eyes. "You're only saying that because you're my best friend. And I'm not going to lie. I appreciate the confidence boost."

"You nervous?"

"Yeah. I want to get it over with. I couldn't eat today. Can you believe that? When I get to dinner, I hope my stomach isn't growling like an angry bear." She throws her hands in the air, then sits on the bed beside me.

I resist the urge to wrap my arms around her and snuggle my face into that soft spot along her neck. I didn't mention the drama with CPS to her, even though it's still weighing heavily on my mind. Being around Jas is enough to lift my spirits.

"Did you send Lennox the details of your date?" I ask, hoping she'd share them with me. Not that I'm planning to stalk out my competition or anything.

"Do you know he showed up at the hospital while I was in the middle of the teaching rounds with the residents and interns? Now all of them know my business. They bugged me all day about the date. It was horrible."

"And did nothing to temper your anxiety." I brush my finger along the side of her face. Her deep brown skin is flawless. She barely wears any makeup because she doesn't need it.

"Nope," she says, then narrows her eyes at me. She lowers her voice as her hand rests on my abs. "Are you alright?"

"What?" I laugh. "Why are you asking me that?"

"You look pensive. Like you've had a crappy day. I've been going on and on about this date and didn't stop to ask why you came by."

"Oh, I need an excuse to visit my best friend now? Is that what it will be like when we're dating other people?"

"Things will change, but nothing is changing right now. You have a key to my apartment. You can come here anytime you need to, so tell me why you stopped by. I know it wasn't to watch me get ready."

Can I hate and love that she's so perceptive about me? The board meeting has me tied in knots. Unfounded complaints from townsfolk to CPS could deprive children with special needs of a rewarding experience. Not that they care about the kids. If they did, they would volunteer for themselves and see the good we're doing firsthand.

Part of me wants to ask her to cancel her date and commiserate in misery with me, watching our favorite reality shows, but I stop myself.

Jasmine frowns, then rises from the bed.

I miss the warmth of her touch and reach for her, but she slips away from my grasp.

I ask, "Where are you going?"

"You'll see," she says, then disappears into the hallway. Minutes later, she returns with a navy cashmere weighted blanket, a set of candles, and a bottle of Elm beer.

A smile spreads across my face.

"If this doesn't get you to talk, I don't know what will," Jasmine says, placing the lavender candles on the bedside table. She turns and wraps the weighted blanket over me, tucking the sides against my body to wrap me in a cozy cocoon. She hands me the beer, then lights the candles. The relaxing scent permeates the air. My eyes never leave her as she walks around the bed and lies beside me.

Only inches separate us, and I want nothing more than to kiss her again. As well as she knows me, I don't understand how she could think this connection we have is a substitute for the real thing.

No one can make me feel like she does.

"What happened today?" Jasmine asks, resting her head against the pillow as she stares at me with radiant brown eyes. Her look is like a magnet pulling me into her orbit. I'm useless to resist her.

"Board meeting for the foundation," I say. "Got some upsetting news, but in the grand scheme of things, it's nothing we can't handle. I'm not going to bore you with the details. You should be focused on your date."

"I will always make time for you, Darren. What was the upsetting news?"

Selfishly, I fill her in on the surprise CPS investigation of our practice sessions. I love how Jasmine gets angrier and angrier as I tell her the whole story. Everything I felt today, I see reflected in her reaction. But she doesn't interrupt me. She just listens. It's one of the things I love about her. The way she cares enough to give her undivided attention to matters important to her, whether that's her patients, her cousins, her brother, or ... me.

"We have no clue when they'll show up or what their findings will be. I hope they don't try to shut the youth football league down before it can get traction. The kids enjoy playing together. It will be so much better when they have other teams to compete against."

"No one is going to stop you from helping those kids, Darren," Jasmine says, then rolls off the bed. "This whole town would band together to help meet any need you have. Find out what needs to be fixed, and we'll get it done."

"We?" I ask.

"You know you need me."

"Always."

Jasmine winks. "I gotta go. Will you be here when I get back?"

I hate that she's leaving to go out with another man. I'm used to Jas spending all her free time with me, not going out on dates with nerdy teachers.

"I'm not budging," I announce, calculating how I can sneak off and do a brief date with Mireille, then get back to Jasmine's apartment before she's home from her date. Telling my best friend how I got railroaded into taking Mirielle to dinner is not an option.

"I'll see you later tonight." She grabs her purse from the bedside table. "Wish me luck."

I wave and smile as she closes the door.

No part of me wants this date to go well.

Jasmine can't get close to any man.

Not before I come up with a plan to convince her to give a relationship with me a chance.

CHAPTER 11

J ASMINE

"WAIT! WHAT ARE YOU DOING?" RANDALL ASKS. HE STARES at the half-torn packet of artificial sweetener in my hand.

I suppress my desired response and take a deep breath. This date is different from what I expected. After luring me with the promise of smoky, delicious barbecue from Baker Bros, Randall changed his mind and suggested we go to a quieter Italian restaurant he loves. Italian is my favorite, which I'm sure Maxwell told him. But my cousin failed to mention to my date that there's only one Italian restaurant in Lasso County I abhor—Spaghetti Western.

The log cabin-style restaurant was built on a concept that is more kitschy than classy. Swinging saloon-style doors lead to the interior, and Italian operas remixed and sung by country karaoke singers blare from a jukebox in the corner.

Faded cowboy murals adorn the walls. Red and white checkered plastic cloths cover the tables. A broken chandelier dangles above a scuffed wooden bar. The outdoor seating area is only slightly better, with iron bistro tables.

The food is mediocre at best. Bad chili passing as tomato sauce. Pasta that sticks together. Hard breadsticks. No wine list. Only beer.

So, why am I sitting in said restaurant now pretending to be excited by what I know will be the worst dinner of my life? Well, I promised myself I would put my best foot forward, which means stifling my usually vocal critic … at least on the first date. I know I can come off as disagreeable and opinionated, so I'm trying to show Randall there is more to Dr. Jasmine Jones than the rumors I'm sure he's heard.

I respond, "They don't have sweet tea here, so I'm going to make it myself." I point to the tall glass of unsweetened iced tea beside my plate.

"As a health professional, you should know better."

"Excuse me?" My neck tenses.

Randall snatches the artificial sweetener packet from my hand and places a packet of real sugar in my palm. "That fake stuff causes cancer. If we're going to be in a relationship, I want you to be around to grow old with me."

I turn my palm over and let the sugar packet fall onto the table.

"Let's not get ahead of ourselves." I force a smile on my face. "As for the misconception that artificial sweeteners cause serious health concerns, numerous studies over the past few decades have proven that to be false. The FDA and dozens of other international health organizations have tested and concluded they are safe for the general population."

Randall shakes his head at me as if I'm playing Russian roulette with my life. Reaching for the container of sweeteners, I grab four of my favorite kind and dump them into the iced tea.

If I weren't insulted, I'd giggle at the look of horror on Randall's face. I need to get the date back on track. Randall had already shown his interest in me, asking tons of questions about why I was inspired to become a doctor as he drove us to the restaurant. It made his insistence to be chivalrous more palatable than feeling trapped in his car for the twenty-minute drive. Now it was my turn to give an effort.

"So, tell me what drew you to becoming a math teacher." I take a sip of my artificially sweetened tea.

"Trigonometry."

"That's a form of math."

"It's a higher-level branch."

"But still math."

Randall grips his tumbler filled with vodka neat. His third so far, downs it, then says, "Well, it started with my passion for sailing and trying to understand how to navigate to different locations. I got obsessed with figuring out the distance between points and angles to know where to sail ..." He looks up at the sky as a commercial airliner sails overhead. A frown creases his eyebrows as he fumbles in his pocket.

I glance up at the plane, then back at Randall. "That was noisy. So did you start to use trigonometry to navigate to locations for sailing?"

Randall doesn't respond. His attention is entirely focused on a small plastic spray bottle. He turns it around a few times in his hand, then begins to spray the liquid over his face, neck, and hands.

"What are you doing?" I try to keep my tone pleasant. It's January, and while the temperature is on the chilly side, it's still relatively mild. There's no need for sunscreen or bug spray as we sit on the outdoor patio behind the restaurant.

"Protecting myself from the chemtrails," Randall says, then offers the spray bottle to me.

I decline.

"Some friends of mine created this antidote that counteracts the effects. You know that trail of condensation plumes is laced with chemical agents designed to limit our life spans." Randall continues, "It's one of the reasons diseases are still so rampant in the world."

"Really?" I say. My mind is reeling. Randall is an undercover medical conspiracy theorist. Of course, I've heard about these bogus claims, but I had never met anyone who believed them.

Randall nods his head enthusiastically. "And you know the main reason."

"I do?"

"Big Pharma." Randall leans his elbows on the table, closing the distance between us. "How do you do it? Stay committed to being a health professional, knowing you're wasting your life. You could be doing something more worthy."

"More worthy than saving lives every week?" I ask, no longer amused.

"There isn't a need to save lives because the pharmaceutical companies have cures for all diseases. They create diseases in a lab. Lace the condensation in planes with them so we keep getting sick, then rake in the profits. Of course, they don't withhold the cures from themselves and their families, but the rest of us suffer."

The waitress interrupts us, thankfully.

"Sorry, it'll be a few more minutes before your food arrives. Here's another vodka neat for you, sir." She hands the glass to Randall. He downs the liquor, then hands the glass back, requesting another.

The waitress looks at me confused, and asks, "Can I get you anything while you wait?"

"No, I'm ... good." I force the words out.

"Glad you are, but I need to go to the little boys' room. Nothing like vodka to make me have to piss like Seabiscuit."

Randall bolts from his seat and leaves me alone with the waitress.

We stare at each other and say in unison, "Seabiscuit?"

I laugh, and she gives me a warm smile.

"First date?" She asks.

"And last."

CHAPTER 12

J ASMINE

I YANK MY PHONE FROM MY PURSE AND TEXT FRANTICALLY.

JASMINE

SOS!!! Help!!! Date is horrible. The guy is a conspiracy kook.

DARREN

Nooooooo

I'm trapped.

Just come home. I'll order takeout for us.

I can't.

Why?

> I was stupid

Ha. Since when?

> Since I went along with Randall's stupid plan to leave Baker Bros and come to Spaghetti Western

You hate that place

> I know! And he insisted I ride with him and leave my car back in downtown Kimbell

I stare at my phone, waiting for the bubbles to start. Nothing.

> JASMINE
>
> I'm stuck

A few more seconds pass.

> JASMINE
>
> Are you going to help me?

Almost a minute passes, and my panic rises. Finally, I get my best friend's response.

DARREN

omw

Knowing the misery will end soon soothes my frayed nerves. I only suffered through five minutes of Randall's rant on the dangers of cell phone radiation when he returned from the restroom.

Darren must have driven a hundred miles an hour to get here so fast from my apartment. The moment he walks onto the deck, the atmosphere shifts, drawing all the attention toward him.

Why in the world did my heart do a flip, then a flop?

He's dressed in a classy navy sport coat, ivory turtleneck, and tan trousers. The picture of sporty elegance, doused with enough sex

63

appeal to set the restaurant on fire. I mean, Darren has always been a handsome man. Incredibly handsome. I'd be blind not to notice.

It just has never affected me like this before.

What's wrong with me?

Evelyn's accusation haunts me.

This is her fault.

Darren's piercing blue eyes flicker with a hint of playful mischief as his gaze finds mine. Smiling, he strides confidently toward my table.

I sit up straighter, wondering what he will do to help me escape Randall.

"Hey babe, sorry I'm late," Darren says.

Babe?

I glance up at him with a raised eyebrow, and that's when it happens.

His face lowers to mine, and his lips crash against my mouth. My mind goes blank, unable to comprehend what's happening.

Darren is kissing me.

Not just any kiss.

A kiss that sends fireworks exploding within me.

His hand gently strokes my neck as he deepens the kiss, taking me down a wonderful path of ecstasy. My heart pounds so hard in my chest I'm afraid it might burst.

Before I realize what's happening, I'm kissing him back.

Really kissing him.

And enjoying every minute of it.

This is bad.

Really bad.

And then, as quickly as it began, it's over.

I look at Darren, dazed, as he pulls back. He gives me a sly wink, grabs a chair from a nearby table, and sits between Randall and me.

"You're Randall, right?" Darren asks, extending a hand toward my date.

Randall's mouth gapes open as he looks from Darren to me and back to Darren. "What? I don't understand." He turns to me. "Are you married?"

"Not married yet," Darren says, then rubs my shoulder. "We wanted to find our third first."

"Your third?" Randall looks confused.

"It took us a while to decide whether our throuple should be two women and me or two men and Jas. I guess you can tell who won," Darren says, then looks at me. "He's a good choice. I think it'll work."

"No!" Randall says, knocking his chair over as he stands. "I'm not into that kind of thing. If I had known, I never would've agreed to this date."

"Try to be open-minded," Darren insists, barely containing his laughter.

I'm stunned at what is happening in front of me.

Randall glowers as he ignores Darren. "I'm sure your boyfriend can drive you home. I'm out of here."

And with that, Randall is gone.

I pick up my napkin and slap Darren across the head. He flinches, then bursts into laughter.

"What was that?" I yell at him.

"A surefire way to get rid of your bad date," Darren chuckles softly, his blue pools twinkling. "You're welcome." He puts a forkful of damp, wilted salad into his mouth, frowns, and looks around for a napkin.

I hand him mine and laugh as he uses it to remove the salad from his mouth. When I have his attention, I say, "I think you could've come up with a plan that didn't involve kissing me again."

"It was more fun that way. I love to see you flustered."

"What if it had backfired? What if Randall was a crazy conspiracy kook who was into throuples? What would you have done then?"

Darren shrugs, then says, "I had a backup plan."

"Which was?"

"I'm not telling you. I may need to pull it out to rescue you from another bad date."

I sigh heavily. "I hope not. This was horrible."

"And it's over now." Darren turns to me with a stern look. "But we need to get one thing straight."

I return his stare, unperturbed by his seriousness. Here comes the lecture.

He takes my hands in his. "Don't ever change yourself to attract a man. You don't need to do that."

"I didn't—"

"Really? You're at a restaurant you hate. And you left your car downtown instead of driving yourself. That doesn't sound like my Jasmine."

"Okay, maybe I subdued myself." I pull away and slump back into the chair. "I'm not the easiest person to get along with. I know that. You know that. The whole town of Kimbell knows that."

"You still have close friends and family who love you just as you are. We don't ask you to change, not that you'd ever consider changing for us anyway."

I snort a laugh, then cover my mouth.

Darren continues, "You want a man who accepts all of you. The hard exterior and the gooey interior."

"Is that your way of calling me fat?"

"I'm talking about your personality, Jas. You're beautiful, even if you don't believe me."

"I have a cute face."

His eyes narrow. "You're sexy, too."

"Stop it."

"Look, don't hide your real self from any man," Darren warns.

"My real self hasn't attracted a man in a long time."

"Past experience isn't a reliable predictor of the future when it comes to matters of the heart. Trust me, I should know."

His words touch me. I wonder what ex from his past may have triggered the slight melancholy in his tone. Darren has had some serious relationships before. But only one woman I thought he'd propose to—Cassidy. But Pippa's accusation against him killed any future the two of them could have.

Cassidy didn't believe Darren when he told her what went down between him and Pippa.

But I believed him. I knew Darren would never force himself on any woman. I wasted no time telling Darren and Cassidy how stupid it was that she didn't believe in the man she claimed to love. I'm not sure if Darren felt the same way or if my vehement response to her lack of trust influenced him. Either way, he ended their relationship within hours of my rant. I've felt guilty for my part in their breakup ever since.

"Anyway," Darren says, playfully punching me in the arm. "Now that you're actively back on the dating scene, things will be different. Trust me."

"Fine," I say, crossing my arms over my chest. "Can we leave now?"

"Yep," Darren says, then adds, "And I already ordered Baker Bros to-go. We'll pick it up on the way back to my place."

"Darren," I say, flinging my arms around his neck and hugging him tight. "You are the best best friend."

CHAPTER 13

ARREN

SOFT HANDS COVER MY EYES, BUT THEY AREN'T THE HANDS I've been dreaming about. The kiss with Jasmine has been on auto-play in my mind since leaving her house last night. Not that the kiss triggered anything different between us ... on the surface. She still insists we are best friends and can't use each other as a substitute for a real relationship. Yet, the kiss at Spaghetti Western was decidedly different from our kiss on New Year's Eve.

The first time, I kissed her. Last night, we kissed each other.

That monumental shift and her bad date with "the conspiracy kook" teacher give me renewed hope and a brand new plan.

One I will share with Wiley the minute I can get disengaged from Mirielle. I lower the sixty-pound dumbbells to the floor, then gently remove her hands from my face.

Wiley pretends he's not watching through the mirror, but I see his eyes on us. Wrapping my hands around Mirielle's wrists, I maneuver her until she's standing in front of me. Her smile is salacious, as if she wants to devour me on the spot. That's not happening. Releasing her from my grasp, I say, "Sorry about last night."

"You owe me a raincheck," Mirielle says with a sexy pout.

Wiley walks over and puts the sixty-pound dumbbells on the rack. Then rolls a barbell with two hundred twenty-five pounds of plates toward me. I'm not fooled. He's inching closer to eavesdrop on my conversation.

Mirielle spins around and faces Wiley. "Are you the friend that made Darren ditch me for dinner last night?"

Wiley frowns. "No, I was—"

I clear my throat loudly and glare at him.

Wiley rakes a hand through his hair, sending it spiking in different directions, then says, "Fine. I'll come clean. I was the friend. But I swear it was important ... right, Darren?"

"Very important. You know, Wiley has celiac disease, and he had a little accident."

Wiley's glare is enough to burn a hole in my head. I shouldn't provoke him when he's doing me a favor. The last thing I need is for Jasmine to find out I ditched dinner with Mirielle to rescue her from the conspiracy kook. She wouldn't like that and might push me away to emphasize we shouldn't be as close as we are.

Wiley says, "I'm gluten sensitive, and I called my good buddy here to drive me home after accidentally eating something I shouldn't have."

"Well, we all know what a great guy Darren is," Mirielle says, rubbing my shoulder.

"So, you were supposed to be on a date last night?" Wiley probes.

Mirielle laughs. "Not a date. I got an article in Texas Monthly about Darren's foundation, and he was taking me to dinner as a thank you."

Wiley nods, then gives me a sly look.

"It's a great article." I maneuver past Mirielle to grip the barbell. Luckily she gets the hint.

"One deserving of a thank you dinner. I'm serious about that raincheck. I'll text you," she says, then saunters away.

"That chick is definitely into you," Wiley says, walking to the opposite end of the bench to spot me.

"Tell me about it. Luke says it's been obvious for a while. I never noticed."

"Because you stopped being able to see any woman as relationship material whose name doesn't begin with Dr. Jasmine and end with Jones.

"Say it louder so the whole gym can hear," I say, then abandon the barbell to face Wiley. "But I have a new plan that might change her mind. Make her more open to considering a relationship with me."

"I take it she was the best friend that sent you the SOS."

"Right. Her date was a disaster and getting worse by the minute, so she texted me for a rescue. I didn't tell her I was going to meet Mirielle at Thorn for dinner. If she knew that, she wouldn't have texted me at all."

"What did you do to help her ditch the guy?"

"Kissed her."

Wiley's eyes grow wide as saucers as he covers his mouth.

"She enjoyed the kiss more this time. Then I told the dude we were looking for a third to add to our throuple."

"I'm your third! Why do you need some other guy?" Wiley asks.

"I'm not talking about friendship …" I say, letting my voice trail off as I hope he makes the connection.

"Oh. Oh!" Wiley says, then bursts into laughter.

"He went running for the door after that. I got to have Jasmine all to myself for the evening."

"Let me guess. Your new plan is to rescue her from a series of bad dates until she realizes you're the one she wants."

"Exactly. So, I need your help to find other guys she could date who would never interest her to make my plan work."

"I'm sure we can figure out something," Wiley says, and I can see his brain churning. "I like this plan, man."

He lifts a hand, and I give him a high-five.

Then I hear Jasmine's laughter.

The sound tickles my ears and causes my spirits to lift, but something is entirely wrong. Jasmine has self-diagnosed herself as allergic to working out. She refuses to step foot in a gym, no matter how often I've tried to coax her to come with me.

So, what is she doing at Chesterton's?

I turn, and it's like I've been sucker punched.

Jasmine is dressed in fitted shorts that cling to her thick thighs and barely cover her round bottom. Her tank top is a V-neck because she knows how that showcases her incredible chest. Her hair is piled high in a ponytail on top of her head. A thin sheen of sweat coats her skin, making her irresistible. I can't help staring at her. She's beyond gorgeous.

But the flirty look in her eyes toward another man has me about to gag. I can't hear the conversation, but her body language says everything. Her face is radiant, and her eyes have lit up like I've never seen them before. She's never looked at me like that.

The truth slams into me.

She's into this guy.

Standing, I move closer, unable to stop myself. Her laughter rings through the air again, and she reaches to stroke the guy's bulging bicep. My bicep is bigger than his, but she's never done that to me.

I absently reach for a dumbbell and do a few curls to hide the fact I'm spying on my best friend. Wiley is right behind me, mimicking my moves.

"That's Troy Renault," Wiley whispers.

"Who is that?"

"You remember the loser who used to work for Zaire? He had a thing for her and quit his job when she and I got together. Now he works for Jimbo Barnes's furniture manufacturing company."

I frown, not liking the sound of this or the scene playing out in front of me. There's no doubt Jasmine is attracted to the guy. Problem is, the feelings seem to be mutual. Troy has moved closer to her, his hand lingering on her hip. They look like a couple who finished working out together.

"Can you hear what they're saying?" Wiley asks, his voice louder.

"I can if you stop talking to me," I whisper back, then strain to hear the conversation.

Jasmine says, "I'm going to have some stern words for our friend, Mya." She tosses her towel over her shoulder and places her hands on her hips. Troy's gaze rakes down her body slowly before returning to her face. Jas continues, "How dare she invite us to try hot yoga, then bail and not show up!"

"Well, she left me in good hands. Happy to have experienced my first hot yoga class with you by my side," Troy says. "Hope it's not the last time I see you."

"I'm sure we can find an excuse to see each other again. One that doesn't involve us drinking gallons of water to rehydrate our bodies from that torture," she says.

Troy laughs and wraps an arm around her shoulder. "You working later?"

"Nope."

"Other plans?"

Jasmine shakes her head and giggles.

She giggles.

Jasmine does not giggle.

Troy says, "Well, you have some now. Dinner with me tonight at Thorn. How does eight o'clock sound?"

Jasmine gives him a smile that weakens my knees, then says, "Eight works."

I watch as she and Troy disappear down the hallway that leads to the locker rooms.

"Yeah, about that plan we discussed ... " Wiley says, then gives me a condescending pat on the back. "Not sure it's going to work anymore."

CHAPTER 14

J ASMINE

THE PUNGENT SMELL OF MOTOR OIL MIXED WITH RUBBER
and metal slaps me in the face. But nothing can bring down my high as
I walk on clouds through the rolled-up garage door of Jones Auto
Repair. The place is my brother's pride and joy. His redo after a series
of mistakes as a teenager landed him in prison for five years.

I walk close to the wall, careful not to trip over the car parts and
tools strewn about and run my hand along the line of chests filled with
every tool imaginable. Four cars are hoisted high above the concrete
floor on hydraulic lifts, while others left overnight for service
tomorrow are parked outside. It feels me with pride how Hendrix has
turned his life around.

A smile bursts on my face, and I clamp my hand over my mouth to
stop giggling. The stars are aligning for my brother and me. He has the

professional success I nailed years ago, and now I'm catching up to him in the relationship department.

All because of Troy Renault.

I squeal, then compose myself.

Pushing through the swinging plastic door at the far end of the garage, marked "Staff Only," and stained with oil smears, I follow the sound of voices echoing from the break room.

"Well, this is rare." I toss my purse onto the counter next to the microwave and fridge, then grab the empty chair between Maxwell and Lennox.

"Only because y'all have intense, crazy schedules," Maxwell says, gloating. Despite the Jones Family's propensity to choose careers serving and helping people, Maxwell is the only one of us who chose one with predictable hours and the entire summer off.

"What are y'all getting into tonight?" I ask, hoping they will pick up on the hint in my question.

"Y'all?" Lennox glares at me. "You're not sticking around?"

"Not tonight," I say and wiggle my eyebrows at him. He frowns back at me. "Ask me why."

Jaxon looks up from his bottle of Elm beer but doesn't say a word.

"Wait, where's my brother?" I ask, not wanting to start the story without him.

As if on cue, Hendrix comes from the bathroom dressed in dark blue mechanic's overall and one sleeve rolled above his elbow. Blood covers his forearm.

I roll my eyes and purse my lips. "What did you do?"

"Nothing my lil sis can't fix," Hendrix winks at me and flashes that gorgeous smile that makes the ladies swoon. He shoves his arm in my face.

I push it away. Hard.

"Owww," Hendrix yelps, grimacing.

"I'm off duty," I say, crossing my arms over my chest. "Don't you have a first aid kit or something?"

"I bandaged it up earlier, but it keeps bleeding," Hendrix says as red drops plop onto the plastic table at a disturbing rate. "Think I need stitches?" A hint of worry flashes over his face. My brother hates needles. I'd have to knock him out cold to stitch him up. Luckily, a quick glance at the wound, and I see it's not serious.

"Stop dripping blood all over the place!" I grab my medical bag from the counter. I turn on the faucet and point for him to rinse the wound. Minutes later, I have him bandaged up, properly this time, and get rewarded with a kiss on the cheek.

"Nothing like having my own personal doctor," Hendrix smiles, then joins our cousins at the table.

"Now that the fake emergency is over." Lennox rolls his eyes. "Why aren't you hanging out with us tonight? Darren is working. You don't have an excuse."

"I have the best excuse in the world." I lift my hands in triumph. "I'm in love!"

Deafening silence slams into the room, and as they say, I could hear a pin drop. Four sets of eyes look at me as if I've lost my mind.

I haven't. I'm just super excited about Troy.

"Hear me out," I say, then fill my family in on my first meeting with Troy at the hot yoga class in Chesterton's Gym, our date at Thorn, and the back-and-forth texts over the past week. "Seriously, he is amazing!" I say, then grab my phone to show them pictures I'd taken of Troy. "Isn't he gorgeous?" I swipe to the next photo. "Look at those muscles." I swipe and zoom in on the next image. "He has beautiful green hazel eyes."

"Jas, you're supposed to tell me who you're dating so we can run a background check on the guy," Lennox says, an edge of anger in his voice. "I can't have you in another situation like what happened with Randall Jefferson." He gives Maxwell a death stare.

"That's unnecessary. Mya vouched for him. I've already spent so much time getting to know him this week," I say, trying to get them to back off. Maybe one date and a few texts don't technically qualify as "so much time," but it's more than I've had in years.

"I don't know Mya. Her opinion counts for nothing. What does

Darren think of this guy? Does he know him?" Lennox interrogates me.

My best friend's response was noticeably tepid as I gushed about all things Troy. Not that he didn't seem happy for me, which he did. I got the sense he thought my excitement was overblown. Who cares! I deserve the thrill of having a man like Troy interested in me.

"He doesn't know Troy," I admit reluctantly. "But he knows Mya. Her recommendation is good enough for him."

"Last name," Lennox demands.

"Renault," I say, knowing I have no choice. Lennox gets up from the table with his phone and leaves the break room.

Hendrix snatches the phone from my hand and places it on the table. "You're attracted to the guy. Fine. He's good-looking and has you all in a flutter. But that's only one part of a relationship. What do y'all have in common? What interests do you share?"

I pause, considering my brother's question.

Troy and I haven't had any deep or long conversations for me to know this yet. The yoga class was distracting, and the date at Thorn turned out to be a quick thirty-minute meet-up for drinks instead of dinner. We have texted, but it's been surface-level pleasantries for the most part. But there's plenty of time to get to deep stuff later.

The most important thing is Troy looks like he walked off the pages of GQ magazine. I never thought I'd attract a man who looked like that. Me, the five foot five, size eighteen nerdy girl. But I did. I almost want to give myself a high five, but that would push my brother over the edge.

Instead, I keep things vague. "We have a lot of things in common. I won't give you a play-by-play of my talks with Troy."

Hendrix drops his head on the table and bangs it softly several times. I reach over and rub the knots out of my brother's neck to get him to relax.

Maxwell says, "I know you were joking about being in love, but shared interests are vital in relationships. That's the first step before you get into the important things. We all want to make sure you're not losing sight of that."

"Important things like what?" I ask, sucking in a deep breath. What could be more important than all the jealous stares I got when Troy wrapped his arm around my waist as we entered Thorn for drinks? I swear, every woman in the place was about to die with jealousy.

Maxwell answers, "Values. Life goals and priorities. Position on social issues. Religion. Family. Kids—"

"I do not want kids," I say, shutting down that line of thought.

"Does Troy know that? Does he agree?"

Hendrix turns his head on the table to look at me.

"We haven't gotten to deep conversations yet. It's only been one week!" I say, then steel my nerves to sneak a glance a Jaxon. The grimace on his face makes my heart drop.

Jaxon's eyes meet mine. "Perhaps you shouldn't jump so fast to saying you're in love, even if you're joking, Jas."

I look away.

"Love is not something to joke about or to enter into lightly," Jaxon says.

"Of course. You're right," I say. Tell that to the butterflies that explode within me whenever I'm around Troy. But I will acknowledge perhaps that's not a sign of earth-shattering love, even though I hope it's the start of it.

Jaxon continues, "You haven't dated anybody in years. Try not to throw all your eggs in the first basket—"

"Second basket," I say.

"No way," Hendrix rises from his chair. "Randall does not count."

Jaxon nods in agreement, then continues, "Like I was saying, don't put all your eggs in the Troy basket too soon. Get out there and date more people. I'm sure Troy is."

"You think so?" The idea almost makes me gag.

Hendrix turns my phone over to show the picture of Troy smiling, green hazel eyes sparkling, then says, "What do you think?"

"Thanks for raining on my parade."

Lennox bursts back into the room and sits at the table. "Check came back clean. No major red flags."

"Well, that's good, at least," Maxwell says.

"Not so fast," Lennox raises a finger, then gives me a stern stare. "You need to be careful. Jimbo Barnes told me why Troy resigned from working with Zaire Kincaid and took the job with him. It wasn't because of professional differences."

"Do I care why Troy changed jobs?" I demand, growing more and more irritated by the minute. At this rate, I will be a moody, annoyed mess when I meet up with Troy at Ultimate Putt Putt Golf.

"Troy wanted a romantic relationship with Zaire. When she picked Wiley over him, he couldn't handle it. So he quit like some punk," Lennox says, pounding his finger into the table. "How do you know this guy isn't on the rebound, looking to use you and toss you when he's done."

"Who cares who he liked in the past? Sometimes things don't work out, and you have to move on. With as hot as Troy is, I'm not upset he moved on with me," I say. Zaire's loss can be my gain. No man could pry her from Wiley, so she's no competition.

Hendrix turns toward me and grabs my hand in his. "Hey, I know it seems we're coming down hard on you."

"Because you are. All of you are jumping on me right when I have my first chance at a relationship in a long time."

"We love you and don't want you to get hurt," Hendrix says. "It's easy to be ecstatic because the guy looks good and probably gave you the best kiss of your life, but ..."

Memories of Darren slam into my head. Dizziness overwhelms me as the softness of his mouth against mine is so clear it's like I'm being sucked back into time. The first kiss was breathtaking, but the second kiss at Spaghetti Western blew my mind.

I squeeze my eyes shut and push the thoughts away. I cannot and should not be thinking about kissing my best friend. Maybe things will be different when Troy and I kiss. Hopefully, he can erase Darren's kiss from my mind, although part of me wonders if that's possible.

"Does that make sense?" Hendrix asks, jolting me from my thoughts.

"Got it. Loud and clear," I say, then glance at my watch. "Y'all have fun doing whatever you're going to be doing. I have to go so I won't be late for my date."

CHAPTER 15

ARREN

TENDRILS OF SILVER-GRAY SMOKE CLIMB TOWARD THE SKY from the smoldering corner of the furniture manufacturing warehouse on the corner of Clayton and Poplar Streets.

I slump down onto the curb next to the fire truck and snatch the helmet off my head. I'm drenched in sweat, despite the cool forty-degree temperatures of the winter night. Fighting the blaze over the past seven hours was like being in the hottest part of a furnace.

A water bottle is thrust into my face. Luke stands over me, looking worse than I feel.

"Can you believe Jimbo Barnes's bad luck?" Luke asks, then collapses onto the grass next to me. Nate and Wiley trudge over, both men shedding the heavy jackets to cool down in the winter air.

"Guy can't catch a break." Wiley shakes his head as he sits on the concrete.

"Can't catch a break?" Nate scoffs. "How about Jimbo uses his head for a change and stops putting his family and employees at risk of burning up in fires caused by his willful ignorance."

As much as I want to have sympathy for Jimbo, I can't deny a pattern is emerging. And not a good one. I nod and gulp the water until it's all gone. "What did Ronan say about the potential cause? Is he going to get Santos out here to investigate?"

The last massive blaze we battled was several months ago at the Elm Street Brewery. Santos Estrada, an arson investigator and the man responsible for Jasmine's father going to prison, discovered the fire was set intentionally by a disgruntled employee. With Jimbo losing his home a few weeks ago, he could be the prime suspect for torching his business to collect insurance money to cover his personal losses.

"You know, Ronan. He's tight-lipped right now. I'm sure he'll fill us in on our way back to the station." Luke leans back on his elbows and stares into the sky. "I'm glad no one was hurt. All the employees got out in time and are safe."

"A few of them are still hanging around in the field behind the parking lot," Wiley says.

"I bet they're worried about their jobs. After Christmas is the worst time to have a financial setback for many workers here," Nate added.

"That's not why we stuck around," a male voice booms behind me.

I turn to see Bubba Hightower crossing the field with a relieved expression. He's one of the facility's longest-tenured employees, having worked for Jimbo's dad before the business was turned over to Jimbo.

"I want to shake your hands, fellas. Y'all fought the bejesus out of that blaze and minimized damage that could have been much worse." He thrusts his meaty hand at Luke and shakes it as if he wants to jerk Luke's arm out of the socket. "We're so appreciative and thankful the fire was contained. Couldn't bear to lose any of the inventory that'll be shipping out to customers over the next several weeks." He moves to Nate and Wiley, shaking their hands before clenching mine in a death grip.

"Any idea how the fire started?" Nate asks, his eyes narrowing.

"Why don't you ask that Ivy Leaguer Jimbo hired to be the new chief of operations," Bubba says with more than a hint of disdain.

My ears perk up. "Troy Renault?"

"Yeah, that's the one." Bubba shakes his head. "He ordered some new-fangled glues and resins that are supposed to speed up the drying time on the construction of some of our furniture. I can't tell you how many of us warned him about storing that stuff in the same room with the drying and curing ovens."

"Why in the world did he do that?" Wiley frowns.

"There was a delay in cleaning the storage space we were supposed to put them in," Bubba admits, a sheepish look on his face. "Then the shipment arrived early." He shrugs, likely resigned to his role in the mistake. "We didn't have any place to put them. Troy insisted it wasn't a big deal to store them with the dryers and curing ovens since it would only be a few days tops before I could get the fellas to clear the other room. I wasn't comfortable with that, but he's the boss. There wasn't any other place to put them."

"Bet y'all are wishing you found another space now," Nate growled under his breath, turning his back on Bubba.

"I thought Troy worked in top furniture facilities in the Carolinas before moving here," I say, remembering the details from Jasmine's texts. "He should know better."

"You're preaching to the choir, my friend," Bubba says, then stiffens. He whispers, "Speak of the devil."

Troy strolls over to where we are sitting, dressed in a meticulously styled sport coat and slacks. He looks like he's arrived for a country club event instead of a man dealing with a major crisis.

"Bubba." Troy pats the man on the back. "Good job getting all the employees out. Top-notch work. Jimbo and I are grateful."

Troy sounds like a disingenuous politician. I stand and face him. Luke and Wiley follow my lead, rising from the ground.

"You weren't here when the fire started?" Wiley asks, crossing his arms over his chest. The tension between Wiley and Troy is palpable, undeniable, and intense.

Troy ignores Wiley and turns toward Nate and Luke. I can't help but notice he's avoiding me as well. I'm sure it has nothing to do with my friendship with Wiley and everything to do with Jasmine being my best friend. As thrilled as she is about this new guy in her life, there's no way she hasn't told him about me and how our friendship is one of the most important relationships in both of our lives.

Rightly or wrongly, a smug satisfaction settles over me at that thought.

"I heard you guys got over here in record time, and that saved our inventory. I can't thank you enough," Troy says, with a fake smile plastered on his face.

I'm over his platitudes.

"How about you thank us by not making stupid decisions in the future," I say, forcing my way in front of Troy. "You're lucky no one got hurt. Storing glues and resins in the same room as the curing ovens is a recipe for disaster."

Troy's smile fades into a scowl as his eyes dart toward Bubba, then settles back on me. His green hazel eyes grow darker. "Of course, if I'd known the team would unexpectedly use the ovens in that room tonight, I never would've stored our supplies there. We haven't used those dryers in weeks. There was no indication we'd do so when I left the office," Troy says, then adds, "to meet up with Jasmine for our date."

The information hits me harder than I expect.

Like a sucker punch.

Jasmine didn't tell me she was going out with Troy tonight.

I take a deep breath, trying to calm down before saying something I regret. But Troy's smug expression tells me he knows his words' effect on me. He's enjoying this.

Troy turns to Bubba and says, "And if I recall, you and I extensively discussed storage areas for the new resins and evaluated several spacing options, isn't that right, Bubba?"

Bubba bites his lip and nods his head slowly. "Yes, I believe we did."

"I would never make a move without consulting more experienced team members like Bubba. I'm new here. I rely on their expertise for these decisions. The shipment arrived early. Given the drop in temperatures, leaving them outside would impact their effectiveness. It was a judgment call for sure, but not one we took lightly," Troy says, the smile returning to his face. "In fact, Bubba was the one who brought up the curing oven room as the area with sufficient space. Isn't that right?"

"Well, yes, I did. But I wasn't sure it was the best move," Bubba says, then quickly adds, "Only because we'd never stored anything in there before."

Troy continues, "But you indicated the location and size were the most effective for temporary storage. I remember you saying that."

Bubba grimaces. "Yes, but I wasn't sure it would be the best move given the nature of the products being stored."

"Right, but you signed off on the risks being low," Troy says with a pointed look at Bubba.

Bubba looks away, then says, "Yes, I did."

"That sign-off is the only reason I approved the decision," Troy says. "Of course, in hindsight, we need to review our safety protocols and ensure proper storage areas are prepared well before flammable supplies arrive at the facility, right Bubba?"

"That's right, sir."

"Now, if you'll excuse me, I need to go make it up to an extraordinary lady for abandoning her tonight." Troy turns on his heels before I can punch him in the face.

"Bubba, don't let that guy railroad you," Nate says.

I say, "He's trying to make it look like this was all your fault."

Bubba raises his hands in frustration. "Sorry, but I'm not billionaires like the two of you. I need this job, and he's my new boss. I got to do what I got to do to keep the peace. Thanks again, though," Bubba says, then heads toward the parking lot.

I glare at Troy as he fiddles with his cell phone, then places it against his ear. No doubt he's calling Jasmine. She's probably happy to hear from him because she doesn't see him for who he is.

"That's the guy dating Jasmine?" Luke asks, resting a hand on my shoulder. "What a jerk."

Nate says, "If you're any kind of best friend to Jas, you'll get her away from that guy. He's bad news."

They aren't wrong.

While Jasmine is convinced we should only be friends, that doesn't mean I have to sit around and watch her fall for Mr. Wrong.

There's a better, more deserving guy out there for her.

I'm going to help her find him.

CHAPTER 16

J ASMINE

THE BRIGHT WINTER SUN SHINES LIKE DEATH-SEEKING
laser beams through the slats of my window blinds, nudging me awake
from the worst night of sleep of my life. I tossed and turned for hours,
mind racing through scenarios that could explain what happened last
night.

How had I gone from a blossoming and exciting relationship with
Troy Renault, a deliciously handsome and successful man, to a dejected
and embarrassed date sitting alone at Ultimate Putt Putt Golf?

Troy stood me up.

And I have no clue why.

I roll over on my stomach and clutch one of the pillows piled
high on the left side of my bed. This one is Darren's favorite. The
faint scent of his cologne, mixed with his pheromones, lingers on the

soft cotton pillowcase, soothing me. I resist the urge to grab my phone.

I'm not delusional.

I didn't miss hearing the chime of a text message coming through.

There's no text from Troy.

He's ghosted me.

And this is why I never should've tried to date again.

My life was fine, focusing on my career, family, and friends. I'm one of the youngest Heads of Emergency Medicine in the country. The people in Kimbell respect my medical expertise and admire me, even if they fear me.

That's what I'm good at.

Dating, not so much.

How dumb was I to get so excited about a few text conversations and a meetup for drinks? I should've known it was too good to be true.

What would a guy like Troy see in me?

While we may be evenly matched professionally, and I dare say I have the edge on him in the education department, he is light years away in the looks department. A man like that can't stay interested in a curvy, nerdy doctor who's dated one man in her entire life for very long. I'm sure he was lured away by someone much skinnier and prettier than me.

And he didn't have the decency to tell me he wasn't interested anymore. If he ever was. Maybe he was being nice to me because Mya is his friend. So he texts me a few times and goes out on a date with me so he can tell Mya we hung out but didn't have any chemistry.

Except I thought we did.

But what do I know?

The last time I went on a date with a man was before my residency.

I was never good at dating. Now, I see how rusty and horrible I am at it. It's the only thing in my life I haven't mastered. Haven't come close. In fact, I fail miserably.

I scream into the pillow.

The one person I want to talk to about this is on shift at the fire station for another two hours. By the time Darren is free to talk, I'll be up to my neck reviewing the overnight patient reports, debriefing with the overnight team before they leave, and kicking off the teaching rounds with the residents and interns.

Though part of me doesn't want to admit being a fool, even to Darren. I was like some dumb schoolgirl crushing over a hot new guy in class. I'm too old to be acting or feeling this way. I'm a doctor, for God's sake.

A glutton for punishment, I grab my phone and scroll to the text thread with Troy. I cringe as I read the texts I sent him last night.

The one after I arrived at the Putt Putt Golf facility.

JASMINE

Hi, I'm here. What's your ETA?

And again an hour later.

JASMINE

Hope everything is okay. Give me a call. I'm still at the Putt Putt Golf, sitting at the bar.

And one last time, two hours later, as I stomped into my apartment.

JASMINE

Not sure what happened tonight. Hope to hear from you soon.

I bang my fists against the pillows and kick them across the room. It's that last stupid sentence I wish I'd never sent.

Hope to hear from you soon.

This guy ditched me, yet I was still giving him a chance to make up for it with that last desperate Hail Mary plea.

I groan and fall back onto the pillows, clutching the phone against my chest as I squeeze my eyes shut. The phone vibrates and jerks against my chest as my alarm goes off.

No more time for a pity party.

I have to get ready for work and figure out how I'm not going to tell my team I got stood up for my date last night. They'll have questions and want details, which I've freely shared when things were good. Now I have to tell them the crappy part and see their sad faces looking at me with pity as they try to console me.

That's the last thing I want, but it's what I know I'll endure today.

I swap the phone for my television remote control and turn on Channel 4 News for You Houston.

I bolt up in bed.

It's unusual for anything in Kimbell to make the Houston news, but there's no mistaking what I see on the screen—the TimberLuxe Furniture facility against the backdrop of night with fire blazing from a back corner of the building.

Wait.

Troy works for Jimbo Barnes as the Chief Operating Officer at TimberLuxe Furniture.

I unmute the volume to hear reporter Ciara Thompson recapping the details of the fire, which happened last night when I was waiting for Troy alone at Ultimate Putt Putt Golf.

Two other fire departments from neighboring towns joined the Kimbell firefighters to tackle the blaze, which took seven hours to put out. All employees were safely evacuated, and no inventory was lost.

I press rewind and watch the coverage again.

A seed of hope sprouts within me.

If there was a fire at Troy's job last night, the last thing on his mind was texting me to cancel our date. He was probably juggling a thousand tasks, ensuring the employees were safe while monitoring the progress of putting out the blaze. His team needed him to be the voice of calm as they watched and wondered if their entire livelihood would go up in smoke.

"Well, that explains it," I mutter under my breath. While Troy was having the worst night of his career, I wasted time being upset with him for not showing up for the date.

I knew there had to be an explanation for his abrupt change in behavior. The thought that he was faking his feelings for me didn't sit well, but I couldn't explain it.

Until now.

My phone rings, and I jump, then glance at the screen.

I squeal when I see Troy's name and face light up on my phone.

I try to calm my racing heart, then answer.

"Hi," I say, sounding more breathless than I'd like.

"Hey, sorry about last night. I guess you heard about the fire," Troy says. He sounds weary and tired.

"I saw the news. You had more important things to deal with than a date with me," I say.

"It was rough. I'd much rather have spent my night gazing into your beautiful eyes than that fire."

I let out a silent scream as butterflies race through my body.

Troy continues, "The firefighters were incompetent. Took them forever to put it out."

My hand clenches into a fist, and I stiffen. Darren was on shift last night. There's one thing my best friend isn't, and that's incompetent. If the fire took a long time to put out, it's because it was more complicated than what Troy realized. I give him a pass on that insult. This time.

"And then I had to deal with Jimbo freaking out. He burned his own house down a few weeks ago. Now he feels like the universe or some crap is out to ruin him. I tried to explain it was an unfortunate coincidence, but he was irrational. Between babysitting him and being questioned by the firefighters and the insurance company, I'm drained. Safety inspectors are coming out to assess the integrity of the building and if it's safe for the employees to return to work. We lose money every day they are away and risk not meeting our delivery commitments. It's a nightmare."

I'm pained at hearing everything he's dealing with. Poor Troy. "I understand," I say, then hesitate. I want to ask for a rain check on our date, but I know it's too soon. I'm lucky he called me this morning to check-in.

"Thanks, I knew you would. I'll call you later when things calm down," Troy says.

"Okay. I hope things get better—"

And then I realize Troy has already ended the call.

I sit on the bed, staring at the phone, utterly amazed that all is right with the world again. Troy and I are back on track for a love match. I bite my bottom lip as a huge smile spreads across my face.

I'm determined I won't be the only one finding love in record time.

It's time for me to help Darren get the love of his life, too.

And I know what I need to do.

CHAPTER 17

J ASMINE

"I'M HAPPY TO HELP, BUT I AM WONDERING WHY YOU wouldn't go to Timmy Quinn to help you look for this person," Odalis Cruz says, a slight frown piercing her face.

I lean over the counter, closing the distance between me and the head librarian of the Kimbell Public Library. "Because Timmy Quinn is a useless, incompetent P.I. and a gossip. I don't want the entire town to know what I'm doing and why minutes after I hire him."

Odalis nods slowly. "Well, I suppose there's some truth in your views about Timmy, although I think he's a decent private investigator."

"Come on, Odalis. He was supposed to find Joe Little after he burned up Elm Street Brewery, and he couldn't do that. He let the cops find the guy first. Timmy's not that good. I'm sure I can do a much better job, with your help, of course."

"Come on over to this side, and let's get started. The library is quiet today. This is a good distraction," Odalis says, beckoning for me.

I walk around the massive circular desk and ease onto a stool beside her. Usually, I grab a quick lunch on the go and review patient files, but I'm making an exception today.

"Who are we looking for?"

"Cassidy Mitchell."

Odalis's eyes grow wide, and she turns to stare at me. "Darren's ex-girlfriend? I thought you didn't like her."

"I didn't like how she responded to the Pippa mess but had no real beef with that girl."

"Why do you want to find her?"

"Because Darren loved her, and I'm kinda sorta partially responsible for them not working out," I say, then give Odalis the run down about our New Year's resolutions and progress so far.

"I heard about you dating that hunk, Troy Renault." Odalis feigns fanning herself with a magazine. "Muy caliente chica."

"Si, si," I say and laugh. "He's so hot. I swear I have to stop myself from drooling whenever I'm around him." I don't mention that it's only been two times—our first setup at hot yoga and the drinks that night at Thorn. Still, I drool over his picture on my phone most days.

"That's surprising," Odalis says, then pulls up a browser and types Cassidy's name.

"Why do you think it's surprising?" I ask, not wanting to mention the obvious gap in our looks. Troy is muscular and buff, and I firmly tip the formula of BMI in the obese category. It doesn't matter that my curves tend to be in all the right places, and my figure is still lovely. I'm very overweight and not the typical look of a woman who should be able to snag a man like Troy.

"Jasmine, your best friend is Darren Manning," Odalis says as if I'm daft. She turns to stare at me. "Darren Manning! The guy is at the top of Mt. Everest of the hottest guys alive. Troy is handsome. I'll give him that. But you've been best friends with a smoking hot guy your entire life. Don't tell me you never noticed."

"Of course, I noticed." Heat prickles up my neck and flushes my face.

Memories of Darren's lips against mine, soft and caressing, cause goosebumps to pepper my skin. This is all Evelyn's fault. I had firmly placed Darren in the friend zone box for my entire life, never allowing myself to think of him in any other way until my mom dropped that ridiculous theory on me on New Year's Eve.

I should not have these thoughts or reactions to a man who has been my best friend for almost twenty-five years. A guy who vomited in the backseat of my car, farts when we're under blankets watching reality shows, and steals food off my plate whenever we're at a restaurant.

I should not feel one ounce of romantic attraction toward him.

Yet, I feel like a dam is struggling within me to hold back a torrent of flood waters of romantic feelings for Darren at the worst possible time.

Troy is interested in me.

I can't muddy the waters by thinking of my best friend in the wrong way.

"Then why would Troy's handsomeness fluster you? You've been super close to a guy much hotter."

"I've been super close to a guy who is not remotely interested in me," I say, although the words don't ring true. Two kisses ago, maybe I could have made that statement more confidently. To convince myself I'm not crazy, I whip out my cell phone and pull up Darren's social media pages. I scroll through the pictures and stop on each of Darren's exes, dates, and flings. "This is the type of woman Darren is attracted to. Women who are the opposite of me—gorgeous, stylish, and—"

"Stick skinny," Odalis says.

"That's why no matter how hot he is, it doesn't matter. He's not interested in me," I say, one more time with conviction. But another memory hits me like a freight train.

There's nothing wrong with how close we are, Jasmine.

Did you feel anything when I kissed you?

I shake my head as if the motion can push those memories straight out of my mind. Darren was drunk on New Year's Eve and feeling lonely.

Evelyn is right.

We used each other as relationship crutches for far too long.

"Makes sense," Odalis agrees, then points at the computer screen. "Looks like we hit a dead end."

"What were you searching for?"

"The easiest thing to cyberstalk someone—Cassidy's social media profiles. But she doesn't have any."

"Well, I could've told you that. The media hounded her like crazy after Pippa Ingram accused Darren of sexually assaulting her. She shut everything down to escape the negative attention," I say, remembering those days too well.

"I always thought they broke up because she thought Darren had cheated on her," Odalis says.

"That's part of it," I say. "He came clean with Cassidy. Sure, he kissed Pippa, but that was it. Pippa was looking for a payday and wanted to hook up with Darren, get pregnant, and cash in. When Darren turned her down, she made up that ludicrous story. But Cassidy didn't believe him when he told her the truth."

"How did you factor into this whole situation?"

I rub my forehead and stare out the expansive windows facing the back of the library. Needles from the towering pine trees flutter to the ground. I've never admitted this to anyone, but maybe it's time to come to terms with what I did and make amends.

"Darren didn't have to say anything for me to know Pippa was spreading lies. I know him. He's not a cheater. If he wanted to be with another woman, he would've first broken things off with Cassidy."

"Still don't get how you had a role in their breakup."

"Because I kinda convinced Darren that Cassidy should've known the truth instinctively as I did. If she loved and knew him, she would know Pippa was lying." I drop my head on the desk.

"And I'm guessing you did it in that know-it-all, matter-of-fact way that only Dr. Jasmine Jones can do."

"Exactly," I say in a strained whisper.

"So Darren was extra hard on her for not supporting him. With her being hurt about thinking she was cheated on, there was no way for the relationship to survive," Odalis says, shaking her head.

"Now you see why I have to make amends."

"Yes. It's crystal clear."

"I know if I can find Cassidy and apologize for my role in their break-up, maybe I can convince her to talk to Darren again. I can't guarantee they'll get back together. But talking would be a great first step. Maybe that's the olive branch that could help them rekindle what they had in the past."

"It's worth a try." Odalis taps her finger against her chin. "Since we can't find her online, we'll have to do it the old-fashioned way."

"And that would be doing what?" I ask, growing impatient. I glance at my watch and realize I've been away from St. Elizabeth's much longer than expected. I have to get back to work soon.

"I'll search public records for her last known physical location. Check for rental records, home purchases, businesses incorporated. Anything required to be filed publicly to track her down."

"Well, she was originally from Philadelphia. But she moved to Pittsburgh to be close to Darren when he was still playing football."

"That's a great start," Odalis says, patting me on the hand. "I will start researching and let you know when I find her."

"Who are you looking for?" An unmistakable male voice interrupts us.

I freeze and look up into the stunning blue eyes of my best friend. I roll my eyes at how handsome he is. Odalis is right. As good-looking as Troy is, he doesn't hold a candle to Darren.

Odalis minimizes the browsers on the screen and flips her notebook over to hide the notes she'd written about Cassidy.

"An old friend from Pennsylvania," I say, which isn't entirely a lie. "What brings you to the library? Shouldn't you be home getting some rest after fighting the fire at TimberLuxe?" I move from behind the desk, giving Odalis another opportunity to turn the computer away from Darren's prying eyes.

I step closer to him, almost lured by his magnificent cologne. I've got to stop this. Now.

"Too wired," Darren says, giving me a smile that nearly stops my heart.

I hate this new effect he's having on me. The only thing that can stop these wayward feelings is being distracted by another man, namely Troy Renault.

He continues, "I'm meeting a couple of my board members to discuss the CPS surprise inspection. It happened earlier today." Darren steps toward me and wraps an arm around my waist. "But you being here is the best surprise. You know this is the first time in years I've gone a whole week without seeing you."

"I know," I say. There's that stupid breathy voice again.

Darren leans over and pulls me into a tight hug.

His face nuzzles against my ear as he says, "I miss you."

Those three words send my heart soaring.

I fight the feelings and push him away. "Whatever, boy. Bye, I got to go back to work." I say, then rush away from him. I call over my shoulder, "Odalis, text me if you find anything."

CHAPTER 18

ARREN

Flipping through my handwritten notes, I force myself to focus on the plan Blossom, Idris, and I have settled upon to address the CPS findings. Four hours of combing through the suggestions and dividing up the responsibilities have us on track to handle all the concerns except one.

"Can you get everything typed up?" I ask Blossom as she stands and steps back from the conference room table.

"Of course." Blossom smiles. "I'll also flesh out a step-by-step action plan for each topic so everyone knows their responsibilities."

"Thank you," I say, then lean back in the chair and stretch. I'm going on fumes after fighting the fire for most of the night at TimberLuxe, then hustling over to the football fields after Idris called to tell me the CPS surprise visit was happening this morning. To say it was a disaster is an understatement.

"There's some heavy lifting we assigned to Mirielle. I think she'll be a lot more agreeable to doing it if you ask her," Blossom says, barely able to contain her smirk.

"Got it. I'll take care of Mirielle." I do feel bad for missing our date-that-wasn't-a-date. I can make up for that and see what other ideas she had to help address CPS concerns. And maybe, just maybe, she can help me to stop yearning for Dr. Jasmine Jones.

I won't lie.

Walking into the library and seeing Jasmine huddled up with Odalis was precisely the prescription for my horrible day. She looked fabulous, wearing a dark green fitted dress with cap sleeves. A wide black belt accented the dress, showing off the hourglass figure I've grown to adore. Her hair fell in loose waves around her face. She was beautiful, as usual, and oblivious to the effect she has on me. But that didn't stop me from wrapping her in my arms. Holding Jasmine always calms me. She fits so neatly against my chest. I love how soft she feels against my body. I wanted to kiss her again but knew that was inappropriate. The hug would have to suffice.

I'm still trying to process why she bolted within minutes of seeing me. Logic says the answer is as simple as she needed to return to work. I know how crazy busy her work days are at the hospital. But a nagging part of me thinks her quick exit could've been related to Troy Renault. Was she leaving to meet up with him?

It's a new harsh reality I have to face.

I can't keep holding on to something that doesn't exist between us.

Jasmine has made it clear we are just friends.

She isn't interested in me romantically.

Jasmine wants Troy.

A guy who is wrong for her in every way imaginable.

I don't have a shot of being with her, but that doesn't mean I should sit by and watch her fall for a guy who will make her regret it later. The guys are right. I have to steer Jas away from Troy and toward a man better suited for her. Even if that man isn't me. But I'm not sure where to start.

"I have to go pick up the kiddos," Blossom says, grabbing her laptop bag and purse. "You coming, Idris?"

Idris squirms in his seat and shakes his head. "No, I … umm … want a few minutes with Darren."

The man looks worried. A frown is etched deep on his forehead as he avoids eye contact with me.

I know what he's concerned about, and he shouldn't be. I don't blame him for what happened today. The surprise inspection ultimately highlighted measures that should be implemented to make sure my youth football league is prepared for the necessities of active special needs children. I'm not trying to cut corners here. I want the kids to have a safe environment to play and learn about being part of team sports.

After Blossom leaves the room, Idris looks at me with apologetic eyes. "I can't tell you how sorry I am about what happened earlier."

"You don't need to apologize. I'm glad we got Quaid to relax and calm down. His safety is more important than anything."

Idris's only child, Quaid, is autistic.

Having Idris involved on the board has gone a long way to help us modify the league to make it safer for autistic children to participate, but we had a pretty major flub today when one of the volunteers played music over the sound system to celebrate the great practice. Not only was it a deviation from the routine and structure we'd established, which many of the kids need, but the loud music triggered Quaid to have a meltdown. Luckily, Idris acted fast to get Quaid to a quiet area away from the other kids to help him recover.

"Not if it results in CPS shutting down the team. He loves playing football with the other kids. He'll be devastated if he was the cause of the team not playing anymore."

"That's not going to happen. CPS recognizes the good we're doing. There are just a few more things we need to maintain a safe environment for the kids."

"Like hiring a developmental pediatrician," Idris adds, his voice trailing off.

"That's the harder part," I say. We tossed around ideas about convincing a developmental pediatrician to work with us full-time. If we were in a bigger city like Austin, Dallas, or Houston, we might have a better shot of getting someone to come on board. As much as I love my hometown, we don't have people clogging up the county roads to move here. "But don't worry. I'll figure something out."

"Don't believe him," a sassy, alto voice pierces the air.

My heart leaps, but I check it as I swivel around in the chair to stare at Jasmine.

"He's always talking about figuring stuff out, but he dumps all that on me. Lucky for him, I'm the best at solving his problems," Jasmine says, then lifts a plastic bag filled with styrofoam containers.

"What're you doing back here?" I ask, not that I'm upset to see her.

"Odalis mentioned you and your board members have been here for hours with no food, so I thought I'd swing by and drop some off on my way back to work," Jasmine walks into the conference room and places the bags on the center of the table between me and Idris. "There's enough here for three, but only two of you …"

"Blossom left to pick up her kids. We're wrapping up," I say, then reach for the bag and untie the ends.

"So I wasted my time?" Jasmine pouts as she places her hands on her hips.

"Of course not. I'm sure Idris and I can come up with something else to discuss while we eat dinner," I say, then glance over at him.

Idris is fidgeting with the papers, trying to organize them into stacks as he sneaks glances at Jasmine. A sheen of sweat has broken out on the man's face, and he looks like … he's smitten with her. What is it with every man in this town wanting to be with my best friend?

Then another thought creeps into my mind.

Idris is the kind of guy who would be an excellent fit for Jasmine. He's a hard worker, serving as the head ranch hand for the Baker Farm for the past decade. A dedicated single father. Cares about people and animals. Goes out of his way to help others.

The opposite of Troy.

Should I try to get Jasmine interested in Idris?

The thought gives me a headache. I force the words from my mouth. "Have you met Idris before?"

She raises an eyebrow and gives me a look that says, "It's about time I found my manners and performed proper introductions."

I laugh, then say, "Sorry. This is Idris Gibson. He works for Colton Baker as the head rancher at the Baker Ranch." I turn to Idris, who looks like he's about to faint. "Idris, this is my best friend, Dr. Jasmine Jones."

He nods at me but doesn't turn to look at Jasmine.

A move she isn't going to tolerate for long.

Jasmine moves around the table directly into Idris's line of sight and extends her hand. "Nice to meet you."

Idris looks up at her with wide eyes, then back down at his hand, which looks sweaty and clammy. He frowns, then rubs it roughly against his shirt before shaking Jasmine's hand.

She gives him a warm smile. It's this side of Jasmine she doesn't show to people often, choosing instead to hide behind her tough, no-nonsense exterior. But it's the Jasmine I've known since I was six years old.

"Me too. Meet you. Nice. I mean, you know." Idris snatches his hand away as if he's been burned, then looks down and says, "It's nice to meet you, too, ma'am."

Jasmine guffaws. "My mother is ma'am. I prefer doctor." She gives Idris a wink. "Just kidding."

Despite his ebony skin, I swear I can see him blush. It's enough to make bile rise in my throat. But if I must choose between Troy and Idris for Jasmine, I'm going all in on Idris. The guy needs to up his game. He'll never get Jasmine or any woman if being around them makes him this nervous.

When Idris doesn't respond to her joke, Jasmine raises an eyebrow at me and frowns, then says, "I'm pulling a double shift tonight." She runs a hand along my shoulders as she passes by. "Hope you enjoy the food. I got your favorite from Gwen's."

"Salmon salad with dressing on the side," I say, then groan with pleasure. "You take good care of me."

"Don't forget it," Jasmine says, then pauses at the door. "I also have a solution for your developmental pediatrician problem."

"How did you find out about that?"

"Darren, when will you learn I know everything about you." Jasmine smiles as she wags a finger toward me. "I'll get you a meeting with Retired Healers Network. It's a group that coordinates volunteer opportunities for retired medical professionals in the community. A partnership with them can secure volunteer developmental pediatricians for your foundation."

"You're joking." I stand and cross the room, stopping inches from her. She looks up at me with those gorgeous chocolate brown eyes and batts her long eyelashes.

"Do I look like a comedian?" She rolls her eyes. "The best part is once we convince them to partner with the Manning Foundation, their services won't cost you a thing."

"Jasmine ..."

"I know," she says, then turns away from me. "Thank me later."

And with that, she's saved me ... again.

Idris clears his throat.

"She's ... magnificent," Idris says, then fiddles with the chain of paperclips in his hands. "I hope you don't mind me asking, but is she single?"

I hesitate, not wanting to answer his question. Then I remember Jasmine's infatuation with Troy, and I blurt out, "As a matter of fact, she is."

"Wow," Idris mutters. "I don't know what I'm thinking. I could barely get a word out around her. She must think I'm some bumbling, country bumpkin. I don't stand a chance of getting her to like me."

"Not yet, but with my help, your chances will improve greatly. Let's talk about it over dinner."

CHAPTER 19

J ASMINE

"Do you need a new car?" I ask, glancing at the gleaming vehicle in the driveway. The early morning sun rays filter through the towering pine trees surrounding Darren's mansion. I tug my cardigan tighter around my body and shiver in the brisk coolness.

Darren gives a nonchalant shrug, his fingers ruffling through his hair. He's dressed to impress in a blue cashmere sweater that matches his eyes and dark navy trousers, like a model who walked off a Ralph Lauren runway. If looks could seal a deal, Darren will snag a developmental pediatrician volunteer at first glance.

He says, "Riley Beaumont opened the first luxury car dealership in Lasso County this week. That's a big deal. I didn't have an electric vehicle, so the timing seemed right."

"Let me guess. You were his first sale?"

He chuckles. "Nate beat me to it."

"Always ready to lend a hand to a friend." I raise an eyebrow and lean against the cool metal of my Audi, my arms folded across my chest.

"I'd do the same for you." He tosses back the quick retort, his eyes meeting mine. "If you'd ever let me. How's it going with the lawsuits?"

I look away, avoiding his concerned gaze.

"Nate said you've depleted your savings," Darren continues.

I stalk over to Darren. "Nate Bell has no business peeking into my financial balances at his Daddy's bank and snitching on me."

"He's concerned. So am I."

"I can rebuild my savings. Hendrix is helping out, too. No new lawsuits have been filed in the past few months, thank goodness."

After my father was convicted, more family members of patients who died under his care have come out alleging negligence. While criminal charges didn't stick in any of them, there is enough for them to pursue restitution in the civil courts.

"The attorneys think most of them will be dismissed, but there are two they recommend to settle out of court," I explain.

"In the meantime, the lawyers are getting rich off you," Darren guesses correctly.

"Basically," I say.

"You don't want to ask Lance for help?"

"Of course not." I cringe and shake my head. I'd never ask my ex to do pro bono legal work for me or my father. It would be too weird and awkward.

I say, "We're ok. Evelyn has the hair salon open twice as much as usual to cover the house and normal expenses."

"I could help out to take some of the pressure off," Darren adds.

Helping out for Darren is code for handing me a blank check signed by him. I stiffen and give a shrug, my foot scuffing at a pebble on the ground. "We have it covered. I'm thankful Santos didn't file a civil suit on top of the criminal charges. With Dad being convicted, he'd get a huge settlement."

Darren steps closer, a hint of fire in his eyes. "I can't stand the guy," he says. "But I don't think Santos wanted money."

No, the grieving arson investigator wanted justice at my father's expense.

I sigh. "I'm thankful he's engaged to one of the town's richest women. That's helping to keep him focused on other things than ruining my dad's life."

"Have you talked to your dad about the lawsuits?"

"I'm sure Hendrix has when he visits him," I mumble, avoiding Darren's steady gaze. "I haven't spoken to him."

"It's been a year, Jas. Don't you think it's time?"

Something about the look in Darren's eyes arrests me. "You've spoken to my dad, haven't you?"

He hesitates, then says, "Maybe."

"Darren!" I gasp, surprise catching in my throat.

"He misses you, so he's called me a few times to find out how you're doing. He thinks he let you down."

"He did," I confess, my voice barely above a whisper. "We don't see eye-to-eye on how to care for patients. He did things I would never do. His medical career is over. He's forced Evelyn to pay for a lifestyle she can't afford. We're all suffering, and it's all his fault. Do you think I should go to Huntsville to tell him that?"

"Yes," Darren says, maintaining eye contact. "It's better than ignoring him. I think it would be good for you two to talk about it. Out of everyone, you're the one person close to him who understands what he did, even if you don't agree. Hearing your perspective might help him."

"He'll be out in a year," I respond with bitterness. "There will be plenty of time for him to hear my perspective then, considering he'll be unemployed."

"Jasmine, let me help you," Darren insists, touching my arm.

I jerk away, a flash of anger sweeping over me. "I don't want your stupid money or bad advice on dealing with my father. You don't see me nagging you about mending the relationship with yours!" I snap.

A flash of hurt crosses his face at the mention of his dad. They haven't spoken to each other in five years since the man paid Pippa an undisclosed amount to drop her assault charges against Darren. While it made his problems disappear, it also made Darren look guilty for something he didn't do.

This is not how I thought this day would start.

We should be going over our carefully crafted pitch to secure a partnership with the Retired Healers Network, which would provide a rotating group of volunteer developmental pediatricians to the kids in Darren's special needs youth league. Not talking about my father, the convicted felon.

"We should go," I say, my voice low.

Darren opens the passenger door, and I get inside. I sink onto the sleek tan leather seats and marvel at the custom luxury and high-end craftsmanship. A captivating array of buttons and knobs surround wide touch screens that emit a soothing glow. Now I see why my best friend indulged. The car is impressive.

"Don't be mad at me," Darren says as he slides into the driver's seat.

I throw my hands in the air. "I'm not mad!" I say much too aggressively.

He pushes a button to start the car, but I notice no change. The interior is still whisper-quiet as he drives down the curved driveway toward the private road that leads off his property. After long moments of silence, he sneaks a glance at me and says, "You know how I feel. When you're going through something rough, I'm going through it, too. It's hard for me to sit on the sidelines and not do anything. Not when I think you need me, Jas. Tell me what to do."

"You're already doing it," I confess, my gaze dropping to my hands in my lap. "Most days, I don't want to think about this or talk about it. But you're the only one I can talk to when I want to talk about it."

Darren absorbs my words, his eyes thoughtful. "You haven't shared this with your new sweetheart?"

I laugh. "Are you kidding? I've only known Troy Renault for a couple of weeks. That's not long enough to share private details about my life."

"Good," Darren says, his eyes softening. "Glad to hear you haven't lost it over him."

I detect a hint of jealousy in his tone.

"So, how's it going with him?" Darren asks, keeping his eyes on the rolling fields and ranches that stretch as far as the eye can see along the country road.

"Amazing, actually," I confess, my face lighting up even though I'm trying to hide how stupid giddy Troy makes me feel. "He's distracted now with the fire at TimberLuxe. Once that's sorted out, I'm sure we'll get back to spending time with each other." I check my phone to see if Troy has texted, but there's nothing. "Your turn. How are things with you and Mirielle?"

"Mirielle?" Darren echoes, looking taken aback. "Why would you think there's something between me and her?"

I shrug nonchalantly. "Because she fell during her barrel racing training and came to the ER to get checked out. That's how I found out about the findings from the CPS surprise visit. She spent the whole time she should've been focusing on her prognosis talking about you."

"Is that so?" Darren asks, amusement glinting in his eyes.

I fold my arms across my chest, smirking. "Yes."

Darren studies me momentarily, then ventures, "You don't like her, do you?"

"I don't have a problem with her," I defend quickly. My voice hits soprano, which causes Darren to laugh. He knows me too well. Not that I would ever lie to him. Still, I know how much my opinions can influence him, and I've learned from the past about oversharing in areas I shouldn't be involved in.

"But you don't want me to date her?"

"Are you interested in her?" I counter, raising an eyebrow.

He grins at me, that easy smile that always seems to be playing on his lips. "Answer my question first."

I let out a sigh. "Fine. It was odd because she gushed about you as if she was a huge fan, not like a woman who's on the board of your charity and knows you. The real you."

"Interesting," Darren murmurs, mulling over my words.

"Is it? I'm not trying to get in the way of anything you two might have. I promise. I'm happy, and I want you to be happy, too. I'm not sure which Darren she's attracted to. Does Mirielle want to know the real you? The guy who spent a whole weekend putting up his Christmas decorations inside and out to make the house look worthy of a competition show? You don't have a housekeeper. You do your yard work. You're obsessed with reality TV shows. And you meticulously track every single thing you eat. I don't believe she's interested in knowing that Darren Manning," I ramble, trying to get him to understand.

Darren chuckles, a grin spreading across his face. "Have you seen those football players who retire and let themselves go? That's not going to be me."

"Yeah, 'cause it's so terrible to be overweight, right?" I snap back, irritation pricking at me.

"I still can't understand how you look in the mirror every day and are unhappy with how you look, Jasmine," Darren responds, his voice sincere. "I wish you could see yourself through my eyes, just once."

His words catch me off guard, my eyes widening in surprise. I let out a weak laugh. "It's not like I think I'm a troll."

Darren regards me seriously. "But you think your size is holding you back from ... I don't know what. It's not. You could have any man you want. You have to decide who that is."

"Whatever," I say, shrugging off his compliment.

"I'm serious. Didn't you notice your effect on Idris the other day?"

"Your board member?" I blink, surprised. "He barely glanced at me."

"Because you took his breath away. He was so nervous he couldn't string a sentence together," Darren reveals, a spark of amusement in his eyes.

"Idris is interested in me?" I ask, astonishment creeping into my voice.

"He asked if you were single. I told him you were since this thing with Troy is still new. He's a great guy but thinks you're out of his league."

"Well, that's silly." My mind drifts to how I had the same thoughts about Troy.

"So, you're keeping your options open?" Darren asks, his voice hesitant.

"There's no ring on my finger. Jaxon told me not to put all my eggs in the Troy basket. I think Troy is great, but there could be other great guys out there I should give a chance," I respond, but not sure I mean it. Idris seemed nice, but Troy has him beat in the looks category. It's hard to imagine I'd ever choose him over the hot man interested in me, but I will heed my cousin's advice.

"I think you'll find a lot to like about Idris. I'll pass on your number to him," Darren suggests, throwing me off guard.

"So much for not wanting to help me find love." I laugh, trying to hide my surprise.

"I'd do anything for you," Darren assures me, his eyes radiating warmth. "You know that."

CHAPTER 20

J ASMINE

THE RETIRED HEALERS NETWORK IS NESTLED IN A MODEST two-story building in the sparsely populated outskirts of Lasso County. A receptionist fawns over Darren as she ushers us through the hallways to the conference room, where the meeting will occur. The organization is less than a year old but has already been inundated with more requests than they have retired volunteer doctors to cover.

The former Head of Emergency Medicine and my mentor, Dr. Sheridan Wakefield, who serves as the network's chairman of the board, devised a way for the group to weed through all the requests. The format is reminiscent of those television shows with wealthy entrepreneurs doling out money to invest in new and different product ideas. Competitive and fierce.

Getting Darren a spot on the list to pitch was the easy part.

Landing the partnership was a different story. That's why I wanted to be here with Darren in person. We are a formidable team.

The receptionist leads us into the packed room, past the crowds of people waiting to convince the Retired Healers Network board to partner with their groups.

She gives a warm smile. "You'll be first to present. Usually, the board members will spend several minutes asking clarifying questions to get more details. The organizations that are a good fit get an answer on the spot. Most get declined, and others rescheduled because they run out of time."

"I guess it's good they get to hear us before all the others, then," Darren says.

"Helps more than you realize." She smiles at my best friend with lust in her eyes. I wonder if he ever gets used to women gawking at him everywhere he goes.

"Thanks," I interrupt before the woman gets any ideas. I need Darren focused on convincing the board to partner with the Manning Foundation. He can flirt later. "Can we get some water?"

"Of course," she says, then saunters away.

We sit in the cushioned seats and huddle close to each other.

"What are my chances?" Darren asks.

"Sheridan was convinced partnering with you was a slam dunk, but he did warn me there was a chance the other board members would like to go in a different direction for volunteer developmental pediatricians. They're in short supply with high demand."

"Well, I guess we'll have to convince them to vote with Dr. Wakefield," Darren says, then sits up straighter as the board members enter the room, chatting and laughing as they take their seats.

I stop myself from gasping as my gaze settles on one board member in particular. The one who hasn't responded to my texts over the past several days.

"Did you know Troy was on the board?" Darren asks.

Troy doesn't look my way as he sits near the middle. I'd forgotten how crazy handsome he is. Heat rushes to my face, and I resist the urge to fan myself.

Swallowing hard, I lean closer to Darren and answer, "Had no idea."

"So he doesn't know you and I will be presenting today?"

I cower at the surprise in Darren's tone.

He expects that I would've told Troy about this meeting and learned about Troy's position on the board. But the truth is that Troy hasn't had time to talk to me since the fire at TimberLuxe. I know he's dealing with a lot. I didn't want to put any pressure on him, even though the lack of communication between us is about to drive me bonkers with confusion.

Still, he hasn't given me any indication his interest has waned, so I have to do what I don't do well—be patient.

"He does now," I say, then smile at Troy as surprise registers across his gorgeous face. He gives me a slight nod of recognition. Then his face turns to stone as his glare drifts to Darren sitting at my side.

Darren, who has his arm draped around my shoulder.

A frown creases Troy's eyebrows. He looks at me, then Darren.

Not a good sign.

Darren frowns. "He doesn't look too happy to see me with you."

"Don't be ridiculous," I say, then slyly maneuver away from Darren's arm.

Dr. Sheridan Wakefield starts the meeting. "Thank you all for coming out today to help Retired Healers Network learn more about your respective organizations and how a partnership with ours can work to produce more good in our community. Unfortunately, due to the limited number of our volunteer retired physicians and their disciplines of expertise, we can't partner with all of you. However, we are actively recruiting more volunteers and hope to be able to make more connections in the future."

The receptionist announces the Manning Foundation and beckons Darren to approach the podium. As Darren and I discussed, I remain seated, giving him a chance to shine as the founder and force behind his excellent work in the community.

I listen with burgeoning pride as he enthralls the board with the activities his foundation has engaged in, the significant impacts the youth league can have on children with special needs in the community, and why partnering with a developmental pediatrician could benefit both organizations. I study the faces of the board members as they listen. It's clear he's won them over. All of them except Troy, who scribbles nonstop on a notepad as Darren speaks. Whenever Troy glances at Darren, his eyes are narrowed in a glare that reeks of hostility and ... jealousy.

As much as I want to be upset by Troy's obvious disdain for my best friend, another part of me loves his reaction. His behavior is enough to quiet all those niggling doubts about his lack of response to my texts this week.

But Troy is wasting his time being jealous of Darren. I decided on New Year's Eve to stop using my best friend as a substitute for a real relationship, and I meant it. I'm committed to finding love, and Troy is at the top of my list.

Darren wraps up his appeal to a round of applause from the crowd in attendance. I hear the hushed whispers of others waiting to do their pitches. Everyone is impressed and believes Darren is a shoo-in for getting a partnership.

"Well, I'm impressed," Sheridan says, then turns to the other board members. "Are there any questions before we put this one to a vote?"

Troy clears his throat, and my heart pounds in my chest.

Darren's strong muscles harden as he grips the podium. Troy leans forward with a challenge in his stare.

"Just a few questions," Troy says. "Mr. Manning, can you explain the incident from a few years back that led to such negative media coverage? Coverage that could negatively impact the impressionable and innocent children who participate in your youth league." Troy's icy tone instantly infects the room with tension.

Darren flexes his jaw, then responds, "I'm pretty sure everyone in this room knows the incident you are referring to, Mr. Renault. There's no need to dredge up the details of that time in my life, but I'm happy to discuss everything I've learned from going through that difficult time with the board. I can also provide more details on the measures I've put in place to ensure all the children we help with my foundation are safe—"

"You expect us to believe children can be safe around a man who regularly engages in sexual activities with those he employs? How many of your current volunteers at the Manning Foundation have found their way into your bed, Mr. Manning? Is that the kind of behavior kids should look up to?" Troy asks.

Before I can stop myself, I'm on my feet. I grab the microphone from the podium as my eyes lock on Troy's shocked expression.

"Your information about Darren is not only outdated but recklessly incorrect. If you insist on getting your intel from gossip rags, you risk leading this board down a path of withholding support from a worthy organization. Withholding support from children who feel like they are less than other kids because of their disabilities," I say, then press a hand on my hip. I turn to the other board members and continue, "I've been friends with Darren since we were six. We've shared all the highs and lows life has thrown at us. Darren cares passionately about children with special needs because he was that child growing up. Born with a disability that affected his ability to walk, he was constantly bullied and ridiculed. As much as he loved football, he never thought he'd play the sport. When he was blessed with a chance to have surgery to correct his ailment, he got the life he dreamed of. But he never forgot about all the other kids that wouldn't get the same opportunity. He wants them to know they don't need to dream of a different life because of their disabilities. They can have the life of their dreams as they are. Ultimately, this decision should be about what your organization wants to do to aid these children. It's not about Darren or his past. I urge you to approve this partnership to improve the lives of children with special needs in our county."

Darren's hand slips into mine as I finish off my impassioned plea. I follow him back to our seats. As we sit down, he clutches my hand to his heart, a look of admiration in his beautiful blue eyes.

Sheridan says, "Very eloquently put, Dr. Jones. And indeed, we are prepared to collaborate with the Manning Foundation. Isn't that correct?" He turns to the other board members and signals for a vote. All hands go up, including Troy's.

"Thank you," Darren says as we stand to leave. "I promise you won't regret it."

But I'm wondering if I should regret my rash response. Not that I take back a single word of what I said to support my best friend. Still, it's painfully apparent a line was drawn in the sand. I showed Troy who takes priority in my life. Maybe it was time for him to know that truth.

Outside the building, Darren lifts me off the ground and spins me around and around. A part of me is surprised he could lift me with such ease. Then I remind myself, it's Darren. A man that could take down an entire offensive line on his own.

I squeal and giggle as I protest, "Boy, put me down. Right now!" But I can't shake how comforting and right it feels to be in his arms.

Darren ignores my demand and says, "I can't thank you enough for what you did back there." His voice chokes with emotion. My heart twinges at the vulnerability in his words. "I can't imagine my life without you."

Darren is more than my friend. He's an integral part of my life, a part I will never, ever let go. The realization is so simple, so profound it leaves me breathless. As much as I want to find the future love of my life, that man has to accept my friendship with Darren.

If Troy can't accept that, he isn't the one for me.

I respond with the only answer I can give. "And you'll never have to."

CHAPTER 21

ARREN

Izzie leans over my table, her boobs on full display in the cut-off t-shirt tied in a knot against her flat exposed stomach. She bats her long dark lashes. Her bright red lips pout toward me. "Did some foolish woman stand you up?"

I laugh as if the idea is preposterous.

Not that a woman wouldn't ditch me on a date because I'm sure that could happen. The reality is I'm not dating anyone until I can exorcise Jasmine from the vice grip she has over my heart. I thought I had a chance until she defended me at the Retired Healers Network meeting. Hearing her passionately protect me made me love her even more.

But that same love reminded me Jasmine wants me only as a friend. Her closest friend, but nothing more. If I love her as much as I say I do, then I must be willing to step aside so she can find the right man for her.

I respond, "No, I'm waiting on Idris Gibson. There was an incident at practice today with the kids."

The text to meet him at Baker Bros came as I was milling around the fire station, avoiding going home to an empty house now that Jasmine was probably spending more and more time with Troy Renault. A guy who tried to stand in the way of my work with the foundation. Part of me hoped Troy's attempt at a hatchet job on my character would've been enough for Jasmine to walk away from the jerk. But she found a way to make excuses for his actions. It's like she's doubled down on him to be the man of her dreams, and I'm not sure why.

"I hope it's nothing serious," Izzie says, sliding into the booth on the opposite side. She makes a show of rubbing the table with a cloth towel as she lingers. "My nephew raves about how much fun he has playing on the team."

"He's a receiver, right?"

Her face lights up. "Yeah, that's right. Didn't think you noticed."

"I make a point to notice all the kids. Show them they matter and are important."

"That's what my sister says." Izzie leans forward. "She's single you know."

"Your sister ..." I don't know how else to respond.

Izzie nods her head vigorously. "I hear you're back on the market. I think the two of you could be a great fit. You're already awesome with her son. Think about it, okay?"

"Yeah, sure ..." I sigh as Idris rushes into the restaurant without his son, Quaid.

"Sorry, I'm late. I dropped Quaid back off at the ranch. He was tuckered out, as you can imagine," Idris says, then gives Izzie a tip of his cowboy hat as she stands from the booth.

"Two beers?" Izzie asks.

"Yes, please," Idris says as he slumps across from me. "I need all the help I can get to erase this nightmare of a day."

"Is Quaid alright? You didn't give me many details in your text."

"Yeah, he's good. A doctor from Retired Healers Network had come by to observe the game and acted quickly to help calm him down. Having them on the team is going to be a huge benefit. But, I still needed to take him to the hospital since they thought he should have an extra evaluation for a concussion from his fall." Idris shakes his head. "He has a nasty bump, but my boy takes a licking and keeps on ticking."

"You took him to St. Elizabeth's?"

"And I ran into Jasmine."

"She's not supposed to be on the schedule today."

"That's what she said. The docs had already cleared Quaid to leave when we ran into her. She came in to check on a patient. When she walked with us to the parking lot, I thought it was a good chance for me to ask her out."

I take a deep breath and glance around for Izzie. I need a beer right about now. No, I need a tumbler of scotch. With time, I hope it gets easier to think of Jasmine in a relationship with another man.

"How'd that go?" I ask, my heart sinking at the notion of Jasmine going out with Idris. While I'm pretty sure she'll see Troy's true colors eventually, Idris is an entirely different matter. He's a great guy and would be a good match for her. I can see that, although I hate to admit it.

Izzie saunters to the table and places the two heaping beer mugs in front of us, right on time.

"You know the rules, fellas," she says, then walks off.

"What should we toast to?" I ask.

"Second chances." Idris grips his mug and lifts it in the air.

We scream the words in unison, then chug the beers until the mugs are empty.

"Alright, so I'm guessing Jasmine turned you down."

"I didn't get to ask her."

"You didn't?"

"I could barely get a sentence out. I was tongue-tied and clumsy. I couldn't get my thoughts straight. Jasmine must have thought I was an idiot. If Quaid hadn't been there to take up the slack of the conversation, it would've been painfully awkward."

"Quaid did most of the talking to Jasmine?"

"They hit it off. He likes her. He told me I should ask her out as I drove him back to the ranch."

"I need details. How bad was it?" I ask.

Idris launches into a play-by-play of his interaction with Jasmine earlier. I try not to, but I find myself cringing and frowning out of embarrassment for him. He's right in his assessment. I'm sure Jasmine walked away from the encounter thinking Idris wasn't worth her time.

"The only silver lining is she gave me her number. Told me if I had any questions about Quaid or autism, to feel free to call her," Idris says with hope in his eyes. Hope I'm not sure he should have. He continues, "I want a second chance. But I'm not sure I can get my act together and talk like a normal person around her. That's why I texted you," Idris said. "Think you can help me?"

"Well, I am her best friend," I start, my mind racing. I do feel bad for Idris. I hate he didn't show Jasmine how great a guy he is in that interaction.

"So, you'll put in a good word for me?"

I grimace. "That's not going to work for Jasmine. She doesn't like to be told what to do. Trust me. The best way to influence her is to drop breadcrumbs and hope she comes to the conclusion you want her to. But it's a good sign she gave you her number."

His face lights up brighter. "You think she's interested in me?"

My face scrunches. "She's interested in Quaid."

Idris's face falls.

"But that's a good start. Jasmine's core identity is tied to being a doctor, but not because of the prestige. Deep in her soul, she loves helping and healing people. Giving you her number is her way of supporting you as you raise Quaid. She doesn't want you to be in a position where you don't understand something he's going through or have questions about what to do. She's willing to help."

"Wow. I think I'm falling in love already."

My fists clench under the table, but I force myself to calm down. This is how I help myself get over Jasmine. Being Idris's wingman is the antidote for my affliction.

Idris leans back against the booth. "But I'm not trying to use my son to get closer to Jasmine. Just feels wrong."

"And she would see through that anyway. I think you should call her and be honest. Apologize for being off-kilter in your conversation earlier. Thank her for offering to be a sounding board for questions regarding Quaid. That's the first move."

Idris nods as I speak. "You're good. That makes sense, but I'll freeze when she answers the phone. What if I make a bigger mess of things?"

While I'd like to dispute Idris, I know he's right. He hasn't been a good version of himself around Jasmine yet. Giving him a roadmap of what to talk about with my best friend won't be enough if the guy can't execute. But what if I can do more?

"You have two cell phones, right?" I ask.

"I do," Idris says. "Why?"

"How about we call Jasmine now?"

"No, I'm not ready for that." Idris waves his arms wildly in front of me.

"Here me out. Call me on three-way so I can listen in to the conversation. I'll text you what to say as y'all talk if you freeze. I'll be like your coach on the sidelines, helping you to make the right play."

"Darren!" Idris yells, a smile bursting on his face. "That's brilliant. I can't believe you'd do that for me."

"You're a good man, Idris. Jasmine is my best friend. I want her to find a man worthy of her. I think the two of you would be a great match. No guarantees, but I want to at least get you off to a better start with her. Give you the second chance you're hoping for."

Idris grabs his two cell phones and places them on the table. "Well, let's give it a go. Let's call Jasmine."

CHAPTER 22

ARREN

I SHOULD FEEL BAD, BUT I DON'T.

Settling under the covers, I reach for the remote to my fireplace and turn the flames higher to warm my bedroom. As I grab my cell phone, it rings in my hand like clockwork, and I answer.

Idris says, "Hey, I can't thank you enough for doing this for me."

This is the fourth call I'm coaching Idris from the sidelines this week. Each time, he thanks me profusely for scripting the words he's saying to Jasmine. At first, we struggled with coordination and had some close calls where Jasmine could've figured out what was happening. But now we've settled into a good rhythm.

For me, I don't notice Idris anymore.

His voice saying my words fade to the recesses of my mind. I'm talking to Jasmine. It's not the same as the conversations we have as best friends, though. Through Idris, I get to talk to her how I would if we were starting a relationship. Tell her what I feel about her and have her open to hearing it.

I know it's working, too.

Each successive call has gotten longer and longer.

Last night, my fingers started cramping from texting for three hours straight. But the conversation was too good. I didn't want it to end. Neither did Jasmine.

If only she knew she was talking to me and not Idris.

Maybe things could be different between us.

Jasmine answers the phone, and Idris does a decent job of handling the initial small talk. I can hear the enthusiasm in her voice. She's been looking forward to this talk with me. Or Idris, rather …

"I would've returned your call earlier," Jasmine begins, then takes a long breath. "But I got home, and Evelyn was in my apartment dropping off leftovers for me to eat for dinner and lunch tomorrow. Of course, we got to talking, and you know how that goes."

I pause, remembering Idris doesn't know who Evelyn is. Another part of me is curious to see how much Jas will share with him about her family. I proceed to test the waters and find out.

I type out a text to Idris.

DARREN

Who is Evelyn?

Jas laughs. A deep, infectious sound I love, then says, "This is going to sound weird, but Evelyn is my mom."

DARREN

You call her Evelyn? Interesting. Is there a story there?

"A long one. I won't bore you. Maybe for another time," Jas says.

DARREN

Come on, don't leave me hanging. Give me the short version.

I swear I can hear Jas weighing the options of opening up. Each conversation has gotten more intimate and profound. I'd be surprised if she didn't.

"Okay, maybe I can share the super short version, which I warn you is still lengthy," Jas says.

DARREN

I'm all ears.

"I should start by explaining Evelyn isn't my dad's first wife. He was married before to a woman named Brenda, but she died from a rare genetic illness," Jas said, explaining things I already know. "It was one of those difficult diseases that slowly debilitates a person and leaves them in a lot of pain. She suffered for a long time before she passed away. My dad and Brenda had one child, my oldest brother, Braxton."

I rack my brain, trying to remember if Jas's secret spy brother, Braxton, has already come up in the conversations. Idris's text answers that question.

IDRIS

Should I know Braxton?

DARREN

Nope. Say, so there's a second brother? I didn't know that.

"Yes, he's a top-secret brother. Braxton was never about that small-town life. He always wanted to get away and see the world. After high school, he got accepted into Hampton, and never looked back. He eventually became a spy."

DARREN

Are you joking? Your brother is a spy?

"No joke. He is a bonafide CIA operative," Jasmine says. I can hear the pride in her voice. She continues, "We don't hear from him much because he's always jetting around the world doing what spies do.

125

Anyway, Braxton was super close with his mom. When Dad married Evelyn, Braxton didn't want any part of having a stepmother. He insisted on being formal and calling her Evelyn. Of course, she accepted Braxton as her own and never wanted him to feel different or left out. After she had Hendrix and me, she made us call her Evelyn, too. She said it was so all her kids called her the same name."

DARREN

I get it. No one would think he wasn't her biological child if all of you called her Evelyn. Your mom sounds like a remarkable woman. Astute, caring, and sweet.

"That's Evelyn. Total opposite of me."

I scoff at Jasmine's misconceptions about herself, then type.

DARREN

I don't believe that for one second.

"Wait until you get to know me better."

DARREN

Happy to have the invitation.

Jasmine giggles, and I know she's enjoying this. It feels good to be the one to make her feel this way. Even if she doesn't know it's me.

Her voice turns serious as she says, "I'm sure you've heard about the mess with my dad."

DARREN

I know about his conviction. He's in Huntsville, right?

"For two long years," she answers, her voice wistful. "I miss him."

DARREN

> I can imagine. From everything you've told me about how he inspired you to be a doctor, I'm sure it's tough for you not to have him with you as a father and as a professional mentor.

"That's it exactly," Jasmine says. "You totally get it. That's why I'm still so angry. He robbed me of time we could have with each other. Robbed all of us—me, Hendrix, Evelyn, and even Braxton. But on the other hand, I think part of the reason he did what he did was because of his experience with Braxton's mom. He couldn't bear to watch anyone else suffer like that."

I pause, surprised Jas shared intimate details about her feelings with Idris. Of course, she'd shared this with me long ago, but Hendrix and her cousins don't know she feels this way. Now, I'm not the only one she's shared her feelings with. She feels close enough to Idris to share them with him, too.

I don't know how I feel about that.

Pushing the thoughts away, I notice an awkward pause in the conversation and realize Idris is waiting for me to tell him what to say next. I type quickly.

DARREN

> As a doctor, I guess you understand better than most.

"Understand, but don't agree," Jas says. "I wouldn't have done what he did, and he knows it. It goes against everything in me. I think that comes from my Evelyn side."

DARREN

> Not so opposite from your mom after all. I told you.

"Wow, I guess you did," Jasmine says. "You're very perceptive. It's a wonderful trait and rare in my experience. Though, I'm pretty rusty with dating and getting to know someone. What are you looking for in a woman?"

DARREN

You.

I text before I can stop myself. It's not what I want Idris to say, but it's too late.

"Boy, be serious!" Jasmine says. I imagine her rolling her eyes.

DARREN

I am serious. Well, I guess I should say the qualities I've already seen in you.

"Like what?"

DARREN

Off the charts intelligence. Not just related to your career and medicine, but you know so much about most topics. Well read, insightful, opinionated, and passionate about history, current events, pop culture. Everything. It's impressive.

"Okay, I won't lie. I like that you started with that one. Most guys would've said something about my looks."

DARREN

I'm not most guys.

I'm the best friend who loves you so much that I'm helping another man make you happy since you won't let me. But I can't say any of that.

"I'm beginning to see that. What else?"

DARREN

> Despite your tough exterior, you can't hide how much you care about people. It's at the core of who you are and something that is evident in all your interactions. The whole town talks about how great you are and how they feel cared for ever since you came back to town and joined St. Elizabeth's.

"I'm sure that's not the only thing they say about me," Jasmine says under her breath.

DARREN

> Most of them are scared of ticking you off, but they also say you're fair. No matter what your personal feelings are, you'll still do whatever it takes to help them. That says a lot about you.

"Wow, you've done your research, haven't you?" Jasmine sounds genuinely surprised by how well Idris understands her. And she should be. There's no way Idris could've figured all this out without my help. I hope the guy is taking notes so he won't botch the connection I'm helping him build with my best friend.

DARREN

> Only because I'm interested. Very interested in you.

"Now I feel bad. I haven't asked around about you."

DARREN

> There's plenty of time for that. No rush. I'm an open book, too. Anything you want to know about me, just ask.

"Anything?"

> **DARREN**
>
> I mean it.

"Do you always put all your cards on the table like this?" she asks, still skeptical.

> **DARREN**
>
> I'm aware I have some competition for your attention.

"Competition?" She sounds surprised. "You mean Darren? He's no competition."

I hesitate, stunned that her first thought was me and not Troy.

Jasmine continues, "Seriously, we're best friends, and we spend a ton of time together, but Darren would never interfere or try to get in the way of me dating someone. We care too much about each other to block each other's happiness. He's an exceptional friend and person."

A smile erupts on my face from the joy I hear in her voice. She may not be in love with me like I love her, but I can never deny how important I am to Jasmine. She's my favorite person in this world, and I dare say I'm hers too.

I quickly get back to my job and text a response for Idris.

> **DARREN**
>
> Yeah, Darren's a good guy. I like working with him at his foundation. But I was talking about the other guy. The one you went on a date with at Thorn.

"A date at Thorn?" She sounds confused, then quickly says, "Oh, right. You mean Troy. Well, that's a new development. Nothing to mention there."

> **DARREN**
>
> That's not what I heard.

"You can't believe everything you hear in the Kimbell gossip mill,"

Jasmine warns with a playful hint in her voice. "Troy and I have had a few conversations, but none as good as the ones we've had."

> Oh, you like our talks? Glad to have that encouragement.

"If you don't feel encouraged, then I'm not doing a good enough job on these calls," she responds with a flirty hint in her tone. It's sexy and about to push me over the edge, knowing she's saying those words to Idris, not me.

Time for me to wrap things up.

> You're fine. It's nice to hear it. That's all. Do you work tomorrow?

I already know her shift at St. Elizabeth's starts at six am. It's half past two in the morning. She should be in bed now, not talking on the phone.

Jasmine groans. "We've done it again. Talked for almost three hours. Yes, I have the early shift tomorrow. I should go to bed."

> Then I'll let you get your beauty rest. Not that you need more of that. If you get any more beautiful, not sure how I could concentrate.

"That's corny ... and sweet."

> And true. Sweet dreams, Jasmine.

"Goodnight ... Idris."

I press end on the call before Idris can say anything to me. I'm in no mood to be thanked for what I've done tonight.

In fact, I'm not sure I should do this ever again.

CHAPTER 23

J ASMINE

"GIRL, I'M NOT SURE I WANT TO GO, AND YOU HAVE ME traipsing through these expensive boutiques I can't afford trying to find an outfit?" I complain as I follow Mya into another store on Main Street in downtown Kimbell.

"I told you he feels bad about ghosting you. He's trying to make up for it by taking you to a fancy dinner at Thorn. Give him a chance," Mya says, nodding like some bobblehead doll.

My interest in Troy Renault waned over the past two weeks as I slowly gave up on connecting with him. I understand being caught up in the aftermath of the fire at TimberLuxe. Troy was busy dealing with insurance companies and repairs. That had to be why he ignored all my attempts to reach out to him. But as one day turned to two, then into a week and another, I'd given up on Troy.

"If he thinks I've been twiddling my thumbs waiting for him to call me back, he's dead wrong," I say, checking my phone for the unexpected, delightful surprise of a man who'd swooped in and filled the gap Troy left behind.

Mya holds up a slinky red dress and shoves it toward me. "Red is your color." She stretches the fabric along my shoulders.

I glance down at the size. "Mya, there's no way I can fit a twelve. Put this back."

She goes through the rack, but her steely gaze locks onto me. "Not twiddling your thumbs, you say? What's that supposed to mean? Have you been going out with another guy and not giving me the tea?"

I stifle a smile, then respond, "I have not gone on any dates you're not aware of but ..."

"But you have met someone else. Someone who is giving Troy some competition?"

I nod my head slowly. It's hard to wrap my mind around my growing interest in the most unlikely man. But I can't deny that not only do I look forward to our phone conversations, I'm eager to go out on a date if we can ever get our schedules to align.

"Yes, that's a true statement," I say.

Mya thrusts her hands on her bony hips and gives me another shrewd stare. I know I can't keep holding out on her.

I ask, "Has Ronan ever taken you to the Baker Ranch? It's run by Colton Baker, the older brother of the triplets that own Baker Bros BBQ. Supplies all the beef and pork for the restaurant."

Mya shakes her head. "You're getting to know Colton?"

"Of course not! Colton is the most rude, closed-off man in Kimbell, Texas. I don't know any woman in her right mind who'd consider dating him." I cringe at the thought. "There's a guy who works on the ranch. I never crossed paths with him before."

"Jas, tell me this guy's name!"

I glance around the empty boutique. Satisfied that there's no one within earshot who could have me as the number one topic of town gossip within hours, I step closer to Mya. "His name is Idris Gibson.

He's on the board of the Manning Foundation, and he serves as the head football coach. His son Quaid is on the spectrum and plays on the team."

"The spectrum?"

"Quaid is autistic. The youth football team has helped him make friends and be more outgoing in school. Idris is so proud of the strides he's made since coming to Kimbell a few years ago."

"So he and Quaid's mother are divorced?"

"Never married. Had a fling when Idris had gone up to Montana to sell some cattle for Colton. He didn't know he was a father until the mom showed up on his doorstep, exasperated by having to raise a "high-maintenance' child. Quaid was eight. Idris stepped up, became a single father, and is working to understand everything about Quaid's condition."

"Wow, Idris sounds like a dream come true. But you haven't gone on a date with him?"

"No." I twist a strand of my curls around my finger. "We've talked almost every night. The conversations keep getting better and better. He's so open and honest about himself. Plus, he's interested in me and seems to get me like ..." I pause, feeling guilty for my feelings.

"Like?"

"Like only Darren does. It's like Idris gives me the best of both worlds. He understands me like Darren but is also attracted to me as a woman."

"No man is this perfect. Tell me his flaws," Mya says.

"Well, if Troy is a ten on the hotness scale, Idris is a solid ... four."

Mya grimaces. "That bad?"

"Generic. Average. Not memorable in the looks department."

"Okay, but a great personality makes up for all of that. Anything else?"

"Troy and I are on the same level from a professional perspective. Idris is a ranch hand. He didn't graduate from high school and didn't bother to get a GED until after his son's mom dropped Quaid on his doorstep. That was the push for him to do it."

"Admirable."

"True." I smile. "The best part is he makes it no secret he's developing strong feelings for me. He wants our new friendship to blossom into something romantic and intimate."

Mya frowns and throws up her hands. "Explain why you and Idris haven't gone on a date."

"That's the part I don't get," I admit, tempering my frustration. "Whenever I suggest we hang out, Idris has some excuse." I pause and hold up my hands. "No, let me stop." I take a deep breath and force myself to give Mya the objective, factual version, not the one tinged with my emotions. "He has a busy schedule like me. We can't seem to get our calendars in sync." I say, then slump down on an ottoman in the corner near a rack of satin dresses I wouldn't be caught dead in. "Now that I know him much better, I think all those superficial things I had focused on before won't matter. I can see myself walking away from Troy for Idris. Is that horrible?"

"What's horrible is both men fail in the dating department. Troy goes radio silent on you for weeks. Then when I tell him you're not upset about how he tried to pounce on Darren at the Retired Healers Network meeting, he gets the nerve to text you again—"

"Wait!" I jump up. "Is that why Troy has been avoiding me?"

"He thought you would rip his head off for the questions he asked Darren. He thought you hated him for what he did," Mya explains.

"Wow, and I thought he wasn't interested anymore."

"Idris isn't the only one you intimidate. That's why I think you should give Troy another chance. See if the two of you might have a spark that is as good or better than the one you feel with Idris."

I walk over to a rack of cocktail dresses and glance at the sizes. Nothing over a twelve. This is not the store for me, but Troy could still be the man for me. There's nothing wrong with keeping my options open, especially since I don't know if the conversational chemistry Idris and I have over the phone will translate to an in-person date. The last time we were around each other, he could barely say a coherent sentence. What if that's still the case?

On the other hand, there's Troy. He's the most handsome man who has ever shown interest in me. He's intelligent and successful and worried he crossed the point of no return when he attacked my best friend. I won't lie. My excitement for Troy waned after that incident. But if Troy is willing to accept Darren's importance in my life, shouldn't I accept his offer to reconnect and rekindle the off-the-charts chemistry we had weeks ago?

"You've been quiet for too long," Mya says, coming to my side. She bumps me with her shoulder. "What are you thinking?"

"I'm thinking I should give Troy another chance."

"Yes!" Mya pumps her fist in the air. "Not that I have anything against Idris. Date them both and see who you have a stronger connection with."

I take out my phone and respond to Troy's text.

His reply is immediate.

"Looks like I'm meeting Troy at Thorn tonight. So, I need a dress, but I'm not going to find one here," I say, heading for the door. "We have enough time to make it to the Cypress Outlet Mall to find something fabulous."

Mya claps her hands. "I'll drive."

CHAPTER 24

D ARREN

GRIPPING THE TUMBLER OF SCOTCH, I STARE OVER THE RIM at a table on the opposite side of the restaurant. Thorn is packed tonight. But nothing can stop me from looking at her.

Jasmine is illuminated by the soft glow of the candlelight flickering from the center of the table. Stunning is the only word that comes to mind as I take her in for the thousandth time. Her hair hangs in loose curls around her face. She's wearing a dress I've never seen before. It's a deep red, accentuated against her deep brown skin. The v-neck plunges toward her chest but maintains sophistication and elegance.

I chug the rest of my drink and push back the thoughts that I should be the one sitting across from her. Not Troy Renault.

I hate that I'm not the only one who can't take his eyes off her. A glance to my left and I read my exact thoughts on the face of Idris.

That's entirely my fault.

I've spent the last two weeks listening to Idris's conversations with Jasmine and texting him all the right things to say to win her over. At first, it was awkward and disjointed. By the third phone call, Idris figured out how to take my words, mostly verbatim, and relay them to the woman I love. And I learned how to text at lightning speed, the words pouring from my heart, hoping Jasmine could tell they were mine. Even coming from the voice of another man who is falling in love with her, I want her to know somewhere deep down it was me and not him.

But she doesn't know. She's starting to fall for Idris. Opening up to him. Telling him things I didn't think she'd share with anyone except me.

Isn't this what I wanted?

I know I can't have Jasmine for myself, so wasn't the next best option to find her a guy that was a better fit for her than Troy? So why am I pissed that it worked?

Maybe because I'll have to let go of my love for Jasmine once and for all. Get out there like she's been pushing me to do and find someone else to fill the void she's left in my heart.

But before I do that, I'm taking the training wheels off with Idris. I've told him what to say in every call he's had with Jasmine over the past couple of weeks. It's about time I extract myself from their relationship. Let Idris handle the next phase on his own.

"Idris, who are you staring at?" Mirielle asks, craning her neck to look behind her.

I stiffen, knowing who has caught Idris's attention.

A goofy grin spreads across Mirielle's face. "Is that Jasmine? I hear she's focused on finding love this year. Maybe, you could have a shot."

Blossom's face lights up, and she squeezes Idris's hand. "I can't believe you haven't told her."

"Told her what?" Luke asks, tilting his head toward me.

I remain quiet. No one knows how I've been helping Idris talk to Jasmine. Not even Wiley.

"None of you know about Idris's late-night conversations with our Head of Emergency Medicine?" Blossom makes a point of looking at each of us, barely able to contain her excitement.

"Well, I don't want to jinx anything. But I guess it's no harm in all of you knowing that the good doctor and I have been getting to know each other ... slowly. I think we're headed in the right direction," Idris responds, but he doesn't look at me.

Mirielle turns to me. "Did you know about this? Has Jasmine told you?"

"If you think I'm going to reveal what my best friend talks to me about, you're crazy." My words are blunt, with a tinge of harshness I can't hide.

"I'm sure Jasmine would knock you out if you did," Luke chuckles and punches me in the arm. He turns to Idris and adds, "You're a much better match for her than that guy over there."

"Doesn't matter because Idris and Jasmine haven't gone out yet," Blossom says. "As soon as they coordinate schedules, I'm sure she'll drop that guy for Idris."

"You better not wait too long," Mirielle warns. "That guy looks like major competition for her heart."

I sneak another glance at Jasmine's table. My muscles tense as the dynamics of the date have taken a downward turn.

Jasmine slowly crosses her arms over her chest and stares daggers at Troy as he rattles off at the mouth. We're too far away to hear what Troy is saying, but I can read the look on Jasmine's face.

She's about sixty seconds away from going off on Troy.

Trouble in paradise?

A surge of adrenaline flows through me.

If Troy has done something to Jasmine, I'll make him regret it. That's for sure.

But I hold off, knowing how much my best friend would be annoyed if I storm over and try to "save" her from a situation she has under control. If there's one thing I know about Jasmine, she doesn't need a rescue. She's more than capable of handling any situation on her own.

"Maybe," Idris says, craning his neck to get a better view. "Looks like the date isn't going so well—"

"Excuse me!" Jasmine's voice booms loud within the restaurant.

Troy raises his voice in response. "All I'm saying is there's a lot of criminals in your family. I wasn't expecting that. No one in my family has ever been to prison."

"Criminals in my family?" Jasmine repeats, but I know it's her way of trying to calm herself down. The worst thing Troy could do is attack the people Jasmine loves most. He's treading on thin ice right now. I can't say I'm sad to see it happen.

But I hate this is the way Jasmine gets to see Troy's true colors.

"Your brother, Hendrix, served time. Your father is in a maximum security prison as we speak. You're being cagey about where your other brother is. How do I know he's not in Rikers for being a mass murderer?"

Luke gives me a shove.

I have to stop things before Jasmine goes ballistic and slams her wine glass into Troy's face. When Jasmine is about to lose it, I'm the one who gets the call to get her out of the situation before she does more harm to herself and whoever is the source of her ire.

The last guy I protected from her wrath was Santos. He got off easy with a Frappuccino splashed in his face before I threw Jasmine over my shoulder and carried her away.

"Go," Luke says.

I nod and push back from my seat.

"Someone needs to get Jasmine away from that guy," Idris says, then glances at me. "You stay. I'll take care of it." He nods again as if to reassure me. "I can handle this."

And with those words, I slump back into my seat and realize it's time to move on from loving my best friend. I may not be able to turn off my feelings overnight, but I can get out of the way and let Idris be the man she relies on.

Idris crosses the room and stops at Jasmine's table. Troy looks annoyed by the interruption, and they exchange heated words I can't make out. Idris extends his hand toward Jasmine. She looks up at him with pure relief and gratefulness as she slips her hand into his.

I drain my scotch as Idris walks out of Thorn Restaurant, hand-in-hand with the woman I love.

CHAPTER 25

J ASMINE

TUGGING AT THE SASH OF MY COAT, I TIGHTEN IT AROUND
my body as a chilly gust of wind blows across the parking lot of Thorn
Restaurant. To say this night is not ending how I expected is an
understatement. All my fantasies of Troy and I rekindling the
chemistry we'd shared before the fire at TimberLuxe and Darren's
presentation at the Retired Healers Network went up in a poof of
smoke the minute Troy revealed his true self.

I should've known he was too good to be true.

The man had everything going for him—highly educated, resume
lined with executive-level positions at numerous companies, and
hotter than August in Texas.

But it's clear why he's a bachelor and might be for the rest of his
lousy life.

Bouncing from one cramped foot in a sequined stiletto heel to the other, I can't stop myself from ranting. "In all the time we'd spent together, and admittedly, when I go back and count up the hours, it wasn't many. Still, he never showed that elitist, judgmental side. If he had, trust me, I never would've given him a second glance. I don't care how ..." I pause, realizing it's not a good idea to tell one man who is interested in me how hot I think another guy is.

Idris is bent over, half submerged in his late model Camry which has seen better days about a decade ago. He lifts a seemingly endless mound of football equipment, discarded jerseys, and sneakers from the front seat.

"Do you know he had the nerve to say he was doing me a favor by ignoring the fact ..." I pause, emphasizing the words to do air quotes Idris can't see. "That I have criminals in my family. Normally, a man with his pedigree wouldn't continue to date someone whose family had done time. Can you believe that?" I press my hands on my hips.

Idris gives me a suitable grunt to continue.

"I'm disgusted it crossed my mind to explain the extenuating circumstances that landed my brother and father in prison. Hendrix was a teenager when he made a foolish and immature mistake. He did his time, and the minute he left prison, he turned his life around. My brother may be an ex-con, but he's also a successful mechanic and businessman. He works for no one but himself running his auto body shop. I'm so proud of him. But do you think any of that mattered to Troy?"

Idris backs out of the passenger seat, his face covered by the mound in his arms. His head moves from side to side, and I know he feels what I'm going through. I don't need to second guess that Idris understands me and would never say something so disrespectful about my family. I've had too many conversations with Idris over the past couple of weeks to know he's entirely the opposite of that jerk, Troy. Idris is more like Darren, which makes him a much better match for me than Troy could ever be.

I follow Idris to the trunk as he ducks back around to the driver's side of the car. "And my father, misguided though he was, thought he was doing the right thing for a patient."

Idris glances back at me with a sympathetic smile, then hauls a mesh bag filled with what looks like dirty laundry over his shoulder and dumps it in the trunk.

"The fact that Troy didn't try to understand what landed Hendrix and my dad in prison shows he and I would never make it. I know I'm not the sweetest person in the world, but I have always given people the benefit of the doubt. I don't hold myself up as being better than anyone else!" I beat my purse against the top of the car.

Idris flinches and then looks at the paint job to make sure I didn't do any damage.

"I didn't mean to do that," I say, then rub my hand over the metal to make sure no damage was done.

"It's okay," he says. Then walks past me to sit in the car. Leaning out, he glances at me, then asks, "You ready to go?"

Before I can respond, he cranks the engine as I stare at the open passenger door. I suppose chivalry is dead, but I shouldn't complain. I'm lucky Idris had dinner at Thorn tonight and rescued me from this nightmare.

I get in the car and almost gag from the stench of body odor and stale sweat. It's like the entire youth football team was trapped in here for hours after their game this morning. But I'm not going to be rude like Troy. I hold my breath and press the button to open the window. A cool, clean, and much needed breeze circulates within the stagnant air.

For the thousandth time, I kick myself for letting a man drive me on a date. When will I learn my lesson?

Idris pulls out of the parking lot.

"This is what I get for going through the trouble of trying to impress a man who has shown me time and time again he's not worth it. Troy and I never have great conversations like we do." I jerk at the seatbelt, trying to get it to cross my body with no success. "Seriously, you're the reason why I realized Troy and I—

"It's broken," Idris mutters.

"What?"

"Seatbelt. Broken."

"Oh," I say, letting it fall to my side.

"Quaid sits in the back. Haven't bothered to get it fixed."

"Well, if the cops pull us over, you're paying for my ticket." I glance his way, but Idris doesn't crack a smile. "Hey, I'm joking. My cousins are cops. They would take care of any ticket for me, not that I've ever gotten one."

Idris grips his steering wheel tighter but doesn't look my way. He nods his head and focuses intently on the road in front of us.

What is up with this guy? I thought all the conversations and details we've shared would get him to loosen up around me, but it hasn't.

From the moment we left Troy back at the restaurant, Idris hasn't said more than a few words to me.

Do I still make him nervous?

Maybe I should be flattered.

But in reality, I'm annoyed. I want to talk about this crazy night. I want to explain to Idris how he helped me to see I need to look beyond a fancy resume and good looks. It's the person on the inside and the connection that matters most. But he won't make eye contact.

"Idris, aren't you going to say anything?"

He clears his throat. "Yeah, I forgot. Did you mention where you live?"

I'm thankful it's dark in the car, so he can't see my heavy eye roll.

"Belvedere on the Lake," I say, although the apartment complex is nowhere close to Lake Lasso, as the name implies. Instead, it's nestled against a manufactured, luxuriously landscaped lake about a tenth of the size.

"Got it." His knuckles grip the steering wheel tighter as he merges onto the county road.

I stare at his profile, wondering what he's thinking. He's never this quiet on the phone. We barely have a lull in our conversation.

His eyes are glued onto the road as if he's afraid a deer will pop out at any moment. And I suppose one could.

I hoped he'd calm me down from my rant like he had done so many times during our phone calls. The only other person better at helping me settle down and think beyond my emotions is … Darren.

But I'm not with my best friend right now. I'm with a man who professes he wants a chance at a relationship with me, but he's not acting like himself. Or at least not the man I know from our phone calls.

I take a deep breath and try not to judge Idris too harshly. I have been spouting venom about another man I was on a date with. I can't imagine that's easy for him, even if I made it no secret I was dating other people and keeping my options open. I guess I should be lucky he came to my rescue at all.

We ride in silence for the next ten minutes until he pulls up to the entrance to the complex. Using my remote, I open the gate and direct him to where my apartment is located. I have the best view of the lake, which Darren insisted I get, even though it meant my rent would be twenty percent higher. He offered to cover the costs, but I wouldn't let him. And I never regretted taking his advice. The sunrise views are stunning and have lifted my spirits many mornings.

"Well, this is me," I say, breaking the awkward tension.

Idris turns to look at me. His eyes are full of compassion as he reaches for my hand. "Have a good evening." The words sound so final that I feel panicked.

"Idris, are we okay? I mean, did this change things for you?"

He shakes his head. "It's late. Quaid. Routine and all. You understand?"

"Of course," I say, feeling like a dolt. "We'll talk later?"

"Yeah," Idris says, but I'm not convinced.

I may have gone from two suitors to zero in one night.

Yay me.

I leave the car and wave goodbye to Idris as he drives away.

There's no way I want to go inside my empty apartment.

There's only one place I want to be.

CHAPTER 26

ARREN

LUB-DUB. LUB-DUB. LUB-DUB.

My hands press the stethoscope hard against my chest as the sound drowns out all other thoughts threatening to send me careening down a pit of despair.

Thoughts like what Idris and Jasmine are doing at this very moment.

After he stormed over to the table where she was arguing with Troy and put the idiot in his place, I spent the rest of the night listening to Mirielle and Blossom swoon over Idris's romantic display.

How many times have I done the same thing for Jasmine? I don't have enough fingers and toes to count, but no one got starry-eyed over my actions.

The only thing keeping my imagination from running wild is listening to my heart through one of Jasmine's spare stethoscopes.

My heart is shattered but still beating.

I told Idris precisely what to say to my best friend on all the phone calls with Jasmine. I'd hoped she would know it was me. Know that I was the one she should fall for, not him.

But Idris played the part too well.

Now Jasmine is falling for him—

The front door swings open. I scramble to my feet, tossing the stethoscope behind the stairs. I need to come up with a lie to tell Wiley about why I'm sitting in the dark.

Until I realize it's not Wiley in my doorway.

Jasmine practically flies into the house. I'm nearly knocked over by the force of her body crashing into mine. I'm momentarily stunned, but then wrap my arms around her with a fierce embrace. If this is a dream, I don't want to wake up.

"My life sucks," Jasmine says, then looks up at me with a pained expression that does nothing to hide how gorgeous she is. Her beautiful brown eyes search mine as a cute wrinkle emerges between her brows. She's still in the sexy red dress that had my eyes bugging out of my head. But her hair is a messy halo of curls framing her face.

I can't resist tucking the strands behind her ears. "I hate you went through that—"

"Oh no! I get that we live in a tiny town, but that disaster happened less than an hour ago. Has the news already spread all over Kimbell?" Jasmine tries to pull away, but I won't let her go. My arms circle tightly around her waist, preventing her from putting any distance between us. Moments like this won't come around much in the future, so I let myself enjoy her.

I chuckle under my breath. "Not yet. I was at Thorn having dinner with my board tonight—"

"So, you heard everything?"

"Yes," I say as she buries her head against my chest. Part of me wonders what Idris did wrong that led Jasmine to my doorstep. Another part of me could care less as the scent of her lavender shampoo intoxicates me. I try to memorize everything about this moment. I know the day is coming when she won't run to me anymore when she's upset.

Jasmine's voice is muffled against my chest. "Go ahead and say it."

I let out a hearty laugh, then rub her back in circles like I know she likes. "No."

"You know you want to."

"I never want you to be disappointed, Jas. I'd rather be wrong."

"But you weren't wrong this time."

"Do you wish I was?"

She leans back and looks up at me with clarity. "No. It's time I stop focusing on all the wrong things and see the real Troy. I hate that I wasted any time with him."

"I would've come over, but Idris ..."

"Wanted to play knight in shining armor."

An edge in her tone sets off alarm bells within me. Did he cross the line? Could Idris not be the upstanding guy I thought? Maybe not the best match for Jasmine after all?

"What happened with Idris after the two of you left the restaurant?" I can barely get the question out.

"Nothing worth mentioning." She inhales a deep breath, then caresses her hands down my biceps until she pulls my hands away from her waist and interlocks her fingers with mine. "He's still nervous around me. After everything that happened tonight, I wasn't going to pressure him. It took a lot to rescue me when he knew I was on a date with another man. Not many men would do that."

The admiration in her voice is like a kick in my gut. She is falling for Idris Gibson.

"So, he took you home and ..."

Jasmine drops my hands to cover her mouth as she yawns, then walks backward toward the staircase. "I got in my car and came straight over here."

As she disappears up the stairs, I jog into the kitchen to grab reinforcements. Freezer first, where I get a pint of Blue Bell Cookies and Cream ice cream. Then I go to the refrigerator for a bushel of grapes and a bag of assorted cheese cubes. With my free hand, I reach for a bottle of Harlow Rose's Cabernet Sauvignon, which Jasmine loves but hates to admit.

With her favorites cradled in my arms, I take the stairs two at a time and join her in the movie room.

A smile plays at the corner of Jasmine's mouth as I place the items on the table next to the couch she's lounging on. I'm surprised she hasn't turned the projector television to the reality shows we binge-watch.

I ease onto the couch, maneuvering my body behind hers. Jasmine inches forward to give me more space to get comfortable. I wrap my arms around her and pull her against me, hoping she can't feel the thumping of my heart against her back.

Leaning my mouth close to her ear, I ask, "Do you want to talk about it or forget about it?"

"Forget," she says, snuggling closer to me.

The space between us feels charged with unspoken feelings. I have an intense urge to kiss her, but I know I can't. I took my shot, and she turned me down. She's falling for Idris, which is a good thing.

"Ready for season four of our show?" I ask, leaning over to grab the remote.

"Yes!" Jasmine says, then claps her hands. She reaches for the pint of ice cream and two spoons, handing me one as I turn the projector television on. "I don't care if you don't want the calories. You have to help me eat this."

I respond by digging a deep spoonful out and stuffing it in my mouth, eliciting her huge grin. As much as I love Jasmine, I don't want to lose ... this. We're so good together. Maybe jeopardizing our friendship for love that may not work isn't a good idea. Not having Jasmine in my life isn't an option.

I reach behind the couch and grab a blanket to cover us. Jasmine snuggles against my chest, getting into a comfortable position. She relaxes against me as I brush strands of her hair away from her eyes.

"Alright, here's the deal," I say as she turns her head to look at me.

I force myself not to get weak from that lovely face. "It's late. You have an earlier start for work than me in the morning."

"Don't remind me," Jasmine says, her face morphing from cute to menacing. "I'll also have to explain to my team how the date with Troy was a disaster. I wish I'd never told them about him."

"You'll be fine. You're tough and strong. You can handle it. Soon, there will be something else that y'all will gossip about, and they won't remember Troy. That guy never deserved you anyway."

"You have to say that. You're my best friend."

Her words seal my fate.

I'm her best friend, and that's all I'll ever be.

"True, but I'm right, too." I gently turn her head back toward the movie screen as the show's opening credits start. "Two episodes max, then you need to get in bed."

Jasmine looks back at me. Her eyes fill with emotion as she rests her hands on my face. "I don't say this often enough." She closes her eyes for a long moment, and when she opens them, I'm struck speechless.

Pure unadulterated want and desire are reflected back at me.

I can't breathe with her looking at me like this.

My heart thunders in my chest, wondering what she will say next.

"Thank you for always being here for me. I can't imagine my life without you, Darren."

Her face tilts up toward mine.

A clear and unmistakable invitation to … kiss her.

I want to devour those lips, wrap her in my arms and never let her go.

It's a dangerous thought.

One I need to push away fast before I say or do something stupid. Like, tell her how I feel about her. How I've felt about her for years.

"And you'll never have to," I say.

CHAPTER 27

ARREN

WALKING INTO THE FIRE STATION BREAK ROOM, I SEE
Ronan and know something is wrong. He looks like a shadow of his
typical confident self. His eyes are troubled as he slumps in his chair
and looks at the ceiling tiles stained brown from water leaks.

"Something happen with the twins?" I ask, glancing at Wiley, then
Luke and Nate, huddled in their usual spots at the table. I drop my
backpack on the couch, then ease into my chair beside Wiley.

"It's Declan," Wiley says. "He's having—"

Nate interrupts, "Declan's having a tough time dealing with his
head injury. Ronan's having a tough time coming to terms with his son
needing to see a shrink."

Luke exhales. "Nate, do you have to be so … "

"Honest? Yeah, I do." Nate snaps back. He turns and locks eyes with Ronan in righteous indignation. "You should've booked an appointment for him weeks ago."

"You think I don't want my son to get better? The problem isn't taking Declan to see a child psychiatrist. I need my brother's help to pick the right one."

"But Connor's not here," I say, trying to recall what Jasmine told me about Ronan's twin brother's departure from St. Elizabeth's Hospital. "Isn't he working with Doctors Without Borders?"

"Yeah, and Ronan's having trouble him," Wiley explains. "Connor's medical team has gone into a remote area and he can't be reached."

"Which means Ronan needs to give up on having Connor co-sign on the psychiatrist and pick one himself," Nate chides.

"And take the chance I do more harm by picking some quack? You think that's best for Declan?" Ronan thunders, rising in his seat.

Nate doesn't back down. "Better than the harm of not getting him help."

Ronan lunges for Nate.

I jump up and rush toward Ronan as Luke jerks Nate backward. I hold Ronan back as adrenaline floods my veins, but he's still seething with anger.

"Hey, stop it. Fighting Nate isn't going to solve anything," I say, trying to calm him down. "His approach needs work, but he means well. You know he wants the best for you and Declan."

"Judging my decisions when he doesn't have a family of his own is a poor way of showing he cares," Ronan says.

Nate looks like he wants to respond, but Luke puts a hand on his shoulder, silently signaling for him to hold his tongue. Fear and pain are etched on Ronan's face. Berating Ronan about how and when he chooses to help Declan won't help. The man is scared and frustrated.

"We know you're going to do what's best for Declan," I say, trying to diffuse the situation.

"Really? Because Nate seems to have a different opinion," Ronan retorts.

Wiley scoffs. "Everybody knows Nate's opinion is not worth a hill of beans. Don't let him get to you."

Ronan chuckles under his breath. I give Wiley a quick nod, thankful he had the antidote to relieve some of the tension in the room.

"I need to finish up some paperwork." Ronan maneuvers around me and heads toward the exit. "Don't waste too much time in here. We need to get the morning assignments done. Nate, you're on bathroom duty."

"Fine with me," Nate says with a defiant nod. As soon as Ronan is out of earshot, Nate says, "Y'all know I'm right."

"Yeah, but there's a right way of making that point and a wrong way," Luke says.

"You chose the most wrong way possible," Wiley rants, pointing his finger in Nate's face.

"Ronan doesn't need us sugarcoating things. He needs a kick in the pants to get Declan help," Nate says. "How much do you want to bet Declan gets that doctor's appointment before our shift is over?"

I shrug, conceding Nate's point.

"If I have to be the bad guy, then so be it," Nate says. "As long as Declan gets to talk to a shrink soon."

"Speaking of bad guys," Luke says, glancing my way. "How's Jasmine doing?"

"What happened with Jasmine?" Nate asks.

I fill Nate and Wiley in on Jasmine's disastrous date with Troy Renault at Thorn last night and Idris going to her rescue.

"She's livid about giving Troy the time of day but fine otherwise," I say, omitting that although she left the restaurant with Idris, she spent the night with me.

"I'm glad she realized Troy is scum before it was too late," Wiley says. "Better to know now before she developed deeper feelings for him."

"Idris being in her life should soften the blow. They looked mighty cozy leaving the restaurant together," Luke says. "I wouldn't be surprised if they become a couple soon."

Wiley raises an eyebrow. "Idris took Jasmine home last night?"

"Speak of the devil," Nate says, flicking his head toward the break room door.

Idris's face is tight with anxiety. He stands rigid as he looks at me. "Darren, can I talk to you for a minute?"

"Of course," I say, ignoring the curious glances from the guys. I lead Idris down the hallway to an empty office. Closing the door behind us, I turn to face him.

"I blew it with Jasmine." Idris paces, the hollow sound of his cowboy boots rhythmically thudding across the tile floor. His wide-brim cowboy hat, usually secured atop his head, now wrings in his anxious grip. "I mean it, Darren. I'm not exaggerating. It was a disaster. Utter train wreck."

My heartbeat slows, the adrenaline rush receding as relief sweeps through me. I thought Jasmine had confessed to Idris about leaving him to get the comfort and support she needed from me last night. I imagined he had put two and two together and come up with I'm in love with my best friend and was going to face off with me about it.

But that was ludicrous.

There's no way Idris could know about my feelings for Jasmine. And what could he possibly accuse me of? Jasmine and I have been friends for decades. Her presence in my home is commonplace. She has her own key and her own room, which the whole town knows.

"And it's worse because—" Idris pauses, drawing in a deep breath. He blurts out his confession, each word like a dagger stabbing me in the heart, "I ... I think I'm in love with her."

"In love ... with Jasmine?" My stomach turns. I should've seen this coming, but the reality lands like a sucker punch.

"Yes."

"Did you tell her?"

His eyes widen. "Of course not! She'll think I'm a certified nutcase. We haven't gone on our first date yet."

"What happened last night?" I ask, trying to remember what Jasmine said about her ride home with Idris, which wasn't much.

Details tumble from Idris's mouth. A play-by-play of the excruciating encounter that I'm sure left Jasmine baffled.

Idris says, "I know I was supposed to say something to calm her down and make her feel better, but I choked. Her closeness, her distress, it was overwhelming. I couldn't think."

"So, what did you do?"

"Nodded as she spoke so she would know I was listening. But I didn't say anything," he admits, shame casting long shadows across his features. "We fell into this awkward, stifling silence as I drove her home. It was pretty bad."

I scratch my jaw, the stubble rough against my palm. I wonder how Jasmine reconciled this quiet, awkward Idris with the confident and insightful charmer she's been falling for over the phone. A guy whose scripted words come directly from me.

I prod, "And how did the night end?"

"I think she wanted to invite me up to her place."

The words, innocent as they may be, ignite a flare of jealousy that I smother before the flames engulf me.

"But I made up an excuse about Quaid," Idris continues, oblivious to my inner turmoil. "I couldn't risk ruining what little chance I have to get her to fall for me," Idris explains. "That's why I need your help."

I level a stern stare at him. "Idris, you need to figure out a way to talk to Jasmine on your own. I can't be there every time. I won't be around when the two of you start hanging out in person."

"I know. I realized that last night." His admission is earnest and forlorn. "So, I studied your texts and practiced the right things to say to her. I'm ready to ask her out. But I need your help for one last thing."

The expectation in his eyes weighs on me. "And what would that be?"

"Plan our first date. Something to blow her away, make her forget last night's catastrophe," He pleads, desperation seeping into his words.

I shake my head, a sigh escaping my lips. "Wouldn't it be better if it was genuinely your idea that impresses her, not—"

"Come on, Darren. Don't bail on me now," he interrupts. "I promise this is the last favor. From here on, I'm flying solo. But I need this one sure shot. Any ideas?"

A plan comes to my mind, something I'd reserved for Jasmine's birthday. But perhaps Idris should be the one to do this for her.

"One last time, Idris. After this, you're on your own."

His face lights up, relief washing away the worry lines. "Deal."

I fish out my phone from my pocket, scrolling to find the number in my contacts. As it rings, a faint echo of disappointment lingers in my heart. I shake it off, and as the call is answered, I say, "Hey, I need a favor."

CHAPTER 28

J ASMINE

"Do I need to be blindfolded?" I ask, thrilled by how much effort Idris put into our first date. I will admit, after he took me home from Thorn a week ago, I had given up on him ... and dating in general.

My heart and mental state couldn't withstand the ups and downs, highs and lows of getting a relationship off the ground with a man. I don't know how other women do it. I'd much rather lose myself in my work, family, and friends—all predictable, consistent, and comfortable.

I didn't feel an ounce of regret about ditching Idris to go to Darren's house. As usual, my best friend knew how to get me past my anger at Troy and that whole debacle. Laying on the oversized couch in his movie room, I basked in Darren's strong arms wrapped around me as I ate Blue Bell ice cream and watched our favorite reality show. It was beyond perfection.

A dangerous thought took hold of me as I was with him.

Maybe Evelyn and my aunts were wrong. Maybe having a substitute relationship with my best friend is better than having the real thing. The whole atmosphere triggered thoughts of the two kisses we'd shared. The next thing I knew, I faced Darren, hoping and praying he'd kiss me again.

Of course, he didn't.

He looked at me like I was the best friend I am, nothing more, and I realized that's all we'll ever be. Still, I can't deny dating Darren no longer seems so far-fetched.

And I don't know if that's a good thing or a bad thing.

So, when Idris texted and apologized for being quiet the last time we were together, I threw caution to the wind.

What's wrong with giving him one more chance like I'd given Troy?

Idris shocked me by suggesting we go on a date instead of having another phone call. I've been hoping for this kind of proactive behavior from him.

Now I can gauge if we have chemistry or if I need to abandon dating forever.

Idris laughs. "I want this date to be full of surprises. Good ones, you know. You wouldn't let me drive you, which I understand. This is my compromise."

I give him a shrewd stare as he grins back at me. He's dressed in a crisp white shirt and dark jeans, cowboy boots that have been polished and shined, and an expensive-looking Stetson cowboy hat on his head. Not the look I'd dreamed of for a guy I'm dating, but I must admit he looks good. More than good. Handsome, actually, for an average-looking guy.

"Alright, Idris. Blindfold me," I say, trying to hide my excitement. No one has ever done anything like this for me except maybe Darren. He's always doing sweet and thoughtful things to surprise me, but he doesn't count.

Idris takes a silky scarf from his pocket that matches the magenta hue of my dress. So that's why he wanted details of what I was wearing. Extra points for that.

As he ties the scarf around my eyes, I can't help but feel a flutter of anticipation in my stomach. Maybe this date won't be so bad after all. I might have a good time with Idris.

"Ready?" Idris asks, his voice low and smooth.

"Ready," I reply, feeling a tingle run through me as he takes my hand and leads me forward.

We walk for what feels like ages, my heart beating faster with every step. The sound of traffic, the murmur of people's voices from the shops and restaurants lining Main Street of Downtown Kimbell, fade away until they're replaced with the soft rustling of trees and birds chirping. My sense of direction isn't that great, but I'm guessing we're on the outskirts of town, where neighborhoods start to blend with the businesses.

"Okay, we're here," Idris says, his fingers tight around mine as he guides me to stop.

"Can I take off the blindfold now?" I ask, eager to see where we are.

"Not yet," he says, his voice teasing. "First, I want you to taste something."

"Taste something?" I repeat, growing more intrigued by the second.

He places a spoon in my hand. I bring it to my mouth and taste the velvety, buttery creaminess of a decadent sauce infused with Parmigiano-Reggiano. My heart soars. Not only do I know what I'm tasting, I know who made it.

"Idris! This is the alfredo sauce from Risveglio, my favorite Italian restaurant," I say, snatching the blindfold from my face.

"I guess you approve?" Idris says, winking at me.

"Absolutely." The stately stone facade of the restaurant covered in vines looms behind Idris. The restaurant's name is etched in simple black letters on a marble square to the right of the door. "But I hate to break this to you," I say. "Risveglio isn't opened on Sundays."

Idris raises an eyebrow as his eyes dance with mischief. "It is for us."

I squeal with delight as he reaches for the door and opens it, beckoning me to enter. I walk through the foyer and enter the main dining room, where all the tables have been cleared except for one. In the center of the room, a table is set with white linen, silverware, and flickering candles that cast a warm glow.

"I cannot believe you did all of this for me."

"You're more than worth it ... but you'll have to work for it."

"Work for it? What does that mean?"

Idris chuckles, then leads me toward the kitchen. "Chef Fiora Moretti will teach us how to make any dish on the menu. Then we'll eat what we made."

"This is a dream come true!" I say as we enter the kitchen. I rush over to the Chef and give her a big hug.

"I'm glad you're looking forward to this experience," Fiora says warmly. "But I must warn you. It won't be easy."

"Bring it on. I know what I want to make," I say, then pause and turn to Idris. "I get to pick, right?"

"Absolutely. Whatever you want." He takes off his cowboy hat and leans against one of the counters.

"Chef Fiora, I want to make your signature lamb rigatoni alfredo and the classic tiramisu. It's my favorite thing to order when Darren and I come here," I say, then slap my hand over my mouth. "I'm sorry, I didn't mean to bring him up. This restaurant is out of my price range. I usually guilt him into taking me."

Idris shrugs. "I understand. I'm sure there are many things you and Darren have done in the past. But hopefully, you and I will start doing those."

"I like the sound of that," I say.

"Well, now that's settled. Let's get started," Chef Fiona announces.

Over the next hour, we chop, sauté, and mix ingredients, all while receiving guidance from Chef Fiora. Idris and I work as a team, our movements in sync as we prepare the dish. The kitchen is a blur of activity as pots simmer, pans sizzle, and the savory aroma of the lamb fills my senses.

Our hands brush past each other, sending electric shocks down my spine each time. I can't help but steal glances at him, admiring how his brows furrow in concentration. The way his biceps flex when he stirs the pot.

Finally, the dishes are ready, and we sit to enjoy our creations. The lamb is tender and flavorful, the rigatoni al dente, and the alfredo sauce rich and creamy. As for the tiramisu, it's a heavenly concoction of espresso-soaked ladyfingers layered with sweet mascarpone cream and dusted with cocoa powder.

As we eat, we chat and laugh, enjoying each other's company, and I realize Idris is more than a great guy who planned a great date for me. He's kind, charming, and funny. I can't help but feel drawn to him in a way I haven't felt before.

Could Idris be my Mr. Right?

Chef Fiora exits the kitchen and clears our plates, disappearing quickly as the soft sound of jazz fills the air.

"You planned everything, didn't you? Who knew you were this romantic," I say, teasing him.

"I know. Impressive, huh?" Idris glances around the room, then focuses his attention back on me. "Care to dance?"

"You're joking." I roll my eyes. We'd look ridiculous dancing alone in this big room. But … I guess who's watching? It's just the two of us, and it's a sweet gesture. "I'm sorry. I tend to default to being difficult."

"I hadn't noticed." Idris laughs. "So, is that a yes?"

I nod, then place my hand in his as he leads me away from our table. We sway slowly and naturally to the rhythm as we look into each other's eyes. His hands slide down my back and rest on my hips as our bodies press against each other.

Tilting my head toward him, Idris takes the hint and leans in for a kiss. I wrap my arms around his neck and pull him closer. His lips are soft against mine, gentle at first but becoming more intense. Idris is a passionate kisser, but I can't ignore the fact I feel …

Nothing.

CHAPTER 29

J ASMINE

DIPPING THE WOODEN SPOON INTO THE BUBBLING CREAMY alfredo sauce, I gather a small taste and walk over to Mya. "Taste this."

"If it tastes half as good as it smells, I know it's going to be amazing," Mya says, reaching her tattooed arms toward the spoon. She places it in her mouth and lets out a moan. "This is divine. I can't believe Chef Fiora gave you her secret recipe."

"Well, she didn't. She didn't let us see everything she was doing. But I memorized as much as possible. I think I came pretty close," I say, pleased with my attempt to recreate the special meal from my date with Idris for my "girls' night in" party.

Mya rises from the chair on the other side of my bar and tosses the spoon into the dishwater.

"You know you're doing all the dishes later, right?" I wave a hand toward the pots, pans, glass bowls, mixers, and utensils strewn across my kitchen.

"Odalis will help. Trust me. Your kitchen will be sparkling clean by the time we leave tonight. If there's one thing I've learned from living with three men and a dog, it's how to make a home sparkle," Mya says, then glances at her watch. "Wonder what's keeping the librarian?"

As if on cue, there's a knock at my door. I turn my attention back toward the pasta boiling on the stove as Mya goes to let Odalis in.

"Ladies, I've brought wine!" Odalis says, clinking two bottles of Harlow Rose wine together.

"Tell me you grabbed a bottle of Cabernet Sauvignon. I hate I love that wine so much," I say, scrunching my nose.

"Got it and the Merlot," Odalis says, marching into the kitchen. She opens a drawer and pulls out my wine opener to pop the cork. "The best part is I got both bottles for free."

"How'd you manage that?" Mya asks, raising an eyebrow.

"Her mom, Qinyang, is the headmaster at Excelsior Prep and came by to donate a bunch of extra books they ordered to the library. I happened to mention I was hanging out with some girlfriends and planned to get some of her daughter's wine for the occasion," Odalis says, grabbing three wine glasses and pouring them almost to the brim. "She was so pleased we loved her daughter's wine that she had a courier bring me two bottles." Odalis squeals. "How cool is that?"

I look at Mya, and we raise an eyebrow, then say in unison: "Rich people!" We bubble with laughter and then take the glasses handed to us by Odalis.

"What should we toast to?" Odalis asks. "Finding love?"

Mya groans, and I join her.

"Oh no, trouble in paradise?" Odalis looks from Mya to me and back again. "Who wants to go first?"

I point at Mya, and she points back at me.

"You're the engaged one. We need to deal with your issue first to stop you from losing your future husband," I say, pressing my hand on my hips. "Plus, this dish still needs my attention. I'll tell my sad story second." I'm not looking forward to admitting the truth to my friends, but I need to talk to somebody other than my brother, my cousins, or Darren about this.

"Okay, before you start." Odalis raises a hand. "I have news for you, Jas."

"What kind of news?" I ask, eyeing her suspiciously.

"I found Cassidy."

"What?" I stalk over to her. "You did?" My heart sinks, and I don't want to admit why. I'd put finding the former love of Darren's life out of my mind with everything else going on.

Odalis nods. "I'm a hundred percent sure I have the right woman. She moved to Vegas after she and Darren broke up and took a job as the head of marketing for one of the resorts there. I have her home address and her work phone number. Her personal number and cell are unlisted." Odalis digs in her purse and pulls out a lavender folded paper.

She extends it toward me, but I hesitate.

"You go, Odalis. Maybe you should give Timmy a run for his money in the P.I. business," Mya says, then sips her wine.

"I plan to become a best-selling children's book author, not a private investigator. I wanted to help Jas out, and I'm glad I did since it led to us becoming friends," Odalis gives me a warm smile. "You still want to reconnect Cassidy and Darren, don't you?" She wiggles the paper toward me.

I can feel Mya's gaze searing into the side of my head. I'm not ready to talk about Darren or the unexpected change in feelings I'm experiencing for him. I clear my throat and say, "Of course." Snatching the paper from her hand, I open it and stare at the contact information for Cassidy. Part of me wishes I'd never got the stupid idea to track her down. Weeks ago, I thought Troy Renault could be the future man in my life. So, it made sense to help Darren find the woman for him. Now, after suffering the disappointment of Troy and my confusion over Idris, I'm not so committed to being the one to help Darren reconnect with the woman he used to love. The woman he may still love.

I stuff the paper in my back pocket, then remove the pasta from the stove. "I will give her a call this weekend. Now, spill it, Mya. What's gone wrong with you and Ronan?"

"I went behind his back and scheduled an appointment with the child psychologist you recommended for Declan," Mya says, then covers her face with her hands. "I am not Declan's mother, yet here I am, overruling Ronan's parental decisions. It was wrong of me."

"Ronan is mad at you for trying to help his son? That doesn't seem fair," Odalis says.

"I don't know. I think you crossed a line," I say.

"Can you sugarcoat the truth one time?" Mya says, shaking her head.

"Why? How is that going to help you?" I ask, then pour the pasta into an oversized mixing bowl.

Odalis winces and points at me. "She's tough."

I say, "You told me Ronan was concerned about choosing a doctor because he couldn't reach Connor to help him. So, I gave you the name and credentials of a great doctor for you to share with Ronan. Not for you to go behind his back and book an appointment for his kid. You know better."

"That's what Ronan said. He appreciated I asked you for help but hates I didn't bring the info to him. Going behind his back was wrong, but I thought he'd make another excuse not to get Declan the help he needs. Who knew he respected you so much and had been thinking of asking you for help?" Mya asks.

I give her a sarcastic laugh. "So shocking. Did you forget I run the ER at St. Elizabeth's?"

Odalis giggles as she maneuvers behind me and adds salad to the plates I have sitting on the counter. She asks, "Where do things stand with you and Ronan now?"

"In reality, we're fine. We talked for a long time, and I apologized. He knows how sorry I am, and I know not to do anything like that again. Still, I hope this incident isn't a dark cloud that lingers over us. I guess time will tell," Mya says.

I roll my eyes. "That man is head over heels in love with you. Nothing is going to make him push you away … ever. That's fake news."

Odalis shifts to the side as I add my version of the lamb rigatoni alfredo to the plates and top it off with a slice of Texas garlic toast.

"If my situation is fake news, then it's your turn. We can tell the food from your date with Idris was fantastic, so what's got you in a mood? How was the rest of the date?"

"That's what I want to know. I was stunned when you texted me everything he did for you. I didn't know a ranch hand made enough money to reserve a closed restaurant and its star chef for a private dinner." Odalis whistles. "I can't imagine how a date that romantic could go wrong."

I look away as I think about what she said. How did Idris pull that off? It was clear he and Chef Fiora met for the first time when we showed up, so how could he arrange such a phenomenal date?

"Hello! Earth to Jasmine!" Mya says, waving her arms. "Was he still awkward with you in person and ruined everything?"

"Actually, no. The date was better than I could've imagined. He seemed more comfortable. We were a formidable team in the kitchen trying to keep up with Chef Fiora's instructions. Once we were eating dinner, the conversation was easy. Not riveting like it had been over the phone, but good enough. I was starting to believe he could be the one …"

"Until?" Odalis asks.

"After we finished dessert, jazz music started playing in the restaurant. Idris asked me to dance," I say.

"Can I send Ronan to this man to take notes?" Mya asks, laughing and clapping her hands.

"Shh! Let her finish. This date does not have a happy ending, and we need to find out why," Odalis says.

"We were dancing close, and it felt intimate and special and nice, and he … kissed me."

Mya and Odalis squeal and make kissing noises until they see the look on my face.

"Oh, he's a horrible kisser, isn't he?" Mya says. "Was it sloppy? Or like kissing a wet fish?"

Odalis screams, "Mya! That's mean." She turns to me. "Was it?"

"No, he's a nice kisser. It was nice," I say, struggling to explain my feelings. "But I didn't feel any romantic ... chemistry."

"Oh," Mya and Odalis say in unison.

Odalis grabs the plates, walks them to my dining nook, and places them on the table. "Not even a tiny spark?" she asks.

Grabbing my glass, I take a few chugs of wine and join her and Mya. "Not a hint of one. I felt nothing. It was the strangest thing. One minute, I think this guy could be the one. And the next, it's like I'm going through the motions as he kisses me. There were no fireworks, no butterflies, nothing."

"Okay, maybe the two of you need more time. It was your first date," Odalis says. "Idris is a sweet man."

Mya asks, "What did Idris do when the kiss was over?"

"He kind of acted like it was the best kiss of his life," I say, then gulp more wine.

"Not good," Odalis says.

Mya nods her head in agreement. "It's one thing if both of you realized the kiss was off. It's entirely different if one of you got the feels and the other didn't. So, how did things end?"

"He was a gentleman and walked me to my car. We kissed again. I felt nothing ... again. Then I drove home," I say. "But here's the worst part."

"Can it get worse than that?" Mya asks.

"I kinda let him believe I enjoyed the kiss as much as he did."

"You did what?" Mya's eyes grow wide. "Dr. Jasmine 'tell-it-like-it-is' Jones wasn't honest with Idris? I can't believe it."

"Neither can I." Taking a deep breath, I stuff a spoonful of pasta in my mouth and allow the decadent flavors to soothe me.

"Why do you think you did that?"

I look away, afraid they might be able to read the truth in my eyes. After a long moment, I say, "I'm not sure."

But that's a lie.

I know why I didn't come clean to Idris.

He didn't stand a chance because I couldn't stop comparing Idris's kiss with the two kisses that rocked my world. The two kisses I can't stop thinking about. The man I want to kiss again.

And he's my best friend ... Darren.

CHAPTER 30

ARREN

I GROAN AS I STARE AT MY REFLECTION IN THE MIRROR.

Mirielle deserves better than this.

Tugging at the faded plaid button-down shirt, I rip it from my body and toss it into a heap on the floor. Swiveling on my heel, I enter my closet. The floor-to-ceiling rows of clothes surround me. I scour the racks for something more suitable. More representative of the man I am, not the man I've been acting like.

Just because I agreed to go out with Mirielle after suffering through an aggravating call with Idris isn't a reason not to put my best foot forward. She deserves a date with an authentic version of me. Not the chump who pushed his best friend toward a relationship with a deserving guy, only to end up simmering in silent envy when the relationship worked out.

A couple of nights ago, I was trapped in a conversation with Idris raving about his date with Jasmine. I didn't want the excruciating details, but that didn't stop him from giving them to me.

Every single last one.

Including the mind-blowing kiss he shared with Jas at the end of the night. A kiss like Idris had never experienced with any other woman. He thought he was in love with Jasmine before, but now he was sure of it. While Jasmine didn't say it, he's a hundred percent sure she reciprocated his feelings.

My response was convincingly supportive. I congratulated Idris on things going well while a storm of resentment brewed within me. All because I knew he was right. Jasmine has gone M.I.A. since the date—a telltale sign she is swooning over Idris. Keeping in touch with me has fallen far from her mind. Plus, we've never shared details of our dating lives with each other in the past. If she's talking to anyone about falling for Idris, it would be Mya. Not me. I'd find out eventually, of course, but not yet.

After rummaging in my closet for a few minutes, I settle on a trusty favorite—a deep red, cable-knit cashmere sweater and dark jeans. A spritz of my signature cologne and a final appreciable glance at the mirror later, I head downstairs.

As I reach the bottom step, my front door swings open.

Jasmine peeps her head in, stops, and gapes at me. She gives me a playful whistle and fans herself, but her antics only add fuel to the fire of my irritation. Shouldn't she be with Idris on her day off instead of in my house? Or had she stopped by to subject me to a retelling of the best date of her life? I've never been more glad to have plans ... with someone else.

"Where are you headed?" she asks, curiosity in her voice as she closes the door behind her.

"On a date." Striding past her, I reach for the ivory bowl that holds various car keys and fish out the ones to my Mercedes. Turning back, I see emotions I hadn't expected in her eyes. "Don't look so shocked. Haven't you been pushing me to get back out there? I'm following your lead." I hate the edge of anger in my tone, but Jasmine doesn't seem to notice.

Her startled expression melts into a softer one. At least as soft as Jasmine gets. She asks, "Who's the lucky lady?"

"Mirielle."

Her forehead creases instantly, a disapproving sneer forming on her lips.

"I don't need your approval. You didn't ask for mine."

"I'm not wrong about her, Darren," Jasmine retorts, blocking me from the door. "She's starstruck. Nothing real or lasting can develop if she's fan-girling around you constantly." She rolls her eyes.

"How about you let me be the judge of that? You didn't listen when people tried to warn you off Troy. You had to see he was a prick for yourself."

Jasmine winces. "Don't you think I wish I had listened to everybody? I don't want you to go through that."

"Well, I'm not convinced you're right about Mirielle. Unlike Troy, everyone else thinks she and I might be a good fit. No red flags or warning signs, so it's worth giving her a fair chance," I counter.

Jasmine's features harden as she gnaws on her bottom lip, seething. "Fine. Go. Have fun."

A bitter chuckle escapes my lips. "Don't worry. I intend to."

CHAPTER 31

ARREN

THE LAST RAYS OF THE DAY FADE INTO TWILIGHT AS WE arrive at the local art exhibit, a popular pop-up space near Conroe that showcases works from various local artists. I chose this place not for its reputation but because Mirielle had once casually mentioned her love for art at one of the foundation board meetings. Tonight, it houses an exhibition called "Rodeo Shadows," a captivating exploration of the unique traditions and history of rodeo culture in Texas.

Stepping out of the Mercedes, a chilly breeze sweeps across my skin as the temperatures plummet lower than expected. I shiver, wishing I'd grabbed a coat, then make my way to the passenger side and open the door.

Mirielle steps out. She's a vision in an ivory wool sweater, tan leather pants, and matching boots. Her eyes dance with anticipation. We talked nonstop on the drive from Kimbell about the foundation, my volunteering as a firefighter, her preparation for the upcoming Houston Livestock Show and Rodeo, then the art exhibit—which she was genuinely excited to see.

Even though I'd had hundreds of past conversations with Mirielle about the foundation, tonight, I got to see a different side of her. One that's alluring and makes me want to see more.

I slip my hand in hers, and we walk toward the modern, glass-paneled building. A soft glow illuminates the interior, with brighter lights cast toward the art suspended in installations from the ceilings and along the walls. The subtle hum of hushed conversations and soft, ambient music fills the air.

"Where do you want to start?" I ask, gazing around the open space.

"There …" Mirielle says, pointing toward a series of sculptures and paintings with horses as the central focus.

We meander through the gallery, immersing ourselves in the artistic stories each piece offers. Mirielle's enthusiasm is contagious. I listen attentively to her perspectives, interpretations, and explanations of the techniques in the artwork.

After a couple of hours, we perused the entire exhibition and found our way to a cozy spot in the outdoor area, adorned with twinkling lights and food trucks selling rodeo fair. I order a turkey leg and Mexican street corn and get a bowl of chili for Mirielle. Sitting on a bench underneath a giant oak tree, I take a moment to watch her. Her pretty face glows under the soft lights, and her eyes sparkle. There's an easy, light, and joyous energy about her. I realize I'm not only enjoying myself but also savoring the company I'm in.

"You know a lot about art," I say.

"It's a hobby of mine. I go to shows like this and dream of the day when I'll have enough money to buy some of the pieces," she says, then looks away sheepishly. "I suppose you don't have that problem."

"No," I admit. As a kid growing up with an iconic college football coach as a dad, there weren't many instances where I was faced with wanting something I couldn't afford. "But your breakthrough is coming sooner than you think. You qualified for the Super Series."

"After years of trying. I'm super nervous. The Houston Rodeo is where we all dream of competing. I hope I don't blow it."

"Why would you say that?"

"Because I was the teen phenom they thought would've been competing at the Houston Rodeo years ago." Mirielle tilts her head toward me. "It's a disappointment that I'm doing it for the first time ten years after everyone expected." Long waves of her chestnut brown hair cascade over her shoulder. "That's why I admire you so much.'

Without realizing it, I reach for the ends of a few strands and rub them between my fingers. "Why me?"

"Fresh off of winning a National Championship in college, you go straight into the pros, when Defensive Rookie of the Year and a Super Bowl. You perform at your best when it matters the most. All I do is choke," she says, glancing up at the heavens for a divine explanation. "It's like I want it too much, you know. So, it never works out for me."

I know what she means, but not with professional sports. What I want so much it hurts is beyond my reach. It would never work out because I harbored those feelings for too many years. Maybe things would've been different if I'd told Jasmine when we were both living in Pittsburgh that I wanted more than friendship. Or after the Pippa mess when we both moved back to Kimbell, I could've pitched us as a couple as a brand new start. But I never made those moves, and now it's too late.

"How did you do it?" Mirielle asks, staring at me intently.

She looks so vulnerable and sad. All I want to do is help her. Show her that, at least with our professions, there's always another chance.

"First," I say, moving closer to her. "You have to know in your heart that the past has nothing to do with the next game. Or the next race for you."

"The whole put it behind you and look forward," Mirielle says. "I've heard that from my coach over and over. Doesn't stick."

"That's only part of it."

"What's the other part?"

"You need to perform for someone or something other than

yourself," I say as a flood of memories wash over me. "During my first Superbowl, I wasn't thinking about the score or winning. The only thing going through my head was not letting my team down. They expected me to give two hundred percent. Every down. Every play. If I did that, it wouldn't matter if we won or lost. I knew I left everything on that field, and there would be no regrets."

"Great motivation when you play a team sport. But it's only me out there when I race. I'm alone with no one to push me ..."

"No one?" I challenge.

"Me and ... Blaze." Marielle's face lights up. "And I guess Jody, my coach, and Harper, Blaze's trainer. Then there's Mitch, who takes care of Blaze's hoofs, Dr. Wilson, the vet, and Mya, my new personal trainer."

"Not on your own, are you?"

"No. I guess I'm not," she says. "I have a team who all want to see me perform at my best."

"That's the focus. Your goal is to perform at your best. Not to win. You have no control over the times and techniques of the other racers. But if you walk out of that stadium knowing you did your best—"

"I have won." Mirielle smiles and grabs my hands, gently squeezing them.

I love the flicker of hope in her eyes and the part I played in putting it there. Mirielle is a wonderful woman. I can't believe I never noticed her before.

"Darren," Mirielle says, twirling her spoon between her fingers. "I'm not sure how to say this, so I'm just going to do it. I've never felt like this before on a first date. It's surprising we've known each other for a while but not really known each other. Seeing this side of you tonight was eye-opening. I hope it won't be our last time."

Her words settle within me, igniting a spark I haven't felt for any woman except Jasmine in a long time. I'm surprised to want to spend more time with Mirielle.

I clear my throat and say, "I had a great time with you tonight. I'm glad we did this."

She smiles at me. "But …"

"No buts. I wasn't very open to new experiences at the beginning of the year. But being with you tonight has changed that."

I remind myself I'm not entirely over Jasmine. I made the mistake of using a woman to try to kill my feelings for my best friend in the past, which turned out to be a disaster. I won't make the same mistake twice. I won't do that to Mirielle. "I can't give you any guarantees, but if we take our time, and take things slow, maybe something special can happen between us."

"Slow works for me. Honestly, I can't afford the distraction of a relationship a month before I'm due to compete. I need all my energy and attention to focus on my training," Mirielle explains.

"Completely understand."

"But I don't want us to lose touch. Maybe we can keep seeing each other in the meantime, but keep it casual for … now."

"Yeah," I say, nodding my head. "I like the sound of that."

CHAPTER 32

J ASMINE

Nothing like waking up at three in the morning and racing to the emergency room to perform surgery to repair internal bleeding, liver, and intestinal damage and set two broken femurs to give a woman clarity about life. Ten hours later, I'm staring at the scans to ensure we didn't miss anything while my mind wanders back to Darren and his date with Mirielle. Again.

I don't understand why the thought of him going out with the rodeo barrel racer irritated me. Darren has dated many women in the past, and it never bothered me.

But that was before Darren and I kissed.

Twice.

Two kisses that are seared into my mind and my heart.

I thought kissing Idris would erase those memories, but it had the opposite effect. Every kiss I shared with Idris on our date was a poor imitation of the kisses with Darren. I know I shouldn't make comparisons, but it's hard not to when one set of kisses nearly buckled my knees, and the other set was a yawn fest. I'm still trying to figure out how we could have a blissful romantic date, but I don't feel anything when he kisses me. No matter how hard I tried, there was no spark.

Luckily, we've both been too busy with work to see each other again. Our phone conversations in the meantime have been fine, but nothing like the engaging conversations we had before. Idris has changed.

Or maybe he hasn't.

Maybe it's me who's changed.

A soft knock on my office door jolts me from my thoughts. Not sure I'm grateful or annoyed by the disruption, I say, "Come in."

A handsome head pokes through the opening, and I squeal with delight. "Get in here."

"You sure I'm not bothering you?"

"Of course, you're bothering me. I'm an extremely busy head of Emergency Medicine who spent the last ten hours in surgery … but I'm always happy to see and make time for my big brother." I get up from my desk chair and cross the room. Hendrix walks inside, looking stunning in khakis, a Polo shirt, and leather jacket. He hugs me as he holds a square plastic container out of my reach.

"What's in there?"

"Avril texted me and said you had a rough morning, missed breakfast, and haven't gone out to get lunch."

"Why am I not surprised that the pretty nurse found some excuse to text you," I say, rolling my eyes.

"Don't start. We're friends." Hendrix gives me a stern look.

"I guess I need to remind Nurse Avril that snitches get stitches. I can wreck her and then patch her back up to cover the evidence of my crimes." Famished, I snatch the container from his hands and pop it open. "Did you make this?"

Hendrix nods as the smell of decadent meatloaf and mashed potatoes fills the air.

"That's not all for you," He warns, tugging at the container. "You must have some plates around here to split it with me."

Reaching for a drawer at the bottom of my desk, I pull out two paper plates, two sets of plastic utensils, napkins, and two bottles of Dr. Pepper. I'm no rookie at working lunches. Hendrix divides the food with precision into equal portions. He hands me a plate and sits on the other side of my desk, where I've cleared space for our meal.

"You didn't go to work today?" I ask, noticing my brother's casual attire. "Who's at the shop?"

Hendrix grins sheepishly, scratching the back of his head. "I guess you forgot with everything going on—"

"Hendrix!" Realization dawns on me, and I smack my forehead lightly. "Your meeting with Zaire. How did it go?"

He leans back in his chair, an air of satisfaction about him. "Better than I expected. Several properties on Commerce Street are available. It's a prime location and ideal for my auto shop expansion." Hendrix leans back in the chair. "Of course, they're all pricey, and I'd have to construct a new building to meet my needs, but I'm optimistic things will work out. Especially since Old Man Bell told me he'd supply the financing."

"I still don't understand your relationship with Nate's dad," I say, shaking my head. "It's weird."

"But advantageous," Hendrix counters, shrugging his shoulders. "I can't help it that the guy admires my grit. His words, not mine. Nothing like the convenience of at-home car repairs to win a person over."

"Does he still call you for that? After you opened your shop?" I inquire, intrigued despite myself.

Hendrix smirks, cocking an eyebrow. "What do you think?"

"Quid pro quo in action," I muse aloud.

"I'm thinking about hiring a couple of guys to start helping me, too," Hendrix says. "I'm crazy busy these days as word spreads about the shop. I guess it's a good problem to have."

"The best kind," I agree, smiling.

Hendrix looks serious. "So, what happened this morning? Anything you can talk about?"

I let out a long sigh. "One of Colton Baker's bulls got loose and gored Smitty Watkins in his backyard. His wife didn't find him until hours later. Lost a lot of blood and had severe internal damage, but I got him stable."

"That's horrible," Hendrix grimaces. "Surprised Idris didn't mention it this morning. He going to make it?"

"Of course, but the road to recovery will be slow," I assure him, then pause. Panic races through me. "Wait. What did you say?"

Hendrix looks confused. "It's horrible?"

"No. The other part ... about Idris." I cross my arms over my chest, leaning forward. "You and Idris were together this morning?"

Hendrix rubs the back of his neck, looking uncomfortable. "He reached out and suggested we meet for coffee since, from what he says, y'alls relationship is getting more serious. Something about the best date of his life and the woman of his dreams. I had to double-check that he was talking about my sister." My brother bursts into a fit of laughter.

"He said all of that," I repeat, my heart pounding.

Hendrix nods, a smile playing on his lips. "And a lot more. You know, I respect a guy who'd reach out to me and introduce himself. He told me how much he admires you and that his intentions are good. I like the guy. He'll fit in nicely with us whenever you're ready."

"I can't believe he did that—" I whisper, my mind racing. Isn't this what I wanted? To meet a great guy and have him fall for me. So why doesn't this news make me happy?

"Before you get all ticked off at Idris," Hendrix interrupts my flustered thoughts. "I want you to know his intentions were good. He's not trying to pressure you into bringing him to meet the family. But he thought he should at least introduce himself to me, given how close the two of you are becoming. Don't be mad at him."

I blink, taken aback. "I'm not mad. I think it's a sweet gesture. Just shocked, that's all."

Hendrix's eyebrows shoot up. "Was the date as good as he says? You like him, don't you?"

I nod. "He got Chef Fiora to open Risveglio on a Sunday and give us a private cooking lesson," I say, hoping Hendrix doesn't realize I'm dodging his second question.

"Whoa." Hendrix whistles. "He pulled out all the stops. How could he afford that on a ranch hand salary?"

"Good question," I reply, perplexed. It was a mystery I was still trying to solve ... without being uncouth and asking him directly. It shouldn't matter anyway. "Maybe he has advantageous friends, too."

Hendrix chuckles, nodding. "Colton must have helped him."

"Maybe," I agree, not willing to delve deeper.

"If you had told me a month ago after you forced Darren to go along with that silly New Year's Eve resolution to find love, that you'd be with Idris and he'd be with Mirielle." Hendrix shakes his head, "I never would've believed it."

"Darren can't be serious about Mirielle," I protest immediately.

Hendrix raises an eyebrow. "Why not? What do you have against her?"

"Why are you asking me like that?" I deflect, feeling defensive. Irritation simmers under my skin. Every mention of her name feels like daggers plunging into my heart.

"Because you always find some issue with the women Darren dates," Hendrix says, matter of fact, which serves to fan my growing frustration. "That's why he doesn't tell you everything he tells us."

"Us?" I echo, feeling my hackles rise.

"Me, Jaxon, Lennox, and Maxwell on our group text," Hendrix replies casually.

"You have a group text with my best friend and not me?" I exclaim, feeling betrayed. "How long have y'all been excluding me?"

"A few years," Hendrix admits, looking away. "After Darren moved back to rehab from his injury."

"Hendrix!" I gasp. "That was five years ago."

"He's light on details," Hendrix hurries to reassure me. "You still know way more about the guy than anyone else, including Mirielle. Calm down."

His words do little to alleviate the churn of … jealousy in my gut. Am I envious of Mirielle? Of course, I am. She's getting Darren's kisses now. The kisses I can't stop thinking about.

"Anyway, Mirielle's a great girl," Hendrix says, taking my silence as acceptance. "I think she'd be good for Darren. Then the two of you could double date—"

His words are abruptly cut off as I launch into a coughing fit. The thought of sitting across from Darren and Mirielle, watching them together, it's too much. I need a moment to collect my scattered emotions and mask the green-eyed monster lurking beneath the surface.

"You alright?" Hendrix asks, looking alarmed.

I wipe my mouth with a napkin. "Yeah. I'm fine."

But my voice is anything but convincing.

CHAPTER 33

J ASMINE

I SWEAR THIS HAS NOTHING TO DO WITH MY CONFUSION about Darren or this pesky jealousy I can't get rid of related to him being with Mirielle. I'm not sure why she rubs me the wrong way, but I can't ignore my gut that she's not the right woman for him.

But who is?

As much as I want to answer, I don't.

I have a remarkable man who adores me and wants to start a relationship. So what if the romantic chemistry is off right now? It could take time for that spark to grow. I felt it in our early conversations with each other. Those late-night talks had me willing to walk away from Troy before I realized he was a Class-A jerk. I know I can have those feelings for Idris.

Did you feel anything when I kissed you?

Darren's words invade my mind.

I didn't lie when I answered him.

But why did he ask me that? And how would he have responded to the same question?

"Stop it!" I scream, banging my hands on my desk. It is too late to go back in time. I can't second guess what happened. I did the right thing. Evelyn and my aunts are still right about me and Darren. We're so close, and the lines between us have blurred because neither of us has been in a relationship for years.

Now, I'm on the cusp of being exclusive with Idris.

I don't want Darren to make a mistake and choose the wrong girl to take his next relationship plunge.

Grabbing my purse, I pull out the folded purple stationery where Odalis wrote Cassidy's contact information. Flipping it open, I stare at the numbers, then grab my cell phone and punch them in.

The phone rings three times before she picks up.

"Hello, is this Cassidy?" I ask when the call connects.

A pause. "Yes, who is this?" the voice on the other end of the line questions. Her voice is calm and distant.

"My name is Jasmine Jones. You may not remember me—"

Her cutting interruption throws me off balance. "I know who you are. Did something happen to Darren?"

"No," I reply quickly, hoping to douse any panic.

"Okay, so why are you calling me?" Cassidy's confusion is palpable.

"Maybe no isn't the right answer. He's fine physically, no medical issues." I clarify.

"Glad to hear it," Cassidy remarks, her voice so dry I can almost feel the desert.

"You know Darren and I have been best friends forever. This year we decided our New Year's resolution would be to find love. Neither of us has dated anyone in the past five years—" I explain, but she cuts me off again.

"Why are you telling me this? Does he know you've called me?" Cassidy's question catches me off guard.

"Well, no, he doesn't. But you were his last relationship. I'm not sure he's gotten over you. I think it's impacting his ability to find someone new," I rush out, trying to make sense of the complicated feelings inside me.

"That is ... surprising." Cassidy's voice is thoughtful. I can almost see her frown on the other side of the phone.

"Putting all my cards on the table, I think he walked away from your relationship when he didn't want to because of ... me," I admit, my heart pounding.

Her response is fierce. "Why? Because you were a judgmental, meddlesome, overbearing busybody who interfered in our relationship where you didn't belong?"

"Wait a minute," I retort, reeling from her accusation. "I'll own up to my mistakes, but I never butted into your relationship with Darren. I was too busy doing my residency to pay attention to what was happening with y'all." I stop and take a deep breath. "But after he got hurt, there's no way I could stay away from him. When the Pippa situation happened, I told him if you loved him, you would believe in him. That's how I felt ... back then. Now, I know it wasn't so simple."

"It wasn't simple at all. Nothing about dating Darren Manning could ever be simple," Cassidy shoots back. "Back then, he was constantly in the media and the object of millions of women's fantasies. On top of that, as an athlete, I dealt with daily accusations of him cheating on me. You don't know what that's like."

"No, I don't," I admit, feeling the sharp sting of her words. "But Darren would never cheat or sexually assault a woman. He's not capable of doing things that heinous."

"I know that now," Cassidy continues, her voice softening. "But when he admitted he'd kissed Pippa and things almost got out of hand, I wondered if losing his football career had changed him. You remember how he was back then. Despondent and distant."

I stay quiet, memories flooding my mind. I recall laying beside Darren in his hospital bed as we talked about everything and nothing.

Darren may have put up barriers with Cassidy, but he never did with me.

"He stopped acting like the Darren I knew and loved. He wouldn't let me help him. The only person he let in was … you. He refused to let me join him in Colorado for rehab even though I was more than willing to. Finding out that leaving me behind gave him more time to hook up with his physical therapist did nothing to help me feel secure in our relationship."

"He never hooked up with her. They kissed, and it was a mistake."

"Then he shouldn't have paid her off. It's like admitting he'd done something wrong. Maybe not everything she accused him of, but he wasn't innocent," Cassidy continues, her voice strained.

"Darren didn't want to settle," I interject, my voice firm. "His father went behind his back and paid Pippa. The publicity was distracting for his dad's run to the national championship, and he wanted it to end. Darren would've fought Pippa in court and won if he'd been given the chance."

"I never knew that," Cassidy replies, sounding genuinely upset.

"Pippa signed a nondisclosure agreement and couldn't talk to the media about the settlement. Darren and his father hit a rough patch and stopped speaking to each other. What good would it have done for Darren to admit what his father did publicly? It was better to let it all die down," I explain.

"Which it did after a few months. But by then, the damage was done. Darren and I were over. I won't lie. It helps to have more insight into what he was dealing with, but it still doesn't change anything," Cassidy counters, bitterness seeping into her tone.

"Maybe it should," I suggest gently. "Darren has avoided relationships since the two of you broke up. But I can't help but think it's because he has some unresolved feelings for you."

I leave out the part about him kissing me. Twice. And how confused I am about it all. Though I shouldn't be. Evelyn is right. Darren kissed me because it's safer for him than dealing with his unresolved feelings for Cassidy. I'm his relationship crutch, too.

188

"I still love him," Cassidy admits, and her candor floors me.

Silence stretches between us as I process her words.

"But no part of me believes we can recapture what we had. It's better to move on," Cassidy adds, her voice a whisper.

"But what if Darren can't?" I venture. "At least not without talking to you. I'd hate to see him make bad choices, either hiding from love or picking the wrong woman because he needs closure with you. Maybe you need closure with him, too."

"What are you suggesting? What do you want me to do?" Cassidy inquires, her voice steadier now.

"Darren's not going to bother you after how things ended. He already thinks he hurt you too much. He would never open up those old wounds," I explain, feeling the truth of my words. "But I can give you his private cell number in case you decide now or later that you want to talk to him. And if you decide not to, that's fine as well. I thought I should at least try."

"Is he going to be upset with you for doing this?" Cassidy questions, her concern genuine.

"Girl, please," I scoff, rolling my eyes even though she can't see me. "Darren can only stay mad at me for a couple of hours before he comes around. I can handle that man. Plus, I think this is in both of your best interests. But no guarantees anything but understanding would come out of y'all talking again. I don't know for sure if he still has feelings for you or not. That's one thing he hasn't shared with me."

"Understood," Cassidy replies. "I'm not making any promises. I need to think about this, but give me his number."

I rattle off the number, the digits feeling heavy on my tongue. "Take care, Cassidy," I say, then hang up.

Leaning back in my chair, I wait to feel at peace for making the move I'd always planned to help Darren.

But all I feel is a torrent of emotions stirred up more than before.

CHAPTER 34

DARREN

UNDER THE MORNING SUN, THERE'S A BLUSTERY CHILL IN the air as I stand on the sidelines of the football field near the back of Bell Park. Parents cheer loudly for the kids, who show off all their hard work in this exhibition game—the Kimbell Kangaroos versus the Grapevine Jaguars. No more practice games with ourselves. This is a real game with a real opponent. If it goes well, I'm hoping I can convince the coach of the Grapevine team to join in on the state-wide special needs youth football league I'm trying to create.

"Let's go 'Roos! Let's go 'Roos!" Chants ring out from the crowd to encourage our kids. They had a lead coming out of half-time, but the Jaguars have come back strong. We're only up by a field goal now, and the kids look panicked. I know I should step in and help Idris with the coaching, but I'm struggling to give the game my full attention.

In the distance, St. Elizabeth's Hospital looms in view. I can't help but wonder how Jasmine is doing after saving Smitty Watkins's life. Nothing worse than a surprise attack by an angry bull. She texted me when the surgery ended yesterday.

> JASMINE
>
> You checking on Smitty?

> DARREN
>
> I'm checking on you.

> That's sweet. I'm fine but kind of hanging on by a thread. It was touch and go. He's critical but stable. Jamie's a mess. I asked Georgia to deal with her because I can't.

> Need me to come by.

> No.

> Should my feelings be hurt?

> Ha! Thanks for making me laugh. If you come by, that thread will break and I can't afford to be emotional. I need to keep that man alive so stay away.

> Got it. If you need anything, call me.

> I will

> Promise?

> Yes, I promise

That was the last I heard from her.

This morning, a text from Avril to me and Hendrix explained why. Smitty had complications overnight. Jas quickly identified the signs of the torn femoral artery and got him back in the O.R. The second surgery was successful. Smitty should be out of ICU in the next day or two.

Jas is probably exhausted and beating herself up for missing the torn artery the first time. I want to go to her, but she won't want to see me. She's in full doctor mode and won't tolerate any distractions.

I feel a tug on my pant leg. I look down at Shane Beauregard, Izzie's seven-year-old nephew, staring up at me.

"I don't think we're going to win anymore. We keep messing up," Shane says.

I bend over and pick the little boy up, then turn my attention back to the game. We got a massive lead because Quaid, our quarterback, nailed passes to Shane, who sped past the defenders to the end zone for three straight touchdowns. I glance at the field and see our offense out there. I wonder why Shane isn't in the game.

"The game isn't over. It's only the beginning of the fourth quarter, and we still have the lead," I reassure him as we watch the next few snaps in silence.

"See," Shane whines. "We keep doing the same thing over and over, and it's not working. Coach hasn't put me back in the game since halftime. This sucks."

I shake my head as I watch the disaster unfolding on the field. The team looks downtrodden and upset. "Hey, run over there and help hand out water to the guys so they don't get too tired. I'm going to go talk to Coach Gibson."

"Okay!" Shane says, then trots toward his teammates.

"Hey, Idris!" I call out, my voice slicing through the cheers. Idris turns toward me. I jog over and pull him aside, out of earshot of the volunteer assistant coaches. "Get your head in the game."

His annoyance is apparent as he says, "What are you talking about?"

I watch the kids on the field, their faces a mix of confusion and determination. "You called the same offensive play three times in a row. Running play to the left side, but that's where their three biggest defenders are. The kids are confused, and so am I."

Idris dismisses my concern with a nonchalant wave. "The kids are fine. I'll call a different play. Unless you want to help out for a change?"

"For a change?" I snort, disbelief in my voice. "You've been our head coach for a year with no issues. We have our first real game, and now you need help? What's going on with you?"

"Oh, I forgot," Idris retorts, a sneer evident in his tone. "You only help when it's convenient for you."

"What are you talking about?" I throw his question back at him.

He looks away. "I texted you three times asking for help with Jasmine last night, and you ignored me."

My eyebrows shoot up in surprise. "Last I heard from you, things were going great with you and Jas."

"I'm not so sure anymore." He sighs, his eyes dropping to the grass beneath his feet. "I feel like something is different between us. That's why I wanted your help. You know, listen in and text me some things to say. Like old times."

"You're joking," I scoff, stunned at his audacity.

"No, I'm not." He meets my glare earnestly. "I need help. I don't want to lose her."

"Do you have her to lose?" I challenge.

"What's that supposed to mean?" His voice is edged with frustration.

I fold my arms, holding his gaze. "It means, who do you want Jasmine to fall for? The real you or you when you're pretending to be me."

"That's low." His words are a whisper in the wind. "I never pretended to be you."

"You took my words and pretended they were yours."

He shakes his head in denial. "Wait a minute. That was your idea, not mine. Now you're mad it worked and refusing to help me again."

"Like I told you before," I continue, my voice unwavering. "You have texts from me for several calls you've had with Jasmine. If you can't figure out how to communicate with her from those, I don't know what else to tell you. I won't give you a script to say to her anymore. You need to be yourself and talk to her with your words and heart. I'm done sneaking around and lying to my best friend about the part I played in the two of you getting together."

"You can't tell her what we did." His voice cracks. "Don't do that to me."

"I'd never do that to ... *her*," I assure him, emphasizing the last word.

"Fine." He deflates, his eyes wandering back to the field. "Maybe I'm wrong for asking you for help again, but I'm worried. She's the best thing that's ever happened to me. I don't want to do anything to mess this up. We've both been busy this week. During the last couple of calls, she was distant and quiet. She wouldn't tell me why and I couldn't say anything right to cheer her up. Did she tell you?"

"Idris." I sigh, running a hand through my hair. "Jasmine is a doctor. Not any doctor but an ER surgeon and head of all the doctors and nurses on staff in that department. Can you imagine the cases that come into St. Elizabeth's every week? How many times she's put in a position to make all the right decisions to save someone's life? Save a life, Idris! Do you expect her to be happy and talkative each time y'all have a phone conversation? Who do you think spent the last twenty-four hours in multiple surgeries to save Smitty's life?"

"It never crossed my mind she was the one operating on him," he mutters.

"Yeah, dragged out of bed in the middle of the night to make sure he lived to see another day with his wife. That's what she's dedicated her life to do," I assert, my tone firm.

"I never thought about it that way," he admits.

"Well, you should," I suggest, trying to instill some understanding in him. "Jas is tough, but she gets emotional about the things she encounters in the ER. Instead of thinking only about yourself and what you want, how about you think about her for a change? Really think about her. The person she is and the things she experiences. In all this time, I can't believe you haven't at least learned that much."

His response is subdued. "If you're trying to make me feel awful, it's working."

"I'm only going to say this one time," I state, looking him straight in the eye. "If you can't be the man she deserves, then walk away and let her find who that man is. Got it? Now get over there and help us win this game."

CHAPTER 35

J ASMINE

"You don't sound excited," Mya says, her eyes glued to me as I finish putting the food I spent all morning preparing into the picnic basket. "You don't look excited either."

"Mya! I thought you were supposed to be my friend?" I throw my hands in the air.

"This is real friendship, Jas. Don't listen to Odalis. She's single. I'm not. I know what it looks like when two people are in sync. It's not what I see in front of me."

"What do you expect me to do? Not give Idris a chance?" Ire crawls through my veins. I regret inviting Mya over and sharing my plans with her. "The man adores me. He went to meet my brother and won him over. Do you know how hard that is to do? Hendrix is super protective. Idris has him eating out of the palm of his hands."

"I'm glad Idris is building a great relationship with Hendrix. But what is he building with you? You're not into this relationship. Why are you pretending to be?"

"I'm not letting a setback change things. We need more time to let that part of things ... develop." I shrug, like it's not a big deal when it is a monumental deal. It's why I'm going out of my way to plan this date with Idris and see if maybe, in his element where he's most comfortable, I'll feel that spark with him again. The spark I felt during our initial phone conversations.

"I thought your brother told you not to change who you are for a man."

"I'm not!"

"You are going out to the ranch where there are animals." Mya looks at me pointedly. "You hate animals."

"Hate is a strong word."

"You're planning to go horseback riding. You're going to touch animals and be out in nature. That's not the Jas I know and love."

"I've done picnics in the park before ..." My words trail off.

I've done picnics in the park with Darren. When we're both on shift, and it's a slower day at the fire station, he'd text me to meet him in Bell Park for a quick snack. Usually something from Gwen's Country Cafe we both love. Those gorgeous blue eyes would sparkle as he teased me about playing hooky from work. Then, he would lay out a blanket for me to sit on and swat the bugs away as we catch up before returning to work. I can't remember how many times we've done that. Too many to count. All of them marvelous.

Why do those memories feel so special and intimate now?

I have to stop doing this.

"Picnics in the park are very different from going to a working ranch," Mya insists.

"When was the last time you were at a working ranch?"

"Never."

"So how do you know?" I give her a pointed stare back. She

acquiesces to my point. "What do you want me to do? Call Idris and cancel. Leave him hanging. Then what?"

"Fine. You're right. But promise me one thing."

"Girl, I'm not promising anything." The only friend I make promises to is Darren. I close my eyes and squeeze them tight. Somebody help me to stop thinking about my best friend.

"Okay," Mya rolls her eyes. "How about this? If you don't feel a spark with Idris after your date today, think long and hard about telling him the truth. You can't force a connection, and you definitely can't force love. It's either there or it isn't."

I reach for the picnic basket and place it over my arm. "Lock the door on your way out."

CHAPTER 36

J ASMINE

AN HOUR LATER, I DRIVE ALONG THE CRUSHED GRAVEL
road stretching like a white ribbon between acres of vibrant green
fields. Majestic live oaks and native pecan trees create a canopy of
shade, their gnarled branches stretching out to touch one another.

Rolling pastures extend as far as the eye can see. In the distance,
the main house looms—a Texas-sized mansion built with native
limestone facades, an expansive wrap-around porch, and a terracotta
roof. I steer the car toward the parking lot near a series of barns
arranged in a semi-circle. A dirt-filled paddock sits in front of the
barns, where various animals run, prance, and play. The whole setup
looks like something straight from the movies.

Not at all what I was expecting.

Pulling into the parking lot, I exit the car with the picnic basket and smile as Idris runs out of one of the barns.

"Hey, let me help you," he says, then leans over to give me a quick kiss. Lacing his fingers within mine, he leads me toward the barn. "I know you're not a big fan of animals, so it means a lot that you're willing to try horseback riding."

I nod slowly as I take in the massive horses meandering in the space. Some are laser-focused on chewing hay, while others are petted and brushed by the workers. "I didn't realize they were so big. I'll need a ladder to get on top of one." I swallow past the lump in my throat. Maybe this wasn't such a good idea.

"Don't worry. I'll help you. I picked the gentlest horse we have. He's well-trained and calm. But most importantly, he knows the trails inside and out and won't deviate. All you have to do is get on him, and he'll do the rest," Idris assures me.

I force a smile on my face and try to ignore my churning stomach.

"Let me introduce you to Nestle," Idris says with a broad smile. He looks so happy here, surrounded by his team and all the animals. All I can focus on is the stench of manure clogging the air and the flies no one notices but me. I can't imagine being out here every day and loving it. But I'm sure Idris could say the same about the hospital. Not many people understand how at home I feel in that element.

I follow him to a stall where a chocolate horse with a blonde mane stands still as if bored with all the activity. Idris rubs his neck lovingly.

"Do you want to pet him?"

"No. I mean, do I have to? Will that make it better for … him?" I ask.

Idris chuckles. "Nah, he's good. I thought we could do the picnic by the bubbling brook. It's about a mile out up the hills and through some of the prettier areas of the property. How does that sound?"

"Wonderful," I say, injecting gaiety into my tone. I do want to make the most of this second date with Idris. After what he did for me on our first date, I want to do something special for him, too. I also want to see if the kiss last time was due to awkward nerves and will be better this time around.

Did you feel anything when I kissed you?

There were no awkward nerves when Darren kissed me. Not the first time or the second. But comparing Idris to Darren isn't fair. I have to stop doing that.

"Ready?" Idris asks.

"I think so."

I follow Idris's directions on how to mount the horse. Ten embarrassing minutes of him huffing and puffing, trying to help me onto the beast later, he relents and gets a step stool like I requested earlier.

Nestle seems unperturbed by my struggles, and we're off across the rolling hills of Baker Ranch. We ride in silence, and I find myself enjoying the gorgeous views. A peaceful quiet surrounds us. The day turns out to be warmer than expected for winter in the Hill Country.

As we stop at the bubbling brook, I inhale the clean, fresh air, then almost face plant as Idris struggles to help me off the horse. I'm not sure how I'll get back on without the ladder, but I don't let myself think about it now.

"What do you think?" Idris asks, waving a hand toward the sweeping views.

I arrange the blanket onto the ground and take out the food, placing it in the center. "It's beautiful. I can see why you like it out here."

"Do you think you could ever get used to being here more? Being in nature, away from the hustle and bustle of the town?"

He sounds wistful and intoxicated by the surroundings.

"No, but it's nice," I say. There's no point in lying to him.

"Maybe it'll grow on you," he responds.

I'm not sure about that, but what's the point of telling him?

We settle into an easy conversation over the lunch I prepared— Caesar salad, lamb stew, yeast rolls, and apple turnovers for dessert. Idris loves everything I made and praises my culinary skills.

But time passes slowly as the banality of the conversation weighs on me. All Idris talks about is the ranch and loving animals and nature, and how much Quaid is improving by living out here. He repeats stories he's already told me three and four times.

I find myself going on auto-pilot, disengaging, and resorting to small talk. What happened to the man who had me up late for hours on the phone after work, riveted from our discussions? Or maybe that's the initial spark that can't help but fade? Perhaps this is the ebbs and flows of dating, and I should be happy with what I have with Idris. Maybe.

"Well, this was the best food I've had in a long time," Idris says, patting his stomach. "You know the way to a man's heart is through his belly. I could eat your cooking every day."

I scoff. "I don't cook every day. Evelyn would flip out if I told her I'm using surgeon hands to make food." I hold up my hands and dramatically turn them.

"Evelyn? Who's that?"

Pausing, I stare at him for a long moment. I can't believe he forgot all the details I shared with him about my mom and why we call her by her first name and not mom, or mama, or mother. Perhaps it slipped his mind. "My mom."

"Oh ... yeah. That's right," Idris says, then hastily packs up the food. "We should head back now."

I'm not upset with this suggestion. "Good idea."

It takes thirty minutes of wrangling, pushing, and hoisting before I can mount the horse again. Idris looks spent and worn out from the effort. I can't help but think Darren would've lifted me with brute strength and gotten me on the horse.

But I'm not here with Darren.

I'm with ... Idris.

As we return to the barn, I use the step ladder to dismount and stand next to Idris. He looks at me admiringly.

"This was the best date ever. Thank you for doing it. I know it pushed you out of your comfort zone," Idris says, slipping his hand in mine.

"You're welcome," I respond and smile. "I had a nice time." It's not a lie. But a nice time doesn't compel me to want to do it again.

"Let me walk you to your car," Idris says, then leads the way.

As we near my Audi, I know what's coming next.

CHAPTER 37

D ARREN

THE SUN CASTS A GOLDEN HUE OVER THE DUSTY TRAINING grounds in a deserted field at the Baker Ranch. I lean against the weathered fence, eyes fixed on Mirielle.

Sitting on her mare, she's a vision of grace and power, deftly guiding the horse around the rodeo barrels with expert precision. Each twist and turn sends a plume of dust into the air as the horse races through the course. My heart thuds with the familiar cadence of competition, watching another athlete practice for an important event. Raw athleticism and determination radiate from her as she approaches the third hour of training. She's as intense as when the session started, and I'm impressed.

"Come on, Blaze," Mirielle urges her horse, sweat dripping off her brow as she leans into another curve. Despite her fierceness, a gentleness in her touch speaks to the deep bond between rider and steed. This unique blend of strength and softness draws me to her. As she navigates the barrels, my attraction to her grows. Something I couldn't fathom feeling a month ago for any woman other than Jasmine, yet here I am. Maybe, I'm turning the corner on that part of my life, just in time.

"No!" she yells as Blaze falters on the final turn, stumbling and costing them precious seconds. The frustration on her face is evident, but I admire how she refuses to let it consume her. Instead, she pats Blaze's neck affectionately, whispering words of encouragement to the tired horse.

As they finish their run, Mirielle looks at me. Her cheeks blush pink. "Hey," she calls out, her voice breathless. "Thanks for coming by to watch."

I push off the fence, brush the dust from my jeans and walk toward her. "Of course." I keep my voice steady and casual. "I couldn't turn down an invitation to watch one of the best barrel racers in action. You're incredible, Mirielle."

"Today wasn't my best," she admits, biting her lip. "But I'm glad you were here." Something in her eyes hints at more than friendly appreciation. "No way I was giving up with you watching."

"Bad days happen to everyone," I reassure her, my voice sincere. "And if this is a bad day, all those other racers don't stand a chance on your good days."

Mirielle's eyes sparkle, and I can see the smile tugging at the corners of her lips. "Well, thank you, Darren. That means a lot coming from you." She blushes and looks away.

"Me?" I shake my head. "I've watched my fair share of barrel races, but I'm no expert."

"That's not why it means a lot." Mirielle looks back at me with fire in her eyes. "I shouldn't say this, but I waited a long time to get you to notice me. You know ... as a woman."

I laugh. "I may be a jock, but I'm pretty sure I always knew you were a woman."

"You know what I mean." She slaps my bicep, then allows her hand to linger there. "You weren't dating anyone. I wasn't sure if you would ever be interested in me. I'm glad you noticed and are giving this a chance."

I chuckle softly, rubbing the back of my neck as I look down at Mirielle's dusty boots. "You know," I begin, "it's kind of strange, isn't it? I try not to let my personal life blur with the relationships important to my foundation. But I was being too strict about it all. Probably because of what I went through …"

"With Pippa."

"Yeah. It made me … cautious."

"But I guess it also gave you a chance to get to know me better without any pressure."

"True, and I like the woman I've gotten to know."

"And now you can get to know me better."

"That's the plan."

Mirielle leans against a barrel, absently rubbing Blaze's neck. "Well, no matter what the future holds, I am enjoying this other side of you, Darren Manning."

"Other side?" I shift my weight from one foot to the other.

"You seemed so larger than life. Before your injury, you were one of the best defensive players the league has ever seen. It was intimidating. But now, I see you're … normal. Not that it's stopped me from being nervous around you."

"Normal is good. Being back in Kimbell grounds me. I'm much closer to the man my momma raised me to be here. And don't worry. I'm feeling pretty awkward myself. In a good way."

Mirielle smiles. "That makes me feel better."

"Let's promise to take things slow," I suggest, extending my hand toward her. "No pressure, no expectations. Just… see where this goes?"

"Deal," she agrees, shaking my hand firmly. We hold the handshake a moment longer than necessary, our eyes locked and smiles lingering.

As we release our grip, I gesture toward the gate. "Want to head out? Maybe grab something to eat."

"Great idea." Mirielle grabs the reins around Blaze's neck and tugs him forward. "I need to get this tired guy back to the barn."

"Lead the way."

I walk next to her as we follow a beaten dirt trail through the expansive grassy field toward the massive stables, which sit in the shadow of five barns arranged in a semi-circle. Mirielle leads Blaze inside, where Harper, the horse trainer, waits to take the horse through its cool-down phase.

"Mr. Manning, nice to meet you," Harper says unabashedly.

I shake his hand and smile at him. "You too."

"Think maybe I could ..."

"Autograph or picture?" I ask, surprised there are still folks in Kimbell who view me as a football star and not a firefighter with a big bank account.

"Both?" Harper says with a grin.

Mirielle leads Blaze into the largest stall while I oblige the horse's trainer. She's back within minutes, slipping her hand within mine. I don't resist or pull away. It feels nice.

"That's enough, Harper. You're eating into my dinner date time with Darren." Mirielle playfully chides him.

"Sorry." He gives a sheepish grin, then heads to Blaze's stall.

"Where should we go?" I ask, leading her out of the stables. We walk toward the parking lot. My gaze is drawn to two people standing a couple of cars away from my truck. They look familiar.

"Some place where we can eat outside unless you don't mind waiting while I shower. There are showers and a full changing room in the middle barn, and it's top quality, very luxurious. Would only take fifteen minutes. Twenty tops."

"I don't mind waiting ..." My voice trails off as I realize who the two people are. Numbness infects my muscles, and I stop walking.

"Is that Jasmine ... kissing Idris?" Mirielle says, excitement in her voice.

My best friend is unmistakable, even at a distance. Her wavy hair blows in the wind. She's dressed in skinny jeans and a form-fitting long-sleeved shirt that makes her curves look incredible. Her arms are draped around Idris's neck as they are locked in a passionate kiss.

"Oh wow! It is! Good for her. Idris is such a wonderful guy. They make a great couple," Mirielle says, her face beaming with delight. "But I guess that's not a surprise to you since you and Jasmine are so close."

"No. Not a surprise at all."

I can't tear my eyes away from the kiss. It's like a bad accident. I'm compelled to gawk even though it's the last thing I want to see. I notice every angle and movement of her body, pressed against Idris. The tilt of her head. The stroke of her hand against his neck.

Did you feel anything when I kissed you?

Boy, you are an amazing kisser, which I'm sure the hundreds of women you've kissed over the years have told you. So, it shouldn't surprise you that I think the same.

But we're friends.

Jasmine never answered my question.

Or maybe she did.

But we're friends.

Focusing on my kissing technique so she wouldn't have to be blunt and tell me it made her feel … nothing.

At least nothing like what Idris is making her feel now.

I wait for the heartache to hit, but it doesn't come.

I've been slowly coming to this place since Jasmine shut me down on New Year's Eve. The place where I don't love her anymore. I'm not entirely there, but I'm far enough along that seeing her kiss Idris doesn't devastate me.

And that's saying a lot.

"Oh my gosh, that's so exciting!" Mirielle gushes, clapping her hands together. "Jasmine deserves it. I've been rooting for her to find someone special for ages."

"Me too."

Mirielle turns toward me. "And I hope you find someone special, too."

Before I know what's happening, her lips are on mine, sealing the deal of our first kiss ... and all thoughts of Jasmine fade away.

CHAPTER 38

J ASMINE

THIS IS THE MOMENT I'VE BEEN WAITING FOR ... THE moment of truth. There's no doubt Idris will kiss me again. My expectations are beyond low, but kissing Idris is why I planned this date. I need to find out if the unremarkable kisses after our first date were a fluke. Maybe we'll have an earth-shattering connection this time, making the less than interesting afternoon I spent with him more worth it. Maybe.

I open the car door, toss my purse inside, and then turn to find Idris mere inches from me.

"You are so beautiful," Idris whispers.

"Thanks ..." My voice is breathy as I look into his dark eyes.

Idris leans down and presses his lips to mine as if on cue. I relax and push all thoughts from my head, giving my full attention to the kiss. It's a sweet kiss. Soft and endearing and gentle. With every touch, Idris shows me how he feels about me. He's more than into me. His feelings are intense. This man kisses me like I'm his entire future and everything he's ever wanted.

But I feel no spark at all.

None. Zip. Nada.

Whatever chemistry Idris and I had in the beginning is long gone. The truth is so blatant I can't pretend there's a chance my feelings for him could change. I'm too confused and mortified to end the kiss too soon. So, I let it continue, although I'm barely focused on what's happening as my mind races.

The last thing I want to do is hurt this man.

Idris is a terrific guy. He's everything I should want, but I don't. They say the heart wants what it wants. The opposite must also be true because my heart doesn't want a relationship with Idris Gibson.

After what feels like a dreadful eternity, I pull back and give a shaky smile. I'm not sure what to say. I need to talk to Mya and figure out a respectful and kind way out of this mess. How do you ditch a great guy? The town is going to have a field day with this one. I'll be labeled the Wicked Witch of Kimbell for breaking Idris's heart.

"I love kissing you. It feels so right," Idris says.

I nod, not trusting myself to speak, but my eyes are drawn to something behind him.

Not something.

Someone.

Darren.

And he's with Mirielle.

Not only is he with her, his arm is wrapped around her waist. She's looking into his face, smiling as if she's the luckiest woman in the world.

In a split second, his eyes lock onto mine.

His face is expressionless, but his beautiful, translucent blue eyes tell a different story. He's happy. Not just for himself. But for what he thinks is happening between me and Idris. He's happy because he believes we're both happy.

But I'm not.

For the first time, everything makes sense.

All the puzzle pieces come together to reveal a picture I never expected in a million years. I couldn't see it before, but I do now. I was too blinded by our past, my misconceptions, and what my friends and family thought about us.

Everything is crystal clear.

I'm in love with Darren …

CHAPTER 39

J ASMINE

"I FOUND HER," HENDRIX ANNOUNCES.

Maxwell, looking a touch more worried than I'd like, turns to us as we enter the living room of his home. "Where was she?"

"In her apartment, still in bed," Hendrix responds, glancing my way, concern written all over his face.

Probably because I didn't speak a word to him after he physically picked me up and dragged me out of my apartment this afternoon. Can't a girl wallow in misery in peace?

I experienced a revelation that has thrown my entire world off orbit.

I am in love with Darren.

My best friend.

Not that I've been harboring romantic feelings for him for years.

Quite the opposite.

I never thought of Darren as anything other than the friend who has been by my side since I was six years old. Until Evelyn, Aunt Mary, and Aunt Lisa accused me of using him as a relationship crutch.

No, that's not it.

Until Darren burst into the movie room on New Year's Eve and planted the kiss to end all kisses on my lips right as the clock struck midnight. I didn't know it then, but that one kiss was the domino that knocked down all the others.

Now, I'm sitting here in a quasi-relationship with Idris, who I've lost interest in, while Darren starts a relationship with Mirielle.

Mirielle, of all people!

He's clearly into her.

The spark I witnessed between them at Baker Ranch this past weekend was enough to set the field on fire. Guess it's a good thing he's a volunteer firefighter.

Why did that have to be when I realized I love Darren?

Why couldn't I have figured this out on New Year's Eve?

"Jas, why didn't you answer our calls and texts?" Lennox demands, jolting me from my thoughts. His face mirrors Maxwell's worry.

Tossing my bag on the nearby chair, I cross my arms over my chest. "Because I didn't want to talk to anybody. Evelyn wasn't freaking out. I don't know why y'all were."

Hendrix sighs, running a hand over his hair. "Because she figured you were at work, but Avril texted me. Said you bailed on work yesterday, and they hadn't heard from you today either."

I scoff, rolling my eyes. "Avril and I need to talk."

"We didn't tell Aunt Evelyn, or she would've had Lennox put out an APB for you," Maxwell admits, sharing a knowing look with Lennox.

"But y'all did anyway, didn't you," I accuse, the statement coming out more as a fact than a question.

Lennox raises an eyebrow, scrutinizing me. "What's with the attitude and the puffy eyes?"

"I think she was crying all day," Hendrix answers for me.

Lennox's eyes soften as he asks, "What happened?"

"Nothing happened," I retort, growing frustrated with their prying.

Lennox isn't deterred. "Did Idris do something? Did he hurt you?"

From the corner of the room, Jaxon, who's been quietly watching from the sidelines this whole time, visibly tenses. The muscles in his arms are drawn taut as he leans closer to hear my response.

"No ... he didn't," I admit, my words strained.

Jaxon rises from his chair. His voice is eerily calm and low as he says, "Let's go."

"No! Stop! Wait!" I rush out, stepping in front of him. "I promise Idris didn't do anything wrong—"

"What does that mean?" Jaxon asks.

"I mean, he doesn't know he did something that upset me," I explain, my heart hammering in my chest.

"You have ten seconds to tell us what happened, or we," Lennox points at Jaxon, "are going to find him."

"Seriously? I'm a grown woman. I don't need my cousins going off to meddle in my private business," I snap, annoyance simmering beneath the surface.

"Four seconds," Lennox warns, unyielding.

Jaxon doesn't say a word, but the look on his face shows he's in complete agreement with Lennox, which sends a shiver down my spine.

"Fine. I went on another date with Idris, and it was ... a dud," I relent, my shoulders slumping.

Maxwell's brows furrow. "What do you mean ... a dud?"

"Lackluster, boring, a chore," I elaborate, trying to keep my voice steady. "That's all. I'm wondering how things could be so different from when we talked on the phone and hadn't had our first date. It's weird. Like he's a different guy. I needed time to think about the situation. Satisfied?"

Lennox looks at Jaxon, exchanging a silent message. "Yeah, we're satisfied."

Jaxon nods toward the door. Lennox walks past me and follows

Jaxon as they leave. I'm alone with Maxwell and Hendrix. My brother grabs me and walks me over to the couch. I sink into the plush cushions as Hendrix grabs a throw and lays it over my legs.

"Where are they going?" I ask, apprehension seeping into my voice.

Maxwell shrugs. "Where do you think? They're cops. They're going to corroborate your story with Idris."

"I can't believe this," I mumble, pinching the bridge of my nose.

"Don't worry. They'll be subtle," Hendrix assures, sitting down next to me, though I find it hard to believe. He drapes his arm over my shoulder and gives me a gentle squeeze.

"Only if Lennox doesn't open his mouth," I counter.

Maxwell chuckles. "He usually defers to my brother in situations like this." He sits on the edge of his oak wood coffee table, facing Hendrix and me. "Okay, give us the details. What was so bad about the date?"

I give them the excruciating play-by-play, careful not to mention anything about Darren. With my current state of mind, I don't trust myself not to blurt out that I'm in love with my best friend. And if I do, it would be game over.

Hendrix would drag me to Darren's house and force me to tell him how I feel, and I can't do that. Not now. Not when Darren is starting to connect with someone. It would be selfish to put him in that situation after blowing off his kiss on New Year's Eve. Maybe he would've been open to it back then, but not anymore.

"Not a horrible experience, but I get why you're not sure about him," my brother says, rubbing the subtle stubble on his jaw. He's growing a beard which will make him more devastatingly handsome. How did he get all the good looks in the family?

Hendrix continues, "Still doesn't explain why that made you cry. You don't ... cry about anything."

"Who said I cried? I didn't cry. I was up all night thinking about it, so my eyes and face are all puffy. It's lack of sleep, not tears," I say, setting the record straight.

"I'm with Hendrix. I feel like you're leaving something out. Tell us," Maxwell prods, keenly observant.

"I cannot believe I'm about to say this," I murmur, a wave of embarrassment washing over me.

"What? You tell us everything," Maxwell says.

"Not about my dating life."

"Until this year, you didn't have a dating life to talk about," Maxwell reminds me. "Now that you do, you need us more than ever. You know we're on your side, so tell us. Get it off your chest."

"Fine. Every time I've kissed Idris, it's been horrible," I confess, the words hanging heavy in the air. I cover my face in my hands and peek at them through my fingers.

Maxwell and Hendrix wince.

"Define horrible?" Maxwell asks, tentative.

"Does he have bad breath? Bad technique?" Hendrix adds, trying to lighten the mood.

"No. It's nice. But I don't feel anything. No butterflies, no excitement, no chemistry. Nothing," I admit, my heart sinking at the confession.

"Explains the tears," Maxwell remarks, his voice softening.

"Boy, didn't I tell you I was not crying!" I glare at my cousin.

Hendrix says, "Now you're wondering if it's worth continuing things with Idris if the attraction isn't there?" His gaze is steady on me.

"By all accounts, everybody in town knows Idris is wonderful. I think he's wonderful. Even you like him, Hendrix," I remind him, looking for reassurance.

"I don't have to kiss the dude," Hendrix retorts with a smirk.

"Would that be a deal breaker for you?" I press on, curious about their views. With Darren warming up to Mirielle and my chances with him being less than no chance, I need to figure out what to do about Idris. "Say you met a great girl, y'all hit it off, but the more you're with her, the chemistry is off or nonexistent? Would you stop dating her?"

"Absolutely," Hendrix confirms, his answer immediate and definitive. Well, he can be because a line of a hundred women is waiting to take her place in his life. I don't have any other options at this point except Idris.

"Hold up. There's more to this." Maxwell looks thoughtful. "You and Idris had great chemistry over the phone, right?"

I nod in response.

"Then you had a great first date and an average second date—"

"Both dates ended with bad kisses, man." Hendrix shakes his head. "It's a wrap."

"Don't forget the conversations I have with him have turned toward the worse, too," I remind Maxwell.

"Right." Hendrix nods his head. "She's in a situation with boring communication and waning attraction to keep her interest. Time to cut him loose," Hendrix concludes, sounding decisive.

I freeze and stare at my brother, unsure I heard him right. "Blindside him and end things now?"

"I don't want you wasting time with this guy. I don't care how nice he is," Hendrix admits, his protectiveness surfacing.

"Wait. Does Idris know how you feel?" Maxwell asks, concerned.

"No. He loves kissing me. Loves hanging out with me. Thinks everything is going so well. I'm trapped," I confess, the weight of my predicament pressing down on me.

Maxwell, serious and sincere, looks at me. "This situation wouldn't be a deal breaker for me, but it is a sign you and Idris must have an honest conversation. If you don't, you might regret it later, Jas."

Hendrix rolls his eyes, crossing his arms over his chest. "What do you think she should do?" he argues, incredulous. "Tell the guy she's tired of talking about horses, cows, and barn duties? He should know not to dominate the conversation. Dating 101—conversations should be a dialogue exchange. Not a monologue."

Maxwell doesn't miss a beat. "But remember, he was nervous about meeting you," he counters. "Some guys take a while to relax when they're excited about a woman. He's probably intimidated and shocked you're dating him. Why don't you tell him how you feel and what you want?"

"What I want?" The words seem strange, foreign even, in my mouth. I don't want anything from Idris. What I want is to go back in time and redo New Year's Eve with Darren. Give a different answer to his question, knowing what I know now, and never suggest the stupid resolution of dating other people.

But that's not happening.

Maxwell nods, resolute. "You know, how you like to be kissed?"

I resist the urge to roll my eyes.

Hendrix grunts, reluctantly acknowledging the validity of Maxwell's point. "I guess it's worth a try," he admits, his tone still skeptical. "But don't give him too much time. Sometimes it's more kind to walk away than to stick around. No one wants to be in a relationship with someone who doesn't want them."

There's a heavy weight to his words, a sad, knowing edge that leaves me feeling like the worst person in the world.

CHAPTER 40

ARREN

I WON'T LIE.

This situation is worse than being caught by military special operatives and waterboarded until the truth is forced from my lips.

Except my captors aren't strangers. They are the four men like brothers to me ... and they want answers.

I lean back on the worn-out recliner in the firefighters' break room as the smell of this morning's stale, abandoned coffee lingers.

Ronan oversees the questioning, leaning against the counter, while Wiley and Luke stand near the pinball machine. Of course, they'd choose Nate to do the dirty work, rifling the first question at me.

"You holding out on us?" Nate asks, crossing his arms over his chest.

I stare back at him with a blank expression. "What are you talking about?" I'm stalling.

"You tried to keep this a secret." Luke, his flannel shirt pulled tight over his broad shoulders, grins and points a fork at Wiley. "No secret lasts long in Kimbell, Texas. Isn't that right, Wiley?"

Ronan scoffs, his eyes twinkling under his red eyebrows. "Secret? Wiley deceived the town with a double lie."

Nate leans back, the rusty chair groaning under his weight. "The whole real, pretending to be fake, pretending to be real epic love of Wiley and Zaire. The ladies in town still mourn that the playboy is off the market now."

Wiley throws up his hands, a baffled expression on his face. "How did this conversation turn to me? I thought we agreed to get the scoop on Darren."

"Scoop?" I question, raising an eyebrow. "Nothing is going on with me."

"Taking Mirielle on two dates in four days counts as nothing. Seriously?" Luke asks, a smirk on his face. "In whose dating playbook?"

"You have a dating playbook?" Wiley's eyes grow wide.

Luke shakes his head, chuckling.

Ronan, however, narrows his eyes at me. "Luke called this love match, but I'll admit I'm surprised. Never pictured you and Mirielle being a couple."

"I could see it happening," Nate interjects. "Why do you think she muscled her way onto the board of his foundation? She's been planning this for a while."

Luke laughs, punching Nate in the shoulder. "Stop it. Mirielle isn't diabolical."

I roll my eyes, getting frustrated with the entire conversation. "Who said Mirielle and I are a couple? We're not. At least not yet."

"But you're open to it? Really open to it?" Wiley asks, his gaze lingering on me in a way I immediately recognize.

The silent question he's asking is if I'm over Jasmine and moving on to find love with someone else.

I respond without hesitation. "Absolutely. I wouldn't have taken her out if I wasn't. But we are taking things slow. No rush. No pressure. She's nice."

"Nice?" Disbelief drips from Nate's voice. "Why is Darren Manning, football legend, wasting time with a woman he thinks is nice?"

"I'm with Nate on this one," Ronan chimes in. "Are you trying to get Jasmine off your back because of the New Year's resolution she forced on you?"

Wiley nods, scrutinizing me. "Good question. Darren, are you trying to find a … *replacement* … for Jasmine now that she's with Idris?"

I glare at Wiley, irritated by his emphasis on the word.

"Jasmine is irreplaceable. But she was right about us. We both need to get back out there and date again. She has Idris. Now it's time for me to find someone."

"Nothing wrong with that," Nate agrees. "My question remains: why are you wasting your time on a woman you think is nice? Walking the dog is nice. A good cup of coffee is nice. Finding your missing sock in the dryer is nice. A woman you're dating … should be more than … nice."

Luke adds, "The man has a point. You know I'm a fan of Mirielle. I wouldn't have suggested you give her a shot if I didn't like her. But I expected you to be a lot more excited than you are right now."

"Don't settle, brother," Ronan advises, serious now. "From the moment I met Mya, I couldn't stop thinking about her. She took hold of my heart before I realized it. All I wanted was to find ways to be near or around her and get to know her better. That's what you want. Do you feel any of that for Mirielle?"

My comfort is fading, replaced by unease. I can't help but wrinkle my nose. "Are we spending the morning dissecting my dating life?"

"It's a slow day. Why not?" Wiley quips, leaning back with a smug smile.

"Answer the question," Nate insists.

"Not really…" I admit, reluctantly.

Ronan raises his eyebrows. "Y'all kissed?"

I nod, and he exchanges a glance with Nate.

"How was it? No details, just the highlights," Nate prompts, earning a frown from me.

Ronan's eyes widen. "Oh, man. It was bad?"

"Not bad," I insist.

"Bland?" Luke offers.

"No spark?" Wiley guesses.

"Forgettable?" Nate throws in.

I reflect on the kiss with Mirielle, remembering the moment.

Absolutely nothing was wrong with the kiss.

The mistake I made was expecting that kiss to make me feel like I felt when I kissed Jasmine on New Year's Eve.

Or when Jasmine and I kissed at Spaghetti Western restaurant.

Because it fell far short of those two moments, I was disappointed. But that's not fair to Mirielle. I won't make that mistake again.

"It was good. No problem with the kiss. It was a great kiss," I maintain.

Ronan sighs. "Who are you trying to convince, Darren? Us or yourself?"

"Get out of that situation immediately," Nate advises, blunt as always.

"Look, we've all been in situations where it takes a while for the spark to show up." Luke tries to defend.

"There's nothing wrong with the chemistry between Mirielle and me," I say, determined to make my point. "The spark, the interest, the compatibility—it's all there. I like her. We decided to take things slow and get to know each other. She's busy training for the Houston Livestock Show and Rodeo over the next few weeks. Plus, there's no rush to force a relationship. We have time."

The guys exchange glances and nod, making me nervous. "What do those looks mean?"

"You're not into her," Nate says simply.

"Nope," Luke agrees.

"Because your heart belongs to someone else," Ronan states.

Looking like the cat who ate the canary, Wiley waves his hands.

"Don't look at me. I didn't say anything to them. Promise. Cross my heart."

"He didn't need to," Nate adds. "It's obvious you have unresolved feelings for—"

My cell phone buzzes on the table, halting our conversation.

We all lean in to see the text that flashes on the screen.

UNKNOWN NUMBER

Hi Darren, it's Cassidy. How are you?

My heart seizes in my chest. Heat pricks at my skin. My face flushes.

Cassidy.

How many times have I held my phone in my hand, my finger hovering over her number?

I've thought about calling her many times over the past five years, but I never did.

I'd put her through too much already. When I suffered my career-ending injury, she was thrust into the spotlight. The media hounded her for intel on how I was doing, my future, and how she was or was not taking care of me.

Things worsened when I moved to the rehab facility in Colorado as the attention shifted to us as a couple. Were we in trouble because she didn't come with me? Was she abandoning me in my time of need?

Then armageddon when Pippa leaked on social media allegations I sexually assaulted her, re-characterizing our consensual make-out session into something more horrible than it ever was.

Cassidy couldn't leave her house without being followed and hounded by paparazzi demanding details.

A part of me doesn't believe I deserve a chance to talk to her again. She's moved on from the life we shared. The best thing I can do is to leave her in peace, even though a big part of me longs to hear her voice again.

I snatch my phone from the table, away from the prying eyes of my friends. My heart races as I stare at the screen. I can't respond now, not with the guys watching my every move.

"Perfect timing, don't you think?" Ronan teases, a smirk playing on his lips.

Nate chimes in, a smug grin spreading across his face. "Now, this is the kind of reaction you should have about the woman in your life."

The guys all nod and agree, chuckling amongst themselves, except Wiley, who looks at me with a concerned expression. He doesn't say a word, just keeps his eyes on me, making me feel more exposed.

Luke whistles, a knowing look in his eyes. "If Cassidy is back, Mirielle doesn't stand a chance."

I don't bother to respond. I stuff the phone in my pocket and push myself off the chair, leaving behind the echo of their laughter. Without a word, I storm out of the break room, the heavy weight of Cassidy's unexpected message bearing down on me.

CHAPTER 41

ARREN

"You bought her a ring," Wiley says.

The winter breeze brushes against our faces as Wiley and I trudge down the near-empty sidewalk toward Gwen's Country Cafe.

"I know," I reply, forcing my cold fingers into my pockets. We shuffle along with our jackets zipped up to our chins.

"You were going to propose to her." His words hit the frosty air, hanging heavily between us.

"I know," I repeat, staring at the cracked sidewalk ahead of us.

"She's the only woman you loved enough to put ahead of Jasmine," Wiley says like it's an undisputed fact.

Yet, I know that's not true.

I don't respond.

Truth is, there hasn't been a time in my life or a relationship I was in where I put someone ahead of Jasmine. I know I should have, but I couldn't bring myself to do it. She's always meant too much to me.

In the past, whenever Jasmine sensed I was getting close to someone, she would back off from our friendship. She would focus on pursuing her career as a doctor, filling up her days until she had no time to do anything. It took the choice away from me.

She always knows what I need and helps me get it, whether it's what I want or not.

It wasn't different with Cassidy.

Jasmine was doing her emergency medicine residency in Pittsburgh while I played professional football there and started my relationship with Cassidy. As Cassidy and I grew closer, Jasmine got busier and busier with her residency. Because Jas didn't have time for me, I spent time with Cassidy. It's the only reason our relationship got as deep as it did.

I won't lie. I did fall in love with Cassidy. I could see a future with her. It wasn't the one my heart wanted the most, but it was the next best thing. And I believed it was attainable, while a relationship with Jasmine was a pipe dream.

Wiley says, "Now Cassidy has reached out after years of no contact between the two of you. The timing coincides with Jasmine and Idris becoming a couple."

We turn and enter Bell Park, crossing the wide expanse of low-cut grass to shave off a few minutes of our trek to the cafe.

"True. I didn't tell you, but I saw them at Baker Ranch yesterday," I admit.

Wiley looks at me, surprise painting his features. "What were you doing at the ranch?" Curiosity sparks in his eyes.

"Mirielle invited me to watch one of her training sessions. After the training, we were heading to the parking lot when I saw Idris and Jas kissing."

"Kissing or *kissing*?" Wiley stops.

I take a few steps, then turn to face him. "Let's say there's no denying how into each other they are."

The image is burned into my memory. Watching Jasmine kiss Idris, his arms wrapped around her intimately, slammed the door on the last shred of hope I had of convincing Jasmine to give a relationship with me a chance.

"Man, I'm sorry," he says, a hint of empathy in his voice.

"I'm not," I retort, the words harder than I intend.

He grips my shoulder and gives it a rough squeeze. We start walking again, maneuvering through the leafless trees blowing and creaking in the wind.

"I needed to see that," I say. "Jas and I have only exchanged a few texts over the past week. I haven't seen her, which you know is unusual for us." I press my hand against my heart and add, "In here, I knew it was because of Idris. She's falling for him more and more every day. She's not trying to ignore me. Her heart makes her choose to spend time with Idris instead of me. I can't be upset about that."

"That may be true, but it doesn't mean anything has changed for you," Wiley says, probing deeper. "Are you over Jasmine?"

"There comes a time when you throw in the towel and realize what you want doesn't have a chance of happening. That kiss sealed it for me."

The truth feels sharp and cold, but I won't deny it anymore.

"Don't get me wrong. A part of me will always love Jas. She's one of the most important people in my life and always will be. But I'm moving on," I declare, finalizing a decision long overdue.

"This isn't how I wanted things to turn out for you, but I'm glad you're not in limbo anymore," Wiley admits.

"Me too," I say, then he hits the nerve.

"Or maybe you still are," Wiley says, giving me a worried look. "Why do you think Cassidy reached out to you?"

I lift my hands in the air. "I never expected her to talk to me again after how things fell apart between us," I confess, memories of our bitter end swirling in my mind.

Our last conversation had been gut-wrenching. Hurtful things were said, bridges burned, and our love for each other was scorched to ashes blowing in the wind. I didn't intend to hurt her, but I did. It's one of my biggest regrets.

"The injury changed me. I wasn't the same man she'd fallen in love with," I confess to Wiley, a sigh escaping my lips. "Cassidy took the brunt of all my grief, sadness, and anger at losing my football career. Then, I got involved with Pippa, which led to another mess. I can't imagine why she wants to talk now."

"Maybe she needs closure," Wiley suggests.

I can only shrug in response. "Maybe."

"There's only one way to find out," he adds.

"Text her back," I agree.

We reach the glass door that leads into Gwen's Country Cafe. The place is emptier than usual due to the dip in temperatures overnight.

"I'll go in and grab the lunches," Wiley says, clapping a hand on my shoulder, then reaching for the door. "Do what you need to do."

Turning away from Wiley, I walk back down the walkway in front of Gwen's and swing a right onto the sidewalk. Slumping down on a frigid metal bench surrounded by planters with dead flowers, I take a deep breath and stare at Cassidy's text. With a shaky hand, I begin typing.

DARREN

Hey, never thought I'd hear from you again. But I'm glad you texted. How are you?

A notification chimes. Cassidy responds, and my chest tightens.

CASSIDY

I'm good. Hope you don't mind that Jasmine gave me your new number.

You reached out to her?

No, she reached out to me

229

A few seconds pass, then another text comes through.

CASSIDY

To apologize. It was nice of her and got me thinking.

I can't help but smile at that. A sense of contentment settles within me. Even though Jasmine was wrapped up in her new relationship, it didn't stop her from being the best friend to me that she's always been. If she's able to do it, then so can I. I will be Jasmine's best friend as she falls in love with another man. I owe her that much.

DARREN

About us?

CASSIDY

Yes. We should talk. Clear the air.

I'd like that

But not over the phone

I can come to you

You would do that?

Of course. Are you still in Pittsburgh?

Nope. Moved to Vegas a few years ago for a job.

Casino management

It was always my dream and now I'm living it

I'm happy for you

Thanks

How about this weekend?

> You don't have plans?

Normally, Valentine's Day in Kimbell was filled with packed restaurants jammed with the who's who of couples around town. This year, the Bell Family was hosting a town-wide celebration of love in Bell Park. Love Under the Stars was creating a lot of buzz, but I have no reason to attend.

DARREN

> Plans? No ...

CASSIDY

> It's the weekend before Valentine's Day on Monday

> Sorry. You must have plans

> Actually I don't

I hesitate, considering the implications of flying off to spend Valentine's Day weekend with Cassidy while quasi-dating Mirielle. Everything with Mirielle is new. I doubt she has any expectations of us being together this weekend. In fact, it's good to pull back to ensure neither of us feels pressured to rush things because of the most romantic weekend of the year.

Still, I can imagine her not being too happy to find out I chose to spend the weekend with my ex-girlfriend instead.

Something inside is compelling me to do this now. Mirielle may or may not understand that, but it's what I need to do. I can't explain why. I know deep inside I need to be in Vegas this weekend.

I text Cassidy back.

DARREN

> So this weekend works?

CASSIDY

> yes

Great. I'll send details once I have them. Talk soon.

I can't wait to see you.

I don't respond, but in my heart, I know I can't wait to see her too.

CHAPTER 42

J ASMINE

M UTED BEEPING MONITORS AND FOOTSTEPS OF FAMILY
members walking down the halls fill the air. I stand by the nurses'
station, leaning against the counter. The morning madness has ended.
Avril and Georgia, two of the nurses on my team, and I are catching
our breath and hoping the busy morning isn't a reflection of what's to
come later in the day.

Although being busy helped me to keep my mind off the only thing
I can think about these days—being in love with my best friend.

"I don't want to hear one more siren," Avril declares, leaning back
in her chair. "Tell the world the ER is closed for the next hour."

"Hour?" Georgia huffs. "How about for the rest of the day? Was
that a record number of patients for the morning?"

"If not a record, it came very close," I say, reflecting on the rash of children rushed to the hospital from an accidental chemical spill at the local elementary school.

"That was nice of Hendrix to come by and drop off food for the worried parents. It helped calm them down," Avril says with a bright smile.

"He wanted an excuse to check on Jas after what went down," Georgia says, raising an eyebrow toward me. "He's not fooling anybody."

"That reminds me. Avril, give me your phone," I demand.

"Why?" she replies, eyes darkening with concern, but hands it to me nonetheless. "What are you looking for?"

"My brother's phone number, so I can delete it." My fingers fly over the screen, hunting for the contact.

Georgia looks up from her monitor with a sly expression. "Why don't you want her to have your brother's number? They're both adults."

Avril's face flushes a deep red as she nervously rakes a hand through her blond tresses. "It's not like that. We're friends."

I give her a stern look as I find the contact. "I don't care who my brother does or does not date. That's between him and the woman. I'm trying to stop you from texting my brother and worrying him about stuff going on with me. It's either delete his number or teach you a lesson a harder way." I hand the phone back to her. "I'd advise you to go with the former."

Avril grins mischievously. "Doesn't matter. I have his number memorized."

"You do?" Georgia and I ask in unison.

"Yes, but it doesn't matter," Avril says, avoiding eye contact. "I'm not his type either."

I know she's referring to the short stint she had trying to date Wiley, the former Playboy of Kimbell, who is now happily in a relationship with real estate mogul Zaire Kincaid.

"Who told you that?" I interject. "My brother's type is … female. That's it."

Georgia pats Avril's shoulder and adds, "Don't sell yourself short, Avril. If Wiley can fall in love, so can all the other irresistible bachelors in this town. Hendrix may not be so out of reach."

"I don't know about that," I mumble, uncertainty threading my voice. My brother has never been in love, and that's on purpose. He's not ready for that kind of connection and is the first to admit it.

"Speaking of settling down," Avril says, changing the topic swiftly, "you hit the jackpot with that man." She nods toward the doors that lead into the ER.

I turn to see Idris entering, holding a massive bouquet of red roses and a paper bag from Risveglio.

This is when excitement should flood me, and I should beam as he walks toward me, looking rather attractive. But all I feel is sadness from this undeserved romantic gesture. I've been so caught up in analyzing my newly discovered feelings for Darren that I haven't thought about how to get out of this situation with Idris.

"Hey beautiful," Idris calls, strolling toward me.

In my periphery, I see Avril fanning herself with a lovestruck goofy look on her face and Georgia with a salacious smirk.

Idris says, "A little birdie told me you hadn't had lunch yet. I thought we could do a picnic in your office. I brought your favorites."

"That's so sweet!" Avril croons.

I turn back to Avril, beckoning for her phone again. Her face scrunches as she hands it over. I scroll through her contacts and delete Idris's number, too.

As I drop the phone back into her hands, I feel Idris's arm wrap around my waist.

"These are for you," he says.

"Those are beautiful," Georgia says.

My heart races as panic crawls over my skin. Thank God Avril and Georgia are responding because I can't seem to force myself to say a single word.

Idris places the bouquet in my arms, then says, "Let's go to your office, babe."

Babe?

My gaze shoots to his face as I inwardly cringe. We haven't discussed being in an exclusive relationship, and he thinks he can start using terms of endearment now.

I push down my rebuke, recognizing my ire is more a function of my unrequited love for Darren and has nothing to do with Idris.

Navigating the hallways, Idris fills me in on the excruciating details of his morning. When we reach my corner office overlooking Bell Park, I close the door behind us, shutting out the world.

Idris doesn't miss a beat, taking the first chance to lean in for a deep kiss. His lips roam against mine in a frenzy. I place my hands on his shoulders to maintain my balance from the unexpected intimacy. Wrong move. He takes that as a sign I want to continue the kiss, which I absolutely do not.

I force a smile on my face as we break apart, even though inside, I'm groaning. I hate that Idris doesn't know my real feelings, but coming clean now during my work day seems cruel. Better to do it tonight when we can be alone.

Idris places the paper bag from Risveglio on my desk.

"Now, I didn't like that dish we made, to be honest. It did a number on my gut later that night, if you know what I'm saying." Idris pulls food from the bag and arranges the containers on my desk. "And it was too fancy with all those ingredients. Who could remember and make it again without the chef over your shoulder? I'm a simple man. Give me some spaghetti and a can of tomato sauce. I'm happy."

I move to the other side of my desk and sit down, grabbing the container that has my initials on them. I'm not hungry since Hendrix brought over a haul of barbecue from Baker Bros, but I don't want to be rude.

Idris rambles, "But I know it's your favorite, and I wanted to brighten your day after the crazy morning you had."

He's not wrong.

Tasting the decadent dish will go a long way toward erasing the stress I've endured today. I lift the container and look inside. My heart drops as I stare at the food. "You got my favorite?"

Idris nods. "Ravioli arrabbiata."

Ravioli arrabbiata?

I tip the container and show it to him. "Does this look like what we made, Idris?"

He glances at it, shrugs. "I guess so. I don't remember. I was too busy watching you, beautiful. But I told them my baby's favorite dish is ravioli arrabbiata. This is what they gave me."

I close the container and push it to the side. "That's not my favorite dish. It's not what we made."

"It isn't? Are you sure?" Idris sounds genuinely surprised.

"Positive," I reply, feeling a rush of frustration. "I don't like spicy foods. Arrabbiata sauce is spicy."

He immediately looks apologetic. "I'm so sorry, babe. Here take my spaghetti. I will eat the spicy pasta," Idris suggests, attempting to diffuse the situation.

I pause, looking at him with disbelief. "Strange that you planned the date but forgot all the details of it a couple of weeks later."

"I didn't plan the date," he says. "I had no clue what I was walking into when we got there. But it turned out real good. You know that chef knew what you would pick off the menu because..."

His voice falters as panic flashes in his eyes.

"Don't stop now," I interject, a knot tightening in my stomach. "So, if you didn't plan our amazing first date, who did?"

He looks embarrassed and admits, "Okay, so the idea for the date wasn't mine, but that doesn't stop it from being great, does it, babe?"

"Who came up with the idea for our date, Idris?" I demand.

He drags a hand down his face, then gives me the only answer that makes sense. "Darren."

CHAPTER 43

J ASMINE

IDRIS STAMMERS, HIS WORDS RUSHING, "I MIGHT HAVE mentioned to Darren that I wanted to impress you. So, he told me he'd take care of it. All I knew was we needed to be at the restaurant by noon, and everything else would be handled."

My heart drops to my stomach at his confession.

This was Darren's idea?

Of course, it was Darren's idea.

Who else knows me well enough to plan a date so meticulously perfect but the man who has been my best friend for over two decades?

The man I'm in love with. The realization brings tears to my eyes that I blink away.

Did you feel anything when I kissed you?

I hear Darren's voice as clearly as if he is standing behind me.

My heart skips a beat in my chest. They say opportunity doesn't knock. The door opens slowly and waits for you to walk through before it closes again.

And I missed my chance with Darren because I was too stubborn to stop and think about what he was asking me, what he wasn't saying with his question. I had one chance where Darren was in the right head space to shift his thoughts about me from best friend to something more.

But I thought I knew everything as it relates to us. How could I be wrong?

But I was as wrong as it gets.

If I had answered him differently or realized the truth sooner, would the private cooking lesson with Chef Fiona have been our first date? Could we be a couple now, happy and in love like Ronan and Mya? Or Wiley and Zaire? Or even Santos and Harlow-Rose, although I hate to think about those two?

A rush of anger and betrayal takes over me. I stand abruptly and point my finger at Idris. "You went behind my back to my best friend and got him to plan our first date? Was any of it your idea?"

"Well, no," Idris admits, looking taken aback by my reaction. "But like I said, I wanted to impress you."

"But you didn't because it wasn't your idea. It was Darren's." My voice echoes in the room, each word a painful reminder of the man I love.

Idris raises his hands defensively. "Ok, calm down—"

"Calm down?" I retort, anger simmering. "Let me ask you this. How much do you think it cost Darren to pull off that date? Have any idea?"

Idris shrugs, a sheepish look on his face. "You know rich people do favors for each other."

"I can't believe what I'm hearing," I mutter, shaking my head in disbelief.

"I don't think it's that big of a deal. He was happy to help," Idris tries to reason, his voice filled with worry.

"Darren cares about me. He wants me to be happy. That's the only reason he didn't turn you down when he should have," I reply, feeling a lump forming in my throat.

"I don't understand. You had a great time on the date," he insists, looking genuinely perplexed.

"Only because I thought you had put your own ideas and creativity into planning it," I confess, my voice shaking. "If I'd known you'd phoned a friend, and not any friend, my best friend, to do it for you, it wouldn't have been as special. I can't believe you used him."

"Okay, I didn't realize this would upset you. I'm sorry, okay, babe."

"Stop calling me babe!" I lash out.

A panic-stricken Idris rises from his chair. "I'm sorry, Jasmine. Please. Don't be mad."

"Don't tell me how to feel," I snap, feeling the sting of my unshed tears. "You know what, it's better if you leave."

He looks stunned. "You don't want to have lunch with me anymore?"

"No, just go," I whisper, barely holding back the rush of emotions.

"Can I call you later?" Idris pleads.

"I will call you when I'm ready to talk again," I say.

Idris slinks out of my office. His face hangs low with embarrassment. The door closes behind him with a soft click, leaving me alone with my thoughts.

With a frustrated growl, I swipe the food containers off my desk. The crash is loud, the sound echoing around my office. The contents spill out in a grotesque display of wasted food and misplaced anger.

A reflection of my messed up life.

CHAPTER 44

J ASMINE

I YANK MY PHONE FROM MY POCKET, MY EYES INSTANTLY drawn to another set of messages from Idris. Like clockwork, they're the usual round of apologies he's been sending the last few days. Ignoring them has become as natural as the chilling breeze blowing through town, where an unexpected winter cold front has swept in.

I find myself in Bell Park, a local gem with winding pathways, mature trees dusted with frost, and a small pond. Passing by a group of stay-at-home moms with kids bundled in coats playing at the playground, I make my way to the centerpiece of the park. A lovely wooden gazebo, painted white and adorned with twinkling lights and festive decorations—red and white for the upcoming Valentine's holiday. Climbing the three steps into the gazebo, I tug my wool coat around my body and warm against the cold backdrop of winter.

Despite the charming scene, my heart feels heavy. No amount of Idris's apologies or the tranquil environment can change the fact that I'm hopelessly, madly in love with Darren.

Not Idris.

I should've told Idris the truth, that I'm no longer interested in pursuing a relationship with him, days ago. There's no saving him from being blindsided by the news. It's not fair for me to let him think I'm open to a relationship when I'm in love with someone else.

But that's why I've been avoiding Idris.

I ease onto the wooden bench seats and stare across the grass at a flock of ducks wading out of the pond.

He will want a reason why the sudden change in my feelings. Blaming it on the first date fiasco isn't an option.

Telling the truth is impossible, though.

No one can know I'm in love with Darren, even if that's the one thing Idris would understand and accept as a reason for me pulling away —

"Hey." A familiar voice rumbles.

I look up, my heart stuttering at the sight of Darren. He's gorgeous in a tight black Kimbell Firefighters t-shirt that showcases his athletic build.

"Avril texted me and said you were out here and might need me," Darren says. "From the look on your face, I think she was right."

"I swear I'm going to punch her when I get back. What is up with her?" I retort, frowning.

"She's trying to be a good friend."

"Good friend?" I scoff. "When did Avril and I become friends?" The pretty blond nurse has become an integral part of my emergency room team since she came to Kimbell years ago, but that's a far cry from being friends.

Darren leans against the entry to the gazebo, his pale blue eyes intense as if he's looking straight into my soul. "Maybe that's what she wants. She looks up to you."

"Fine, whatever. You didn't have to come, you know. I'm okay." But my protest falls flat, even to my ears.

"Do you think I'd get that text and not drop everything to find you?" Darren counters. His words, combined with the concern in his eyes, pull at my heartstrings.

Suddenly, we both say, "I miss you."

The silence that follows is thick and heavy, filled with emotions neither of us want to acknowledge. Darren moves closer, hesitates, and sits on the opposite side of the gazebo from me. He doesn't have to say a word for me to know the reason. Darren is trying to respect what he believes is my new relationship with Idris.

The distance is needed for an entirely different reason, but it feels too far away for what my heart wants.

"Glad I'm not the only one," I say, breaking the silence.

"You're not."

"Things are complicated now."

"I know. But we'll figure out how to still be us and not make Idris feel put out. Trust me, I learned from the best over the years."

"I don't know that I did that great of a job, in hindsight," I confess, looking down at my hands.

"You did," Darren assures me with a smile that sends another round of butterflies skittering through my body. "It was me who couldn't let go of our closeness. It caused a strain in my relationships, but I didn't care. I'm not going to make that mistake with you and Idris. That's why I've been keeping my distance. I don't want to give him any reason to be insecure."

"There are plenty of reasons for that man to be insecure, not that he's observant or intuitive enough to realize it," I grumble, feeling a surge of frustration at the thought of Idris.

Darren leans forward, muscles tensing. "What happened? Talk to me."

"I guess I should thank you for the date Idris and I had at Risveglio?" I ask, a hint of sarcasm seeping into my voice.

Darren cringes at my words and leans back on the bench, shaking his head. "He wasn't supposed to tell you."

"I wondered how he could afford it, but thought he got help from Colton Baker. It never crossed my mind that the entire idea wasn't his. He stole it from you."

"Stole?" Darren asks, rising. He crosses the gazebo in four long strides and sits next to me. Warmth radiates from his muscular body, and I long to lean against him.

"Is that why you're upset?" Darren asks. "Because I planned the date, not him."

"How much did that set you back? Ten thousand? Fifteen?"

"The money doesn't matter. You're worth it."

"Idris doesn't appreciate what you did. I should've known he couldn't come up with something tailored precisely for me. But you could."

"I was going to do that for your birthday, but he needed help, and I knew you were starting to like him. Don't be mad at Idris. Be mad at me. I'm the one who should've told you."

"I could never be mad at you."

"Oh, you have selective amnesia now?"

"Boy, shut up. So you gave Idris your plans for my birthday?"

"I did."

"Now, my birthday will suck?"

"Already came up with something better," Darren replies, a mischievous twinkle in his eyes.

"I can't believe you. How did I get so lucky to have you in my life?"

"Because I got lucky first. You came to my rescue, remember?"

"Best three punches I ever gave, and I didn't get caught." I recall the memory with a small smile.

"I don't want to be the reason things are strained between you and Idris," Darren says, his voice pained. "He's a good man, and y'all are good together. When Mirielle and I saw y'all at the ranch this past weekend, it was obvious how perfect you are together. Don't push him away to defend me."

"How are things with you and Mirielle?"

"Changing the subject, I see."

"I can't make any promises about Idris, Darren."

"Why not? So what if he didn't plan the date? He was there with you, and y'all had a great time, right? I didn't do that part. He did."

"Are you having a great time with Mirielle?" I ask, unable to stop myself.

Darren gives me a knowing look as I avoid continuing the discussion about Idris.

I continue, "Rumors are floating around town about y'all." I hold back from telling Darren my envious theory that Mirielle is the one leaking details of their dates to put all the other women on notice she's staking her claim on him.

A claim I want to stake but can't.

"I like her, but there are some things I need to figure out first," Darren says, then brushes a lock of hair from my face. A touch that instantly warms me.

"Thanks to you, I can do that," he says.

"Me? What did I do?"

"You found Cassidy."

I nod, hoping to maintain a pleasant look amid my disappointment.

"She told me you were the one who convinced her to reach out to me."

"Oh ... that. I wasn't sure she'd call you."

"We texted but realized it's better if we talk in person."

"In person? You're going to Vegas."

"Yep, this weekend."

"Valentine's Weekend?" My words are a high-pitched croak. "Are you going to be back for the Love Under the Stars Valentine's Day event that Old Man Bell is putting on?"

"I'm not sure," Darren says, shrugging. "I don't want to wait. This conversation has been years overdue. I chartered a jet and leave in the morning."

"You excited?" My voice is so low I'm surprised Darren heard me.

He nods. "And nervous. I'm not sure what's going to happen. This weekend could change everything for Mirielle and me. What she and I have is so new and ..."

"What you and Cassidy shared was the real deal."

"Yes, it was."

"I hope you get everything your heart wants this weekend, Darren."

Darren pauses to look at me, an expression I can't read in his gorgeous, faint blue eyes. "Me too."

"I gotta go." I choke out, my voice barely above a whisper. Seeing the hope in Darren's eyes about reconnecting with Cassidy makes my heart feel like it's splitting in two. I can't be around him anymore. He would know something is wrong. "I've already been away for too long," I add, standing up abruptly. Darren follows suit.

I attempt to sidestep Darren and continue my escape from this torturous scene, but he's quicker than I am. He intercepts me, his arms snaking around my waist to pull me back toward him. His touch sends electric shocks through my body, causing my heart to thrum wildly in my chest. I can't fight his gravitational pull over me, nor do I want to. I succumb, melting into his welcoming embrace, clinging to him like a shipwrecked sailor to a life raft.

The gazebo is quiet around us, the soft hum of the winter wind rustling the leafless trees and the distant laughter of children playing in the park our only soundtrack. Darren's hold on me is firm but not suffocating, creating a cocoon of comfort and affection that sends my heart spiraling. An intense, silent exchange of emotions ricochets between us.

This isn't a friendly hug, not from my side, at least. As I bury my face against his hard chest, I pour every ounce of my love for Darren into the hug, hoping he can somehow feel the silent confession echoing from every cell in my body. His scent fills my senses, a comforting mixture of fresh winter air, his familiar cologne, and the underlying musk that's uniquely him.

The bitter irony is he doesn't know the depth of my feelings and how they've changed since New Year's Eve. That's my fault.

With a final squeeze, I let go and step back, my fingers lingering on his waist for a fraction longer than necessary. I throw a weak smile in his direction, hoping it masks my inner turmoil. The gazebo feels too small, too intimate. I need space, distance. I need to breathe.

"I... I've been away for too long. I should go," I stammer, making a beeline for the gazebo's entrance.

Darren follows me. "I'll let you know how it goes," he promises, his reference to the Vegas trip not lost on me.

"Okay," I respond, forcing a smile.

The moment I step out of the gazebo, a gust of cold wind hits me, snapping me out of the bubble Darren and I were in.

I take one last look at him, his ice blue eyes still sparkling with an emotion I can't decipher. With that, I leave, carving a solitary path through the park, my heart heavy with the weight of unspoken words and unexpressed feelings.

After all, how can I burden him with my truth, especially when he's on the verge of reconnecting with his past?

CHAPTER 45

J ASMINE

"If this is a bad time ..." My gaze drifts across the modest log cabin nestled on the opposite side from Colton's massive mansion at the Baker Ranch. The early morning sun shines brightly onto the porch, and I'm thankful the temperatures have improved from the frigid cold yesterday.

Idris shakes his head but never takes his eyes away from his cell phone.

After waking up late on my day off, I texted him. A sense of urgency to cut ties with Idris overwhelmed me emotionally. Or was it the text from Darren that pushed me over the edge?

DARREN

On the G5 now. Staying at Bellagio suite and coming back Sunday night. Wish me luck.

WANTING MORE

Good luck

I had to force myself to respond because I knew this trip would change everything for me. I couldn't help but feel crushed. But I'm not letting my lousy mood stop me from doing what's necessary with Idris.

His fingers swipe quickly across his phone screen as he steps back into the house. I wait a moment to see if he will look at me. When he doesn't, I stifle my impatience. I want this break-up to be over painlessly. Even though we never explicitly discussed being exclusive, the entire town has concluded we are in a relationship. In Kimbell, sometimes that's all it takes to become shackled to someone, regardless of whether it's what either person wants.

"Idris." My voice is loud enough to crack through his cell phone-induced haze. He looks at me.

"You want something to drink? I have coffee, tea, soda," Idris says, then turns his attention back to the phone.

"No, I won't be here long enough for that."

This gets his attention, and his eyes jerk up toward me. "Why not?"

I take a deep breath. "I think you know what I'm going to say."

"No." Idris shakes his head and closes the distance between us. "Wait, let me apologize, okay? I can fix this." He scrolls more on the cell phone, eyes glued to the screen.

"How can you fix this when you can't give me your undivided attention from your stupid cell phone?" I demand, snatching it from his hand.

"Wait, don't look at that," Idris barks, eyes full of panic.

He wrestles the phone from my hand until it flies into the air, landing with a thud near my foot. I grab it, glancing at the screen to see a string of text messages from Idris to … Darren. The dates on the messages are from a month ago, when Idris and I first started talking over the phone. I scan the first message.

DARREN

> Now tell her — I apologize for acting off earlier.
> Make sure you say apologize and not sorry.
> Jas hates it when people say I'm sorry.

> Try something like — Yes, Dr. Jones (don't call
> her Jas until she invites you to). I've heard a lot
> about you. Your reputation as a brilliant doctor
> is known all over town, just wasn't expecting
> you to be so beautiful.

> Now say … It threw me off. Don't want you to
> think I'm rude or not a gentleman, because I
> definitely am.

"Give me my phone," Idris says, his voice hard and cold

I hold up a hand, warning him to stay back. "What is this?"

Idris is quiet as his shoulders slump. He turns his back on me and walks into the kitchen.

"Idris," I repeat. "Why did Darren text you these things?"

The memories become clearer in my mind.

My first phone call with Idris.

"Is this Dr. Jones?"

"Yes, it is. I don't recognize this number. Who am I speaking with?" I ask.

"Idris Gibson. I met you earlier this evening at the library."

I remember him, decent looking guy with no social skills. "Oh, yeah. You're one of Darren's board members at the foundation."

"That's right."

"Well, I hope you enjoyed the dinner," I say, wondering the reason for his call. Perhaps it has to do with his son, who is autistic.

"It was good. Thank you for bringing it."

"I'm glad to hear it. Did you call to thank me for the dinner?"

"No. I actually called to apologize for acting off earlier."

"Apologize?"

"Yes, Dr. Jones—"

"Please, call me Jas."

"Okay, Jas. I've heard a lot about you. Your reputation as a brilliant doctor is known all over town, just wasn't expecting you to be so beautiful."

I laugh, face flushing warm from the unexpected compliment.

"It threw me off. Don't want you to think I'm rude or not a gentleman, because I definitely am …"

"What is this?" I scream at Idris.

Idris stands rigid in front of the kitchen sink, gazing through a small window that overlooks the rolling hills of Baker Ranch.

I continue to scroll, recognizing in each text from Darren things Idris had said to me during our many late-night conversations. I don't know what to think about any of this.

"You need to start talking now, or I'm calling Darren to get answers," I threaten. It's an empty threat since Darren is on a three-hour flight to sin city.

Idris turns. His expression is full of shame. "I think you need to sit down for this."

"I'll stand." I glare at him. "Explain all of these texts from Darren."

"When I first saw you in the ER, I thought you were the prettiest woman I'd ever seen. I tried to talk to you but couldn't get a few words out. Thank goodness Quaid was there and helped things not be so awkward," Idris begins.

"I remember. So what?"

"When I met Darren at the library, I told him what happened and how I wanted a second chance to make a better impression on you. Then you showed up, and the same thing happened again." A pained expression crosses his face as he continues, "Darren saw how much I was struggling. So, he offered to help coach me until I got comfortable enough on my own."

"Coach you? What does that mean?"

"You see the text messages."

"I want to hear you say it."

"He gave me pointers on what to say to you during our phone calls."

"But how could he know what we were talking about?"

"I called him first, then called you on three-way—"

"Darren was listening to our conversations?"

Idris nods.

"We talked for hours, many times for two weeks. He listened to all those calls?"

"Yes."

"So, he heard what I said to you, and then what? Texted you how to respond?"

Idris nods.

I turn my attention back to the phone, reading with lightning speed all the texts from Darren. The words I thought were Idris's, the ones that wooed me, had all come from my best friend.

They had all come from the man I'm in love with.

I swallow hard, then throw the phone at Idris.

It hits him in the chest and clatters to the floor.

"I'm so sorry, Jas," Idris says.

"Don't you mean I apologize? That's what Darren told you to say to me, right? He gave you the script to make me fall for you, and it worked."

"It wasn't my idea! Darren was the one who suggested it. He thought it was the best way to help me."

"So, not only did you lie to me about our first date, but all of our phone conversations were lies."

"Just the early ones. After our first date, Darren refused to help me anymore. It was time for me to stop relying on him. Since then, it's been one hundred percent me."

"You think that makes this better? Darren made a boneheaded move, and I will talk to him about that," I explain, blood boiling. "But what you did was so much worse!" I point my finger at him. "You were only thinking of yourself and what you wanted. You had no problem deceiving me into thinking you were someone you were not."

"I am that man—"

"No, you're not. The man I wanted to go on a date with was the man who captivated me with engaging late-night conversations. But you weren't the one talking to me. Darren was. You were reading a script." I throw my hands up. "I couldn't figure out why our conversations were so different in person than over the phone. This explains why."

"You're saying you didn't enjoy the time we spent in person?" Idris looks crushed. "You weren't attracted to the man you talked to after that first date? When it was all me with no help from Darren."

"It was ... different," I admit.

A scowl crosses Idris's face. "So, what would've happened if you'd talked to the real me on the phone? Would you have given me the time of day? Would we have started dating?"

"I don't know. I can tell you our conversations lately show me we aren't compatible like I thought we were. But it makes sense because I was talking to my best friend on those early calls, not you."

"What about our kiss? You can't fake that connection."

"Idris ..."

"What is it? Oh, you didn't enjoy the kiss either?" Idris asks, voice rising. "So who's been deceiving who? Do you see what you're doing?"

"What I'm doing?" I press my hands on my hips.

"Everything is always Darren this and Darren that. You can't open up and give another man a chance because you're so wrapped up in Darren. But you lie to yourself and claim he's your best friend when you want more," Idris lashes out. "Why don't you admit it?"

"You're right," I say, gaze locked onto his.

"I am?" Idris asks, confusion and anger battling in his eyes.

"My feelings for Darren are much deeper than I ever realized. Those texts prove why. He gets me like no one else ever has. We have a special bond that can't be broken, no matter what. He's the most important person in my life."

"Wow." Idris drags a hand down his face. "Darren has no clue how you feel."

"Of course, he doesn't. Do you think he would have helped you if he did?"

"You think he feels the same way about you?"

"No." I shake my head. "Not at all. But if he knew I had these feelings for him, the last thing he'd do was pressure me to get into a relationship with someone else. He'd want us to discuss it and figure out how to salvage our friendship despite my feelings."

"Sounds like Darren."

"Doesn't it."

"You know him pretty well, too." Idris crosses his arms over his chest. "How long have you felt this way about Darren?"

I sit in the chair across from Idris at his dining room table. "Since I saw him kissing Mirielle at Baker Ranch after our date."

"I guess my kiss didn't rock your world, and you realized it's because you wanted the kiss Mirielle was getting from Darren."

"I never meant to hurt you, Idris."

"I know. Part of me wishes I'd never gone along with the stupid plan, even though I'm sure I would've ended up in this same spot regardless."

We are quiet for a long moment, knowing his assessment is accurate.

Idris breaks the silence. "Are you going to tell Darren how you feel?"

"No way." The words tumble from my lips. "He's on the way to Vegas as we speak to reunite with his ex, who was the love of his life. Probably still is. After they broke up, Darren was different. He didn't want to date and spent all his time with me. It's like he didn't want to put himself out there again. I think it's because he was still in love with Cassidy."

Clearing the air with Cassidy will be hard enough for Darren. The last thing I will do is burden him with my unrequited feelings for him.

I love him, and I know I have to set him free to love who he wants. And that woman isn't me.

"Makes sense, but if you ask me, he's a fool for not seeing who he has right in front of him."

"That's nice of you to say, considering."

"Think you can forgive me ... for everything."

"Honestly, in a way, I understand why you did what you did, and I'm flattered," I say, grabbing his hand. "And yes, I forgive you."

"Maybe we can be friends?" Idris asks.

"Maybe," I say, then exhale loudly. "The only reason I told you how I feel about Darren is to help you understand why I couldn't connect with you. But I don't want anyone else to find out about this. I need you to keep this a secret, Idris."

"Of course, I won't tell anyone. I promise," Idris says, squeezing my hands. "We may not seem like a good match now, but who knows what the future holds, right?"

I bite my bottom lip and fight back tears. "Who knows ..."

CHAPTER 46

J ASMINE

THE LATE AFTERNOON SUN FILTERS THROUGH THE LACE
curtains of Evelyn's house, casting an intricate pattern of light and
shadow on the old worn-out wooden floor. The familiar scent of home
lingers in the air—a blend of the lemon furniture polish she's
obsessed with and the leftover aroma of the lasagna she'd prepared for
lunch.

Evelyn stands in front of me, hands on her hips, while Aunt Mary
and Aunt Lisa lounge comfortably on the overstuffed couch, a favorite
family heirloom.

"Why aren't you at work?" Evelyn asks, her forehead creased in
worry.

I let out a humorless chuckle. "It's nice to see you, too, Evelyn."

Aunt Mary chimes in, her voice soothing. "Oh, Jas. Your momma didn't mean it that way. It's unusual for you not to be at work in the daytime."

Aunt Lisa adds, "Or nighttime. Sweetie, you work too much." Her lips press into a disapproving line. "That, as well as those extra pounds you're carrying, is stopping you from getting a man."

A sudden hush falls over the room as Aunt Mary drops a tidbit, her voice laced with mischief. "Word on the street is Jas has found a man."

"Not the right man," Aunt Lisa mumbles, shaking her head.

Evelyn shoots Aunt Lisa a look that immediately silences her.

I clear my throat, eager to set the record straight. "For the record, despite what the Kimbell town gossip is, I'm not dating Idris Gibson. At least not anymore."

Evelyn looks relieved, too relieved. "You're not. Thank goodness."

Aunt Lisa looks at Evelyn and immediately clamps a hand over her mouth.

I narrow my eyes at her, more confused than ever.

Curiosity getting the better of me, I ask, "What's wrong with Idris? He's a nice man."

"He is. A hard worker and very accomplished. I hear he's also a great father, stepping right up when his baby momma dropped that precious little boy on his doorstep a few years ago," Aunt Mary offers, her voice filled with fond respect.

"That doesn't mean he's the right man for our Jas," Aunt Lisa protests. "So, what happened with you and Idris?"

Evelyn sternly scolds Aunt Lisa, "Stop being nosy. My child doesn't need to explain anything about her personal life to us."

I swallow the lump in my throat. "It's okay. I need to talk to someone about this."

"You do?" Aunt Mary asks, her eyebrows raised in surprise.

"And you came here?" Aunt Lisa chuckles. "This has to be serious."

"It is serious," I confirm, my voice barely more than a whisper.

Evelyn grabs my hands and leads me to my dad's oversized recliner. How many times did I sit on the edge of the armrest and pour out my problems to him?

Too many to count.

He always helped me figure out what I needed to do without explicitly giving me advice. Deep inside, he knew I hated to be told what to do, so he helped me to figure things out on my own. It's times like these that I'm more angry at him for getting himself thrown in prison.

"Sit," Evelyn commands, her tone gentle yet firm.

I do as I'm told, and Evelyn sits on the armrest next to me.

"Where do you want to start?" she asks.

Voice trembling, I confess, "I broke things off with Idris this morning. I found out he lied to me and misrepresented himself. But even if he hadn't done those things, I still would have stopped dating him."

"Why, Jas?" Aunt Mary prods, concern etching her features.

"Do you remember our talk on New Year's Eve?" I ask. They nod their heads, leaning closer toward me. "Well, y'all were partially right."

"Is this about Darren?" Aunt Mary ventures, her eyes gleaming.

I nod, unable to find my voice.

"Partially?" Aunt Lisa asks. "What part did we get wrong?"

"Y'all thought I was using Darren as a substitute for a real relationship, but I wasn't. I didn't realize it back then, but I want to be in a real relationship with Darren," I confess, my heart pounding.

There's an exchange of glances I can't decipher. Taking a deep breath, I plunge ahead. "I'm in love with Darren." My voice hits a high octave that annoys me.

The reaction is immediate. Evelyn jumps up and skips over to Aunt Mary and Aunt Lisa. They exchange high-fives and hugs as they dance around each other. I watch in stunned silence like I've stumbled into an alternate reality.

"What are y'all doing?" I stammer, my eyes wide in disbelief.

"Honey, we are celebrating you getting a clue of the obvious," Aunt Lisa replies, her laughter ringing through the room.

"I don't understand," I say, feeling lost.

Evelyn explains, "Ever since you convinced Darren to move back to

Kimbell to reset his life after the Pippa debacle, we all could see the two of you were in love. Both of you were too blind or stubborn to realize it." Her eyes shine with a combination of satisfaction and relief.

"So, we hatched a plan to get y'all to see what was right in front of you," Aunt Mary chimes in, a mischievous twinkle in her eyes.

Aunt Lisa interjects, "It was my idea. What better way for the two of you to realize you're meant for each other than to send you off to date other people."

"And it worked!" Evelyn exclaims triumphantly.

I hold up a hand to stop them. "Not so fast." I'm reeling from this manipulative revelation. They all fall silent, looking at me expectantly. "There's nothing to celebrate." I blink back tears that threaten to spill over. "I wish y'all had found another way of helping me see the light."

Evelyn crosses the room and wraps her arms around me. "This is what the two of you needed. Now you can be together."

"No, we can't," I say as stupid tears roll down my face. "I said I'm in love with Darren. I never said he loved me back. He's on a plane right now to rekindle his relationship with Cassidy. And that's my fault. I pushed him to find love with someone, and he decided that person was the one who got away five years ago."

"Darren is going to see Cassidy on Valentine's Weekend? Oh, this is not good." Aunt Mary wrings her hands in worry.

"So Darren doesn't know how you feel about him?" Evelyn asks, her voice soft and gentle.

"Of course not. There's no way I can tell him now," I reply, feeling my heart breaking again.

"Why not?" Aunt Lisa demands, looking puzzled.

"Are you joking? He's in love with someone else. Why should I spill my heart to him and put him in a position to let me down? He wouldn't want that. I don't want that," I retort.

"He still needs to know, Jas," Aunt Mary says firmly. "You can't hold these feelings inside. That's not like you. The truth is going to come out. You won't be able to keep something this important from him."

Aunt Lisa nods in agreement. "Listen to your Aunt Mary. You need to take a plane to Vegas and tell him how you feel. Then let him decide."

Evelyn joins in, the concern evident in her voice. "I agree. Do you think you can keep this from Darren for the rest of your life?"

"I don't know," I admit, feeling defeated.

"You can't," Evelyn declares, shaking her head. "We all know that. It's not in your DNA to not speak your mind, especially with Darren."

"Mary, go grab that laptop and start looking for a flight for Jas to take to Vegas in the morning," Aunt Lisa instructs. Her eyes are fiery, igniting a spark of fear in me.

"No... I can't. Maybe when he gets back," I stammer.

Evelyn interjects, her voice stern. "That will be too late."

"You say that like there's a chance Darren has romantic feelings for me. He doesn't," I say, my voice choked with sadness.

Aunt Mary's hand envelops mine in a warm grip. "Are you sure about that?"

Did you feel anything when I kissed you?

Darren's question haunts my memories.

Why did he ask me that?

What answer was he hoping for?

I fall silent, my conviction and confidence shattered.

Aunt Lisa laughs lightly, seeming to find my silence amusing. "See, you're quiet! That's enough to convince me there's hope. Mary, book a flight for Jas."

"Sweetheart, go home and pack your best outfits," Evelyn advises. "The ones that will make that man's eyes pop right out of his head. You go to Vegas and tell him the truth."

Aunt Mary speaks up again. "You and Darren have been friends your entire lives and closer than most married couples. The two of you know each other inside and out, flaws and all, and still want to spend every chance you get with each other. On the off chance—"

"Extremely unlikely chance," Aunt Lisa interjects with a smirk.

"That Darren doesn't share your feelings," Aunt Mary continues, ignoring Aunt Lisa, "he's going to do everything in his power to save your friendship."

"The two of you will always have a bond, whether romantic or not," Evelyn assures me.

"You have nothing to lose, Jas," Aunt Lisa states firmly.

Mary looks up from the laptop she's been furiously typing on. "Flight is booked. You're on the 8:30 am out of Bush Airport in the morning."

Evelyn turns to me, her eyes hopeful. "What do you say, sweetie?"

CHAPTER 47

ARREN

BENEATH THE ELECTRIC GLOW OF VEGAS' NEON LIGHTS, Cassidy crosses the street and heads toward me. I stand near the edge of the crowd clustered around the dancing fountains in front of the Bellagio Hotel.

"Hi," Cassidy says. Her face flushes pink as her eyes rake over me. Her hair shimmers gold beneath the streetlights as dusk fades into the night sky. She's prettier than I remember, dressed in a white tank top and fitted jeans.

"Hi," I say, then take her into my arms for a long hug. The feeling is familiar, like throwing on an old sweatshirt from college.

"You look great. The years have been good to you." Cassidy smiles.

"Right back at you." I chuckle, then point toward a restaurant. "I made reservations at Spago."

She glances in that direction. "Can we walk along the Strip?" There's an unmistakable edge in her tone.

"Of course," I respond, hoping to reassure her.

We both know this conversation won't be easy, but it is necessary. I don't blame Cassidy for not wanting to be trapped in a restaurant if things get emotional.

I fall into step next to her as we maneuver past the throngs of people. Laughter, music, and the distant chiming of slot machines are the soundtrack to a long overdue conversation.

No point in wasting any more time.

"We've known each other too long for small talk," I say with a nervous laugh.

"Totally agree. Do you want to go first?"

It's not a question but a request to which I oblige.

"I'm sorry for how things ended between us. I blamed you for things that weren't your fault. I wasn't supportive of what you were going through. I never stopped to think about how difficult that time was for you, too. I should have handled things better," I say.

"Were you planning to propose to me?" Cassidy asks, her voice surprisingly steady.

The question is like a bomb detonating, and I stop to gather my thoughts. The ring I bought for Cassidy had been a hasty decision.

Jasmine had been in Pittsburgh for a couple of years, working on her residency. It was the first time we'd lived in the same city for almost a decade. I tried to ignore my feelings, but I failed miserably. All those old feelings wouldn't be contained. I made up reasons to pop in on Jasmine at her apartment and the hospital, unable to stop the insatiable need to be close to my best friend.

The ring was a reminder that I'd already built a good life with Cassidy. Risking my friendship with Jasmine for love wasn't wise, no matter how much my heart yearned for her.

But I never gave Cassidy the ring.

I didn't know she knew about it.

Cassidy stops walking and turns to face me, her eyes searching mine. She takes a deep breath, and I brace myself for what's coming.

"I found the ring in the back of one of your drawers months before you got hurt and waited around for you to propose, but you never did," Cassidy explains. Her words hang in the air between us. "Why didn't you give it to me?"

I swallow hard, feeling the weight of my past mistakes. I look away, staring at the ground littered with discarded flyers and crushed beer cans.

"Because I didn't deserve you," I admit, my voice barely audible above the noise of the Strip. "I couldn't bring myself to make that commitment when I knew I wasn't being honest with you or myself."

Cassidy's expression softens as she studies me, giving way to something more akin to understanding. But I can still see the hurt in her eyes, and it tears at me that I caused it.

"Are you being honest now?" she asks, her voice wavering.

"More than I've ever been," I reply, meeting her gaze again. And as we stand there, surrounded by the whirlwind of Vegas nightlife, I hope my words can somehow mend the fractures I've left in our hearts.

I take a deep breath, the scent of street food and car exhaust mingling in the air. "Before that game," I begin, my voice thick with emotion, "I stopped lying to myself about who I wanted." I pause, struggling to find the right words.

Cassidy's eyes widen, but she doesn't say anything.

"I was so distracted, trying to figure out how to break things off with you. My head wasn't in the game. I made a ton of mistakes. The next thing I know, I'm blowing past one offensive lineman and almost at the quarterback when I get slammed to the ground. I never saw the other lineman barreling toward me. A mistake I hadn't made since I was a rookie, and it cost me my career. It changed the trajectory of my life," I say as the memories play in my mind. "I was on the football field, and I couldn't move. Couldn't feel anything. The medical team lifted me onto a gurney, and the only thought flipping over and over in my mind was … I need Jasmine." I drag a hand down my face. "I'm sorry for only coming clean with you now."

A myriad of emotions flickers across Cassidy's face. "All the time we were together, you wanted to be with Jasmine."

"I'm sorry," I repeat, sounding like a broken insensitive record.

"Don't apologize for how you feel. Was the ring for her?"

"No, I bought it for you. I just couldn't go through with it."

"Because you were in love with Jasmine?"

"Yes." There is no point in denying it.

Cassidy shrugs. A sad smile on her lips. "Part of me always knew your relationship with Jasmine wasn't just friendship, at least not for you. When she came to Pittsburgh for her residency, everything shifted between us. I didn't understand why, but now it makes sense."

I nod, my worries ebbing away with each passing second. "Yeah, I know."

For the first time in years, I feel a sense of peace settling within me, and I hope Cassidy feels it too.

Cassidy peers into my eyes, searching for the truth beneath the surface. "So," she begins, her voice laced with curiosity, "has anything changed between you and Jasmine?"

"It's ironic. The woman I want is the one I can't have." I exhale, the burden of my secret tightening its grip on me once again. "Jas is in a relationship with a great guy. A friend of mine. I helped them get together. It's getting serious. Watching her fall for him has helped me let go of her. I won't jeopardize her happiness or our friendship by telling her now. And besides," I add, forcing a smile onto my face, "I'm over her."

Cassidy's eyes narrow, scrutinizing my expression like an art critic examining a masterpiece. "You're a liar, Darren," she accuses, her tone firm but not unkind. "You are as much in love with Jasmine as you've always been. Don't try to deny it."

A flicker of irritation courses through me, but I push it aside. "You're wrong," I insist, meeting her gaze squarely. "Jas will always be important to me, and I love her, but it's not that kind of love. Not anymore."

Cassidy looks at me, her skepticism evident in the arch of her brow, before she relents with a conceding nod. "Alright, if you say so."

"I'm in a new relationship," I say, giving details Cassidy may not want to hear. But it's important she knows everything I wanted with Jasmine is in my past. I'm ready to move toward a future with someone else. "Her name's Mirielle. She's a rodeo barrel racer who has been on the board of my foundation for years. We started dating a month ago." I pause, watching Cassidy for any signs of hurt or betrayal. Instead, her expression remains open and curious.

"A rodeo barrel racer? That's a change from what you were used to," she remarks, a hint of amusement in her voice. I can't help but chuckle at the truth of her statement.

"Definitely different. She's incredible," I admit, feeling a warmth spread through me at the thought of Mirielle. "But before I can open my heart to her, I need closure with you. I won't ever treat a woman like I treated you back then. I regret so much what I did. Can you forgive me?"

Cassidy's gaze softens, her eyes shimmering with unshed tears as she processes my confession. She reaches out, gently touching my arm, conveying her understanding and acceptance. "I forgave you a long time ago. It took a while, but I knew how much you were hurting. I also realized I wasn't the one you wanted to help you through the hurt."

"And for lying to you about my feelings for Jas. Can you forgive me for that, too?"

Cassidy looks away. The kaleidoscope of Vegas lights shines bright against her face. When she turns back, sincerity in her gaze touches me. "Yes, I forgive you for that, too. I'm sorry you didn't get the happy ending you wanted with Jasmine. Life is funny that way. But finding someone new who makes you happy is a good start to moving on."

"Thank you."

"Darren ..."

"Yeah."

"Be sure you're not lying to yourself. Mirielle deserves better than that. Be sure she's the one you want." Cassidy leans in, hugs me, then walks away, disappearing into the crowd.

I stand alone near the curb, as I reflect on the significance of her words.

CHAPTER 48

ARREN

"Where are you?" There's a shrill edge in Mirielle's disembodied voice booming through my cell phone.

The room is bathed in inky blackness.

After talking to Cassidy, I couldn't get back to the hotel suite fast enough. Closing the blackout shades on the window, I crawled onto the massive king-size bed and stared at the ceiling for what felt like hours. My mind raced through the encounter, settling time and again on Cassidy's last warning to me.

Be sure you're not lying to yourself.

Alone in the room, I searched my heart and found Jasmine still had a firm hold on it. I don't know how I tricked myself into thinking I no longer loved her. Or rather, that my love for her was merely platonic.

It's deja vu.

But this time, I'm doing the right thing before it's too late.

"Vegas," I say, keeping my voice calm.

"When did you leave? I didn't know you weren't going to be in town this weekend. Not that I had any expectation of us spending Valentine's or going to the Bell's Love Under the Stars event together. I mean, all of this is too new ..." Mirielle rambles, her voice shaking.

"I flew out yesterday," I respond. I originally planned to fly back to Texas to be home on Valentine's Day, so Mirielle wouldn't think I was spending the holiday with Cassidy. But that was before I realized the truth. "I'll be here for a few more days."

"Football season is over," Mirielle says, an accusation in her tone. She knows I didn't sign on to do any analysis or commentary for the playoffs or Superbowl. I've only been working on my foundation and at the fire station since the last game of the professional football season. She continues, "Are the guys with you? Nate and Luke? Wiley?"

Time to put us both out of our misery.

"I came alone ... to see Cassidy."

"Cassidy? Your ex-girlfriend?" Mirielle's voice hits a higher octave. "I didn't know the two of you were still in contact with each other."

"We weren't until recently—"

"Is this break up call? Because if it is, get it over with," Mirielle demands, anger lacing her words. "Don't drag it out."

"Technically, we're not a couple," I remind her.

"Whatever. So, what? You don't want to date me anymore? After talking to your ex, you realize I'm not who you want?" Mirielle peppers me with questions.

"Mirielle, I'm not trying to hurt you. But I do need to be honest with you. You're not going to get what you want from dating me. This won't lead to a relationship or a commitment. I'm not going to mislead you," I say, choosing my words carefully but knowing they all come out wrong. Too harsh. Too unfeeling. Even though that's not my intent.

"What changed? Are you and Cassidy getting back together?"

"No."

"But you want to get back together with her?"

"No."

"Darren, I don't understand. Then why can't we continue to date? We both agreed there would be no guarantees. We enjoy each other's company—"

I interrupt her. "Mirielle, I'm in love with someone else."

The silence that follows roars in my ears. I wonder if the line has been disconnected. I check my phone and see the timer on the call still ticking by.

Mirielle sniffles, then says, "Oh."

"That's why it's not fair for me to continue to date you. My heart isn't in it."

"Does she know you love her?" Mirielle asks.

"Who?"

"Jasmine." She says my best friend's name like something vile in her mouth. "Did you tell her?"

"What makes you think I'm in love with Jasmine?" My heart pounds in my chest. If Mirielle has figured out my secret, who else knows?

And how on earth will I survive Jasmine's wrath if someone else tells her and not me?

"I've noticed how you look at her when you think no one is watching. You find ways to touch her when it's unnecessary. She's never far from your mind. You talk about her all the time. She comes up in every conversation," Mirielle says.

I'm quiet.

"But you know she doesn't want you, not like that. You are a friend to her. Nothing more," Mirielle continues, her words slicing through me. "You are wasting your time if you think she will develop romantic feelings for you. She and Idris are solid. You can't shake that."

"I'm not trying to," I say through gritted teeth. "The most important thing to me is for Jasmine to be happy. If Idris makes her happy—"

"If? If? He does make her happy. She doesn't want you to be her man." Mirielle taunts, plunging the knife deeper.

Anger simmers within me, threatening to boil over. I bite my tongue before I say something I'll regret. I suck in a deep breath, then respond, "I'm well aware."

"But you still are putting your dating life on ice for ... her."

"Yes, I am."

"You're such a fool. You will regret this, and when you do, don't call me," Mirielle says with resolute finality.

I stare at the phone as the call ends.

What I regret is not telling Jasmine how I felt on New Year's Eve. She knew what I was trying to say but didn't want me to say it. She believed we were using each other as relationship crutches. She didn't think the feelings I have for her could be real.

I should've done more to convince her of the truth.

If I had, would we be together?

Or would she have let me down easily, explaining why my feelings weren't reciprocated?

Either way, I know I'd be better off than I am now.

I wasted weeks helping another man get close to Jasmine.

Idris and Jasmine are in a relationship, and that's my fault.

I drag a hand down my face, then grab the pillows from the bed and hurl them across the room.

How on earth am I going to deal with this?

A beep emits from my cell phone. I glance at the illuminated screen.

JASMINE

Are you at the Bellagio hotel?

I rise and grab my phone.

DARREN

Yeah

271

JASMINE

Penthouse suite?

Yes, why?

I sent you a gift. Thought you might want it now.

What kind of gift?

Boy, open the door and find out.

They delivered it to my door? I didn't hear a knock.

Argh! You are so stubborn. Open the door and you'll see it.

A smile plays at the corner of my mouth.

I can't deny how satisfying it is that on Valentine's weekend, when Jasmine should only be thinking about Idris, she took the time to send me a gift. I'm on her mind as much as her new man is. I shouldn't read into that, but I can't help myself.

DARREN

Alright. I'm going to the door. Stay by the phone.

JASMINE

OK

I jog to the door and swing it open.

The phone falls from my hand as I stare into the gorgeous brown eyes of Dr. Jasmine Jones. She's dressed in a red satin floor-length dress that hugs those delicious curves. A glittering red sash is tied in a bow around her waist.

I open my mouth to speak, but no words come out. She's so beautiful I'm speechless.

"Surprise," Jas says, her voice low and breathy.

"Are you ... my ... gift?" I force the words from my mouth, hoping for the answer I long for.

Jasmine steps closer, reducing the space between us to mere inches.

"Yes," she says.

Before the word is out of her mouth, my lips crash against hers in a passionate kiss.

CHAPTER 49

J ASMINE

FIREWORKS.

Not the literal fireworks popping off outside the hotel as the Bellagio fountain show ends.

The fireworks erupting inside of me as Darren's kiss goes deeper, touching me to my very soul. My heart races, my mind is a blur, and I'm consumed with euphoria. I've never felt this way about any man before.

I love Darren Manning.

In my wildest dreams, I couldn't have asked for a better welcome to my impromptu crashing of his trip to Vegas to see Cassidy.

I don't bother to think about what happened between them.

Or what could happen next between Darren and me.

All I want is to enjoy this moment as if it's the only thing in the world.

As Darren's lips caress mine, my body surrenders. The electricity between us is palpable. I wrap my arms around his neck, pulling him closer. His hands reach my waist, tugging me until no space separates us. The kiss has taken on a life of its own, leading us to pure pleasure.

I can't help but feel we've come home ... to each other. Every ounce of love I have for Darren is reflected from him to me. This is something real. Something worth risking everything for.

Darren breaks our kiss too soon for my liking, and I'm left panting and breathless. As I look into his stunning soft blue eyes full of longing, desire, and love, I know this is the beginning of something special. Something I've been waiting for my entire life. I rest my hands on his muscular arms and smile.

"I'm sorry. This was a mistake," Darren says, pulling away from my touch. An icy chill slices through the air as the A/C kicks on.

What?

No, this can't be happening.

I know I'm not hearing him right.

"Mistake?" My heart reaches tachycardia, and I feel nauseous.

"I shouldn't have kissed you," Darren says firmly with no hesitation. He swipes a finger across his lips, removing the last remnants of my lipstick. Erasing the phenomenal kiss we shared. "It won't happen again. I wasn't expecting ..."

I stand in the middle of the room dumbfounded.

Darren smiles, but it doesn't reach his eyes. "It doesn't matter." He squeezes the bridge of his nose. "What are you doing here? Did you and Idris plan to celebrate Valentine's Day in Vegas?" He's injecting a casualness into his voice that is disjointed and out of place.

I shake my head. "Idris?"

"Your boyfriend. Hope you weren't expecting to do a double date with me and Cassidy because that's not happening," Darren says, walking toward the luxurious king-sized bed. He taps an electronic keypad and the entire room floods with light. "She forgave me for how things ended with us, so that's as much as I could hope for."

"Are you disappointed?" I croak, confused by his sudden change in behavior. It's like he can't get far enough away from me.

"Disappointed?" He frowns. "No, not at all."

"But you came here to …"

"Clear the air," Darren says. He leans against the wall next to the window, as far away from me as possible. "I wasn't trying to rekindle anything between Cassidy and me. Is that what you thought?"

"I wasn't … sure," I say, then take a deep breath. "No. Yes. That's what I thought. Isn't that why you haven't had a serious relationship in five years?"

My courage wanes, and I can't ask if he wasn't dating anyone because he wanted to be with me. Especially not minutes after he declared the new best kiss of my life as a mistake.

"That's not why," Darren says but doesn't elaborate. "Where's Idris?"

"I don't know," I retort, irritation creeping into my voice.

"You don't know?"

"I'm sure he's back in Kimbell at the Baker Ranch licking his wounds," I say, pacing the room.

How did everything go from being so phenomenal to bizarre?

I'm not sure what to say next.

When have I ever been at a loss for words with Darren?

This is unchartered territory.

Stupid love messing everything up between me and my best friend.

"Licking his wounds? Did the two of you get into an argument?" He asks with more than curiosity in his tone. Is it a hint of hope? Or am I hoping that he's hoping?

"We broke up. Not that we were ever an official couple, despite what the Kimbell rumor mill cooked up." I stop pacing and stare at Darren.

"You going to tell me why? What happened?"

"You happened."

"Me?" He raises an eyebrow. His eyes flicker with amusement as they rest on my face.

My skin flushes hot. Thank goodness there's no way he can see me blush under my deep brown skin.

"Don't look at me like that. I know what you did behind my back." I press my hands on my hips. "The coaching you provided to Idris on what to say to win me over."

Darren's face falls, and he looks away. "Jas, I was only trying to help."

"Well, you shouldn't have. You should've stayed out of it and let Idris and me figure out we're not compatible. There's only one reason I thought we were, and it's because his words were yours!" I point an angry finger at him, then step out of the strappy stilettos cramping my feet. "I saw all the text messages. The romantic conversations I thought I was having with Idris. But they were with … you." I look away. "I hate you know me well enough to trick me into falling for something that was never real."

His presence envelops me before I look up to see the distance closed between us.

Darren looks into my eyes. "You know I would never do anything to hurt you. Maybe it was wrong, but I thought being with Idris would make you happy."

"It was wrong, and you were wrong."

"I apologize."

A bitter laugh escapes my lips. "I bet you do. That's Jasmine 101, isn't it? I was such a fool."

"I'm sorry. If I could go back and erase what I did, I would. Trust me." Something about the conviction in his words tugs at my heart.

I glance up and see the regret in his eyes.

"I guess you're the only one with a love match now." I fight back the tears threatening to spill down my cheeks. "You're flying back in time to spend Valentine's Day with Mirielle, right?"

"We broke up," he says with a mirthless chuckle. "Not that we were a couple despite what the Kimbell rumor mill cooked up."

My mouth drops open. "What? Why?"

"She deserves and wants more than I can give," Darren shrugs. He takes a step back and sits on the bed. "More than I … want … to give … to her."

The smallest seed of hope springs within me.

"Darren," I say, then let out a shaky breath.

"Yeah."

"Did you feel anything when I kissed you?"

I bite my lip and feel like an eternity passes before he responds.

He doesn't look at me as he says, "Yeah."

"What did you feel?" I ask, then swallow past the lump in my throat.

His head hangs low as I walk over to him. I rest my hand on his neck, stroking his hair until he gazes at me.

"I'm in love with you, Jasmine," Darren says.

All the air escapes my lungs, and I can't breathe.

"You love me?" I try to hide the smile spreading across my face.

He squints as he looks at me. "Madly, passionately, deeply. You are my best friend, but I found myself wanting more. So much more."

I giggle, then clamp a hand on my mouth. Once I regain control of my emotions, I say, "Boy, I have good news for you."

He gives me a smile that sends my heart soaring. "What's that?"

"I'm in love with you, too," I say, then kiss him gently.

When I pull back, I feel his arms wrapping around my hips.

Darren asks, "You sure? I don't want you pretending to love me because I'm a substitute for a real relationship."

I wave my arms in the air. "Do you know Evelyn, Aunt Mary, and Aunt Lisa told me that to trick us into realizing we should be together?"

"Are you serious?" Darren's brows crease.

"They thought convincing us to date other people would help us realize we want to be with each other. Can you believe that?" I wrap my arms around his neck. "But I guess they were right."

"Jas, this is a big step for us." His words turn serious. "We've been close our entire lives. I can't lose you. My life doesn't work without you in it. So, if any part of you thinks a relationship between us might not work and could end our friendship, then maybe we shouldn't try."

Easing down on his lap, I stare into his eyes. An idea formulates in my mind. "I have no doubts, and I can prove it."

"Prove it how?" he asks.

A giddiness bubbles inside of me.

"Marry me, Darren. Tonight!"

CHAPTER 50

J ASMINE

"DO I NEED TO REMIND YOU I SAID NO TO YOUR PROPOSAL?" Darren asks, his hand laced with mine.

"So what if you felt like, as the man, you should be the one to propose to me? Who cares about the formalities? All that matters is we are getting married." I laugh. "And it was my idea, not yours."

"This line is so long. Who knew so many people would want to get married at midnight on Valentine's Day?"

"It's Vegas. I'm guessing this isn't unusual. Every chapel we went to was busy." I lean into Darren's arms.

We are quite the pair. I'm dressed in a red ball gown and stilettos, and he's in an old faded Pittsburgh football t-shirt, black jogging pants, and flip-flops with socks. But I wouldn't have it any other way. I ignored all his protests to change into something more traditional and forced him out the door. I may have let an opportunity pass me by on New Year's Eve when Darren kissed me at midnight, but I wasn't going to make the same mistake on Valentine's Day Eve. No matter what, I wanted to ring in the holiday of love as Darren's wife.

"Evelyn is going to kill me," Darren moans, kissing me on the head. "You know she's going to be mad she's not here to see her only daughter get married."

"She'll get over it," I say as we shuffle forward a few feet. "I'm more worried about Hendrix. He's going to punch you when we get back."

"Think we should hold off?" Darren leans back to look at me. "Maybe do a big wedding in Kimbell where everyone can be there?"

"Nope." I shake my head.

An elderly lady dressed in a sequined minidress that shows off her wrinkly legs approaches us with forms on a clipboard. Her voice has the rasp of a pack-a-day smoker when she says, "Fill this out and have your IDs and credit card ready."

"Yes, ma'am," Darren responds, like a good Texan.

As he fills out our paperwork, I want to pinch myself. I cannot believe this is happening. It's a dream come true for both of us. I can't imagine why we didn't realize how perfect we are for each other years ago.

"Sign here," Darren instructs.

I grab the pen, then hesitate.

"What's wrong?" Darren asks, rubbing his hand along my back.

"Do I need to sign a prenup? Protect your money and all that?"

"Absolutely not."

"But my father has a lot of legal bills …"

"If you recall, I offered to help cover the legal expenses when we were just friends," Darren says. "You're going to be my wife. I want to share everything with you, Jas."

"Okay, if you're sure." My hand hovers above the clipboard.

"I'm sure. Sign, woman."

I laugh and put my signature on the form.

After thirty minutes, a one hundred fifty dollar ceremony fee, and a few thousand to bribe other couples to let us skip in line to ensure we are married as the clock strikes midnight, we've made our way inside the chapel as the couple facing the minister.

"Any guests?" The minister asks.

"No," Darren and I respond as we hold hands.

"Let's get the two of you hitched," the minister says, then turns toward the elderly lady in the minidress. "My mama will be your witness, take the Polaroid picture of the two of you after you're married and process the license once the ceremony is done. Should take around ten minutes total. Sound good?"

I nod my head as butterflies erupt within me.

"Sounds great," Darren says. His hands caress mine. He whispers, "You ready?"

"Definitely," I say, becoming choked with emotion.

As the minister begins to speak, I feel a tear roll down my cheek. Darren notices and wipes it away.

"We are gathered here today, under the vibrant lights of fabulous Las Vegas, to unite these two souls in matrimony. Marriage is a promise, not just between the couple, but to the community around them, that they will stand together, come rain or shine, luck or bust."

Darren and I laugh as I grip his hands tighter. I ignore the excitement racing through me and focus on this moment. I don't want to forget a second of my wedding to the love of my life.

The minister turns to Darren. "Please share your vows with your soon-to-be wife."

"Vows?" Darren says, stalling for time.

"Yes, you know how much you love me and can't imagine your life without me," I tease.

The minister's mom says, "Honey save that for your own. You're up next."

I give her a wink. "Good point."

Darren pulls me closer to him and looks into my eyes. "From the moment I saw you in Ms. Patterson's first-grade class, I knew you were special. It didn't take long for us to be inseparable. Honestly, I can't remember a time when I wasn't in love with you. It's been as constant with me as breathing."

More tears roll down my face.

"I've wanted this moment with you, just like this—"

"Like this?" I wave a hand toward the chapel decorated in kitschy decor.

"Stop interrupting me," Darren warns, giving me a gentle shake. "As I was saying. I've wanted this for so long but never thought I'd get it. The fact that you are standing across from me, ready to commit to living the rest of your life as my wife, is the greatest gift I could ever receive." Darren smiles at me. "I promise to cherish you, respect you, protect you, laugh with you, and comfort you for all the days of our lives. Most importantly, I will always love you. This is my vow to you, now and forever."

"Good job, my man," the minister says, slapping Darren on the back. "Now, your turn, Miss Lady."

"Wow," I say, my voice shaking. "Thank God I came to my senses and realized how I feel about you before it was too late."

"Amen to that," Darren says.

"I love you so much and can't imagine my life without you," I say, beaming.

"That's it? You're done?" Darren teases.

"Yes, short and sweet and true," I say.

"Beautifully said," the minister adds. "Now, do we have rings?"

"Shoot," I say. "No, I can't believe I forgot about rings."

"I got you," Darren says, reaching into his pocket. "I grabbed this off the nightstand before we left the hotel."

He opens his palm. Resting in the center is his very first Superbowl ring.

"There's no way you're giving that to me," I say, forcing his fingers closed over what I know is his prized possession. "We'll skip the ring part."

"No, we won't." Darren insists. "I'll get you a proper ring when we return home, but... I want you to have it. There's no better symbol of my love for you than to place this ring on your finger."

I cover my face with my hands as more stupid tears fall.

Darren wraps me in a tight hug, whispering, "I love you so much."

I look up at him. "I love you, too."

"Now that's settled, can we move on?" the minister asks, nodding at the line of couples waiting behind us for their turn.

"Yes, of course," I say.

"Please place the ring on the bride's finger and repeat after me," the minister instructs.

The Superbowl ring is enormous, but with a few cotton balls supplied by the minister's mama, we get it to stay on my ring finger.

Darren says, "Jasmine, I give you this ring as a symbol of my love and faithfulness."

The minister nods, then looks at me. "Do you have a ring hidden in your pocket too?"

"No ..." I say, then open my small clutch purse and dig around until I find something that could be a substitute. My fingers brush across a neon green rubber hair tie. I jerk it out as if I've found a pot of gold. "But I can use this." I fold it until it's small enough to roll onto Darren's finger without falling off.

"That's perfect," Darren says, laughing.

"Darren, I give you this ... ring ... as a symbol of my love and faithfulness." I laugh as Darren holds his hand up and nods appreciatively at my ring workmanship.

The minister says, "By the power vested in me, in the great city of Las Vegas, I now pronounce you husband and wife. You may kiss the bride."

"I love you, Dr. Jones," Darren says.

"Mrs. Manning," I correct him.

"You're taking my last name?" He asks, surprised. "Or Jones-Manning?"

"Nope, just Manning. Jasmine Manning. Sounds good, doesn't it."

The minister clears his throat. "The two of you should be kissing right now."

"How many seconds until midnight?" I ask, glancing at the minister's mama.

She gives us the official countdown. "Five, four, three, two ..."

Darren leans down and kisses me.

"One."

~

Want more of Darren and Jasmine? Get their swoon worthy marriage reveal bonus story delivered straight to your email inbox!
https://BookHip.com/QKLWQGT

Next up to find love in Kimbell, Texas is Darren's friend Luke Diamond. When news reporter Ciara Thompson comes to town to cover a devastating fire, she stumbles upon a secret that good guy Luke wants to keep buried. Luke is wary of the beautiful reporter, but finds himself unable to resist her even as she could turn his life upside down. Does he have a hope of keeping his secret and getting the woman he wants?

Check out the next book in the Kimbell Texas Sweet Romances ...
CHASING HOPE!

ABOUT THE AUTHOR

Angel S. Vane never imagined she'd stumble into becoming an author. An avid fan of books her whole life combined with an active imagination were the right ingredients to embark on a single goal of completing one book.

Now she's written several books and has tapped into her love of Jane Austen novels by writing her own brand of satisfyingly sweet romances. Learn more at Angel's website.

ABOUT THE PUBLISHER

BONZAIMOON BOOKS

BonzaiMoon Books is a family-run, artisanal publishing company created in the summer of 2014. We publish works of fiction in various genres. Our passion and focus is working with authors who write the books you want to read, and giving those authors the opportunity to have more direct input in the publishing of their work.

For more information:
www.bonzaimoonbooks.com
info@bonzaimoonbooks.com

facebook.com/BonzaiMoonBooks

Made in the USA
Coppell, TX
15 September 2024